Memories of the Alhambra

...a novel of the Chicano heritage myth and a man's search for his roots.

Jose Rafa, nearing retirement, leaves his ninety-five year old father's funeral in New Mexico with a burning obsession. To search for his true 'Spanish' origins as a descendant of conquistadors.

He disappears, leaving no word with his wife. A part of their retirement savings has been replaced by a receipt for travellers' checks, a cancelled check, and a business card from a shyster geneologist who preys on Mexican-Americans in East Los Angeles. Jose's first destination is Mexico, a way station on the Rafas' seventeenth century migration to the New World.

Woven through the realities of Jose's search are the memories. Jose's own. Of his wife, Theresa, who pushed him from the farm into the modern world of California. Of their only offspring, Joe, now a middle-class, college-trained scientist. Of what it meant for a modern pioneer to migrate from the ranchitos of the Rio Grande Valley into the modern American world.

Final destination: Spain, birthplace of conquistadors, where destiny awaits Jose Rafa.

Bilingual Press/Editorial Bilingüe

General Editor
Gary D. Keller

Managing Editor
Karen S. Van Hooft

Senior Editor
Mary M. Keller

Editorial Board
Juan Goytisolo
Francisco Jiménez
Eduardo Rivera
Severo Sarduy
Mario Vargas Llosa

Address
Bilingual Review/Press
Hispanic Research Center
Arizona State University
Tempe, Arizona 85287
(602) 965-3867

Memories of the Alhambra

by Nash Candelaria

Bilingual Press/Editorial Bilingüe
TEMPE, ARIZONA

ISBN: 0-916950-32-8

Also available in a hardcover edition. ISBN: 0-9601086-1-0

Library of Congress Catalog Card Number: 76-26410

PRINTED IN THE UNITED STATES OF AMERICA

Third printing, April 1987

Acknowledgments

Quotation from "Little Gidding," in *Four Quartets* by
    T. S. Eliot, copyright 1943 by T. S. Eliot; copyright 1971
    by Esme Valerie Eliot. Reprinted by permission of
    Harcourt Brace Jovanovich, Inc.

Lyrics from "Over There," copyright © 1917, renewed
    1945, Leo Feist, Inc., New York, New York.

We shall not cease from exploration

And the end of all our exploring

Will be to arrive where we started

And know the place for the first time.

T.S. Eliot
"Little Gidding," FOUR QUARTETS

1

The patriarch was dead. But Jose Rafa had felt a vague, hovering uneasiness even before his brother had telephoned to tell him that their father had died. It was a feeling that had nothing to do with the old man's death—a feeling that he, Jose, was on the precipice of a crisis.

The feeling had intensified on the drive from Los Angeles to Albuquerque, New Mexico. Jose and his wife, Theresa, had been driven to the funeral by their son, Joe. Jose Rafa, the first of all the Rafa's to finish high school, driven by his son, the first Rafa to graduate from college, back to the country suburb of what had once been a small town. Back to Los Rafas, New Mexico, in the northwest section of Albuquerque.

The drive down Route 66 had been a blur. Albuquerque was no longer the place Jose remembered from his childhood some sixty years ago. It was a metropolis. His brothers, sisters, in-laws, cousins were familiar but slightly changed, older versions of what he remembered.

One thing had not changed. The dust. The wind was blowing the morning they rode to the cemetary. Sitting between Theresa and Joe, he trembled, watching the brown specks settle onto the shiny black surface of the limousine. The limousine ahead turned and the headlights flickered pale, bleached by the morning sun. As their limousine turned, the hearse winked into view, then disappeared. His sister, Juana, began to cry silently, while his other sister, Gregoria, sat rigid beside her. From the rear view mirror, the chauffeur's eyes looked back noncommitally. A fleeting reflection showed Jose's hair streaked with white, the dark face fleshy and ashen.

'Pobre. Pobre, papa.' Juana was building up to hysteria again. Her quiet sobs unnerved Jose. She could not forget for a moment. The fact of death was shock enough. Why must she lacerate herself and others with it?

Now, for the first time since they had left the church, Gregoria stirred. Twice she cleared her throat, then lapsed into silence. Jose turned and stared at her as if to say: All right. What is it?

After clearing her throat once more, she forced the words out. 'I should have ridden in the front car. They have no right to put me in the second car. He was my padre, too.'

'Mama and Carlos and Eufemia are in the first car,' Jose said irritably.

'There was room. Did you see that, Juana? Did you see? There was room for all of us.'

'What difference does it make?' Jose asked.

'It's not fair. We were cheated. Eufemia is up there. You don't see her in the second car. Isn't that right?' Juana sniffed her tears and nodded.

'Maybe you should have ridden in the hearse,' Jose said. 'They could have put a chair for you right alongside the casket.'

'You don't care. You weren't here all the time he was sick. You were in California getting rich. So why should you care whether or not you're in the first car?'

Jose rubbed his temples, and his face flushed. His hands closed and unclosed, a sign that he wanted a cigarette. But a funeral procession was no place to disobey doctor's orders.

'Yes,' Juana echoed. 'Why should you care? You weren't here.'

Jose looked out the window, peering vacantly at the people on the sidewalk who watched the procession with disinterest. He glanced past his wife with a fleeting look of desperation, of frustrated entrapment. 'Shut up! Goddamn it! I'm tired of your nonsense. Who cares what car we ride in? Who cares if someone said the rosary too loud and another not loud enough? He's dead! How can your foolishness help that?'

Juana began to wail hysterically—like this morning at church —like the other night at the velorio.

'Let's try to be a little calm,' Jose said in a quieter voice. 'Let's try to have a little respect for the dead.'

Juana's attempt to hold back her tears sounded like slurping soup. 'Please,' Jose said as he handed her a handkerchief.

Jose looked toward Theresa. They had passed the park where the sunbonneted statue of the Madonna of the Trail looked west, then turned out of traffic toward the outskirts of the city. At the first dirt side road Jose closed his eyes. He knew where the limousine was going. Past a few more dirt roads to the turn onto a rutted way so covered with dust that you would not believe it was ever paved. A road one did not see. A road that one could feel and breathe.

Well, Jose thought, the family was still the same. True, his father had died. But that had been expected daily for the past ten years, so that his death was not so much a change as a realization. And—like always, after a day or two here he became jumpy. He and Theresa had left Albuquerque forty years ago, just before Joe was born, to get away from all this. Yet the place would not let them alone. It kept pulling them back to rehearse for their own time, which would be soon enough.

'We're there,' Gregoria said.

The limousine pierced through the dust into the cemetary, moving along the trimmed green lawn and the painted white crosses and engraved headstones. 'Good,' Jose said. 'It will be a relief to get it done with.' Juana began to sniffle louder.

During the ceremony voices could be heard above the intonations of the priest— like dogs quarreling over a bone. The Widow Rafa held on to her two sons. The others were beyond, mouths still open though their whispers had faded at Jose's glance that swept back and then hesitated on his brother. There was avarice on Carlos' face. Even his feet rested tenderly on the ground so as not to despoil the precious land which seemed more valuable than life to him.

Jose became impatient as the priest droned on. He wanted to get to the limousine quickly so that they would be the first to get away. Then they would get to his mother's house before the vultures got there and picked the place clean.

When the service ended, Jose turned toward Juana and Gregoria to urge them on when a hand on his shoulder stopped him. He narrowed his eyes, leaning toward the apologetic, accented voice, trying to pierce the layer of years that covered the familiar voice with this alien flesh.

'Jose. It's Herminio. Herminio Padilla.'

Jose shook his head in bewilderment. Herminio? His cousin. His best friend from school days. No, Jose's expression seemed to say. This can't be. Not this frail, gray-haired old man. Then he remembered his own reflection in the limousine mirror, and his eyes widened in fright.

'Herminio. Herminio.' Jose clasped the stranger's bony shoulders.

'Compadre. Primo. How long has it been? Twenty years? Has it been that long—to finally come to this?' Jose averted his eyes, the tears welling up—not just for his dead father, but for Herminio and for himself who one day soon would be resting in a place like this.

'Twenty years,' Jose said.

'Que lastima, su padre.'

'He had a long life. May we all live to be ninety-five.'

Herminio shifted awkwardly from foot to foot, tears in his eyes as he looked sadly at Jose. 'Come see me if you have time. I'm still at the same old place. Alone now, you know. Where Indian School Road meets the river."

Jose nodded, knowing that he would not make it, knowing that Herminio did not expect him to. They shook hands and clasped shoulders. Jose felt the touch self-consciously, seeing the rich texture of his suit in contrast to his cousin's calloused paw and threadbare sleeve. 'The same old place,' he said. Herminio nodded and disappeared into the crowd.

'There you are!' Jose turned in the direction of Juana's voice. 'Come on. The others are already gone.'

Jose muttered a curse under his breath. 'Where's Gregoria?'

'She went in the first car. They wouldn't let me go because it was too crowded. Now we'll be late.'

'Late for what?'

Juana flushed a deep purple. 'Nothing.'

'You mean they'll steal everything before you get your hands on a share.'

Juana climbed into the limousine stiffly, brushing past the chauffeur who held the door open. Jose followed, smiling, to let her know that he knew. She looked away from him. Thieves, his expression said. Goddamned Indian thieves.

The others were already there when they drove in back of the adobe house and parked under the huge cottonwood tree. Even before the handbrake had been set, Juana had leaped from the car and hurried through the screen door.

Jose opened the door with deliberation, letting Theresa and Joe in, then let the screen slam, hooking it shut to keep out the flies. As they went into the kitchen, the cacophony of voices died down. The family turned and looked silently at Jose—everyone except Widow Rafa, who sat on a straight back chair staring into space.

Carlos nodded abruptly. 'Jose. Junior. Theresa.'

Jose nodded at each in turn—at Carlos, at Eufemia and Gregoria and Juana and their husbands, Jose's brothers-in-law. Then Jose went to his mother and put a hand on her shoulder. After an awkward silence, his presence no longer seemed an intrusion, and they continued their talk.

'You'll move in with us,' Eufemia said. 'We can pack a few things now, then come back for the rest when you're ready.'

'We have more room,' Gregoria said quickly. 'Your great-granddaughters have doubled up like they've wanted to for so long. They cleaned and decorated the extra room for their favorite great-grandmother.'

Carlos nodded gravely at the old woman. 'Remember what I told you. We should keep the land in the family. Before you sell it to anyone, talk to me.'

Eufemia moved toward the closet. 'Which of your things do you want now, mama? I can start packing.'

'No, mama. We have the room. Your great-granddaughters have made it ready for you. Don't listen to her. You know her cooking. Her frijoles swell you up like a balloon.'

Jose's face flushed with anger as Juana walked quietly to one wall and took down an old framed photograph of his father. Then she eased to the niche in another wall and took a small wooded statue of the Virgin Mary.

'Stop it!' Jose shouted. 'Put those things back, or I'll call the police."

The family froze in silence, focusing stonily on Juana with arms full. 'I was just going to take them for safe keeping,' she said meekly.

'Put them back.'

She rehung the photograph on the wall and replaced the statue, turning it so it faced out properly. Jose scrutinized the others

—Carlos, whose avarice could be seen in the pinched squint of his eyes as he glanced through the window at the tiny apple orchard —Eufemia and Gregoria, planting their feet as if for a tug-of-war where each would grasp one of the old lady's arms and tear for the larger hunk. Once again Juana's eyes were wide with desire as they flitted from object to object. All the while the Widow Rafa sat staring, unaware of the quarrel.

'Why don't you all go home,' Jose said. Gregoria gasped. Carlos' folded arms reacted, ready to lash out, the authoritative reflex of the older brother. But that was long ago, another age, another life, and Jose looked past the now meaningless reflex as if he didn't see it.

'Well!' Eufemia said. 'Well!'

'I think mama needs to be left alone.'

'So you can take what's ours,' Juana said. 'So you can pack your car with our things and go back to California.'

Jose was infused with a calm that surprised him. As he looked at them, he spoke quietly so only Theresa and Joe could hear. 'These are not my sisters, my brother. Look at their brown, greedy faces. Listen to their accented speech. We're not members of the same family. We're not even members of the same race.' Then aloud to the others: 'Leave!'

Juana edged to the door, hesitating after each step to see if anything had changed, to see if it had all been a mistake, to see if someone would smilingly call her back. Jose stared at her darkly, and she continued through the kitchen.

Eufemia said, 'Well. Well,' then moved toward the door, Gregoria following.

'You're just tired,' Carlos said. 'We're all tired. Come by the house before you go.' Jose nodded. Now they were alone with his mother who was still staring out the window, far away, all alone.

Jose put a hand on her shoulder. This was how it ended—the old widow numb and uncomprehending. Soon it would be his widow's turn. And he had never traced back to the root of things, to the beginning—back to the conquistadors—back to the hidalgos, hijo de algo, son of someone. These pretenders he had thrown out of the house were not his family. Not his siblings. He was more than that. He was *someone*.

Jose looked past his mother, through the window, past the apple orchard toward the river. But his thoughts carried him farther. Across the ocean to the source, the beginnings. To a place he had never seen that was some secret, essential part of himself. And it was then that Jose knew what he must do.

2

The Rafas and Trujillos, Theresa's family, had lived in New Mexico for over two hundred and fifty years. Since before the founding of Albuquerque in 1706. Yet Theresa did not feel that it was home.

Over the years the trips to Albuquerque had become more o-dious, and it was with acute relief that she returned to Los Angeles this time. Ironically, their grown son drove them back over the same road that she and Jose had travelled on their first trip to California forty years before, when she had been carrying the unborn Joe.

Jose had headed for East Los Angeles where many refugees from the Mexican revolution of the early 1910's and 1920's had settled. It had seemed that the signs in the shop windows should have read "English spoken here" instead of "Se habla espanol." These were not their people, these latter day migrants from below the Rio Grande River, these Chicanos who huddled protectively under the shelter of common language and common appearance in this part of the city. Yet the pull to live there, the ambivalence, had drawn them newly married to the familiarity that Spanish-speaking East Los Angeles had offered to a young couple fresh from the Albuquerque farm.

'Why do we have to rent this one?' Theresa protested in a whisper. The dark, squat, shirt-sleeved landlord held open the front door with a smile, exuding a stale aroma of beer. The little house itself was a disappointment, hidden modestly behind a larger

13

front house like a shyly smiling young girl with a tooth missing behind a taller, more beautiful sister.

'The rent is cheap. Muy barato,' the landlord said. 'It's very clean.' They stamped their shoes of yard dust on the worn mat and followed the strong smell of disinfectant into the small linoleum floored living room.

Immediately Theresa's eyes narrowed as she checked the base boards and corners for vermin. The smell reminded her of a hospital. Of disease and dirt. In the tense stillness a fly's buzz amplified into the angry whine of a squadron of airplanes. The landlord smiled weakly at the stiff and scrutinizing Theresa and shrugged. The rims of her eyes were red as her eyelids flickered at the welling tears.

'It's only a few dollars a month,' Jose said.

'Es muy barato,' the landlord echoed.

'No,' she said—quietly but firmly.

'Let me show you the kitchen. It's been freshly painted.'

Jose had patted Theresa's arm reassuringly. 'Freshly painted,' he echoed.

The kitchen was two strides across the linoleum to one corner where the wall color changed abruptly just in front of the tiny stove and dripping faucet.

'No,' she repeated.

The landlord turned as if he hadn't heard. 'With a little paint the bedroom would be just as nice. In fact,' he said to Jose, 'I'll buy the paint for you. All you'll have to do is put it on.'

The landlord put his arm around Jose's shoulder and led him to the other room. 'See the bedroom? It hardly needs paint, but for you, compadre— You say you're from Albuquerque? I have a cousin there. He loves it. Wonderful people, he says. I'm from Chihuahua. Almost a blood brother.' Theresa stood waiting at the front door; she had not even looked into the bedroom. The two men looked at her, then at each other. 'Been married long, joven?' Jose shook his head. Then the beery whisper. 'You got to let them know who's the boss. Who wears the pants in the family. Who's got the balls, hombre."

'It looks good,' Jose said aloud as if to no one in particular.

'No,' came the answer.

'Maybe I could adjust the rent. Down a dollar or two a month.'

But Theresa had left the house, and Jose followed. 'Don't forget,' the landlord said. 'Let them know who's boss.' Then a final volley. 'How about three dollars a month less?'

She sat stiffly in the Model T, the hat pulled down over her bobbed hair so that the dark eyes peered out from under as if from a cave. 'Give me a cigarette," Theresa said. Jose stood beside the car, immobilized by his emotions. He was angry at her dismissal of the little house, even more angry that she had ignored his authority in front of the landlord, and now she had brazenly asked for a cigarette—one of the many sources of criticism from his sisters and sisters-in-law. Only hussies smoked and disobeyed their husbands.

'Will you give me a cigarette?'

'No. Goddamn it! My mother doesn't like it!'

'Or your sisters,' she answered stiffly.

'Yes. All three of them.'

'They don't like me chewing gum or rolling my stocking or painting my lips red or boop-boop-te-doop.' But the words belied her true feelings, for again her eyes reddened and tears welled up. 'Give me a cigarette. Please.'

Jose took a pack of Lucky Strikes from his shirt pocket, giving it a quick forward thrust and sudden halt that popped a cigarette part way out of the torn corner of the package. With trembling hand, Theresa held it to the center of her pursed mouth while Jose fumbled for a match. The silent tears trickled down her rouged cheeks.

'You didn't want them to build us a house either,' he said. She didn't answer. 'My father and my brothers had the plans all drawn.' Still no answer. 'Goddamn it! Say something.'

She stared straight out the windshield, trying to control her tears, trying to keep from choking on the cloud of smoke that emanated from her cigarette. 'They didn't ask me,' she finally said. 'They just came over one night with the drawings. It was supposed to be my house, and I didn't have anything to say about it. It wasn't what I wanted, and it wasn't where I wanted it.'

'In the old days it had to be built before we could get married. That was the custom.'

15

'These are not the old days.'

'Goddamn it! What do you want? It was a free house. Built from adobe from our own land. Near the rest of the family. Right in Los Rafas.'

'That's just it. It wasn't our own house. It was the family's house. So they could walk in and out as they pleased—tell us what to do or not do. Can't you see that? Why are we in Los Angeles if it wasn't to get away from your family?'

'All right. All right.' From the corner of her eye Theresa could see the landlord close the front door of the little house and look down the dirt driveway at them. 'But what about his house?' Jose asked.

Theresa exploded into tears, her twisted mouth emitting such frightening sobs that Jose trembled. Finally the words came, disjointed, between sobs, 'I don't want... our child... to grow up... here. I want more!' to be dissolved again in wailing sobs.

'What child?' Jose said, looking at her abdomen. Her wailing continued. Gently he took the burning cigarette from her fingers and threw it into the gutter. 'There,' he said, patting her shoulder. 'We don't have to live here if you don't want to.'

'It's... got to be... better. Not... the ranchitos... like Albuquerque. Not... Frijoles Flats. But with... everybody else. We're as good... as everybody else. Better!' The landlord had passed by, shuffling his feet and whistling.

Theresa smiled now as she remembered that scene of forty years past. She looked across the seat of the car toward Jose, who had slumped down asleep. He had gotten more than he bargained for, she thought. A girl who had refused his family's gift of a house. Who talked back. A flapper—a Chicana flapper, which was some kind of mutation in itself. No longer content to be a brown-skinned chula of the ranchitos, but a modern woman. Whatever that meant. Jose could be so angry with her, and yet she knew he loved her. Hadn't forty years shown that? 'Till death do us part,' the words of the ceremony had gone. And it was true.

3

Joe Rafa, Jr., sat in his suburban ranch house and stared at the telephone that he had just hung up. "What is it?" his wife asked from the kitchen.

He walked slowly into the aromas left from dinner and the hum of the automatic dishwasher. 'My mother,' he said. 'My father has disappeared.'

'Wha—at?'

'I'd better go over there, Margaret.'

'I'll go with you.'

Minutes later they were on the freeway heading from the beach toward the senior Rafas' home in Whittier. The telephone call had reawakened a premonition that had been with Joe for much of the past month—ever since he had driven his parents to New Mexico for his grandfather's funeral. A feeling that something drastic was about to happen.

He remembered his father's state at the funeral. Whatever it was had started there. But it had nothing to do with despair over the loss of a parent. It had more to do with Jose's reaction to his brother and sisters—Joe's aunts and uncle. And with Jose's ambivalence about them and himself.

Joe understood his father's feelings about the family. Hadn't he had them too? He could remember the boyhood summers when a feeling would work its way up from some deep hidden place during their annual pilgrimage to Albuquerque. For there would be his country cousins, browner even than he, with their Spanish-accented English. They would keep secrets from him, speaking in Spanish which Joe little understood, slyly pointing and laughing. And every summer Joe would be goaded into matching his prowess with one cousin in particular; he was a year older, slimmer and taller and hard as rock. One summer Joe earned a bloody nose from boxing. Another summer an abrasive pinning to the dirt in a wrestling mismatch. Each summer he would return to Los Angeles with the feeling: Who are these—these creatures that torment me so? What have they to do with me? The same feeling he had heard his father express after Grandfather Rafa's funeral.

Theresa Rafa was trying to look calm as she told them about the disappearance. She had waited for a telephone call—from Jose, from a hospital, from the police—but no call, and suddenly it was the third day.

Joe watched her eyes, puffy with strain, as she talked. It had taken him years to recognize her tremendous self-control and the price she paid for it. Theresa had once been a strong woman— very strong. With age she gradually attenuated into ill-health like the ultra-slow motion film of a house roof collapsing.

Theresa was shaking her head as she talked. 'Your father had been acting strange ever since your grandfather died. He was more nervous than ever. Talked about retiring and moving to Spain.' Conquistadors! Joe thought. Son of conquerors. Bullshit! Theresa looked at him as if she were reading his thoughts. 'You know how your father is," she said. 'I—I guess I haven't paid enough attention to him lately. I have my own problems. So he left.'

'Was there a note? Anything?'

'Just this.' She slid their savings account passbook across the table. It showed a withdrawal of three thousand dollars dated two weeks previous, leaving a balance of twelve thousand. Tucked inside was a folded paper, a carbon copy of a receipt for two thousand dollars in travellers' checks.

'He knew what he was doing,' Joe said. Theresa nodded. He thought he'd try to lighten the leaden atmosphere. 'Do you think he ran off with some chick?'

'Who'd have the old goat?' But instead of smiling, the tears finally began to flow. Both Joe and Margaret placed their arms around her shoulder. 'After more than forty years you'd think I could almost read his mind,' Theresa continued. 'The old fart. He's been planning it for weeks. He who wouldn't go to the drug-store without me by his side. God! I hope he knows what he's doing.'

'I think he does.'

'Finally there's this,' Theresa said, sliding a business card and cancelled check toward Joe.

'Geneology,' it read. 'Coats of arms. Historical consultant. Senor Alfonso de Sintierra.' In the upper left corner was a coat of

18

arms nesting in a tree of kinship like that used in geneological charts. The check had been for three hundred dollars.

'He's a crook,' Theresa said. 'He has an office in Boyle Heights. I hear he got his start selling printed copies of the Declaration of Independence to Mexican migrants for ten dollars. He used to tell them that it was a law. If they didn't buy, the immigration officials would ship them back.'

'What did Jose get for three hundred dollars?'

'He never mentioned it. Just like he never mentioned taking part of our savings.'

Joe put the card in his pocket and resolved to visit Senor de Sintierra as soon as possible.

The office was on Whittier Boulevard next door to the Mexicatessen from which wafted the aroma of posole. The neatly painted gold letters in the window said 'Alfonso de Sintierra. Historical consultant,' just like his business card. As Joe pushed open the door, chimes rang out the first five notes of 'La Cucaracha.'

Sintierra did not look up. Back to the door, he hovered over a table piled with books and papers, searching rapidly through them. The desk, too, was covered with papers, some on the top tattooed with brown ringed memories of cups of coffee.

'Momentito,' Sintierra said. In contrast to the table and desk, the wall behind stood ordered and impressive. Framed certificates and manifestos with words too small to read and a variety of seals in gold and silver hung prominently in view. 'Ah, here,' Sintierra said, thrusting an onion skin sheet from one pile to another. As he looked up his eyes narrowed, scrutinizing—the scales already on knife edge to weigh the possibilities for profit that had walked into his small office. On seeing Joe dressed in sport coat and tie, rather than denim workclothes, the furrowed squint relaxed and Sintierra stood and offered his hand.

'Alfonso de Sintierra. A sus ordenes.' His manner was friendly, equal to equal, rather than the brusque authoritarian manner he might have used with some of his clients. The emphasis was not on his first nor his last name, but on the bridge between. On 'de.' de meant of—of someone, of someplace—being at once a sign of affectation and of historical significance, perhaps even of status as in the minor peerage of the Anglos.

'Joe Rafa. Pleased to meet you.'

Again the narrowed eyes. Joe, he could almost hear Sintierra think. Not Jose. English, not Spanish. 'Ah, Senor de Rafa. It's a pleasure to deal with a man of substance. Not like some of these—' He didn't say the word, just rotated his hand impatiently.

Joe lowered himself onto a chair. 'It's Rafa,' he said firmly. 'Not de Rafa.'

The answering smile was forced. 'What's in a name? It's what you see in the quality of a man. Is that not so?' The man's fluttery, oily manner annoyed Joe, but Sintierra filled the silence before it stretched to an untenable length. "You are a professional man I take it?"

'A chemist.'

'A scientist. Yes. Yes. I could see it at a glance. de Rafa. Your family must be from—let me guess.' Joe almost smiled, thinking: New Mexico ranchito, next to the pueblo. But he found himself looking at Sintierra, trying to place him the way his father would try. Cuba? Argentina? What was that slight accent? Paraguay? But no answer came. For unlike Anglos whom his father always placed by name almost intuitively—Morris, English Jew; Haupt, German; Tuzinski, Polish—these Latins were hard to figure. 'Yes,' Sintierra mused. 'de Rafa. Sevilla? Barcelona? Madrid? No. Barcelona.'

Now Joe did smile. Beanfield, New Mexico. By way of Tortilla Flats, California. 'I was born in Los Angeles. My parents are from New Mexico.'

'But before that—Barcelona. It shows. You cannot hide what is in one's blood.'

Sintierra, Joe countered in his thoughts. Guatemala? Ecuador? His father could always place those he met automatically because Jose always felt so placed—often incorrectly. *Mejico? No, Spanish.* Sintierra? The inability to place the man would have disturbed his father. Would have given him the kind of uneasy vibration that he often felt with someone new and unknown. Not so much a failure in a guessing game but more an unanswered mystery about something vital to his own sense of knowing where he stood. *Mejico? No, not Mejico.*

20

'Well, Senor de Rafa. What can I do for you?'

'My father was a recent client of yours.'

The expression on Sintierra's volatile face went limp. It reminded Joe of the old tomcat they had when he was a boy. When threatened by the family dog or by the wrath of one of his masters, old Gato went limp. His face eased to a benign innocence that bordered on falling asleep. But underneath, Gato was like a drawn bow waiting to launch himself to safety.

'No,' Sintierra said innocently. 'I remember no de Rafa.' His innocent face and his bold lie angered Joe. Undecided between spearing him with the truth and gently helping his memory, Joe could not speak for a moment. But the glare of his eyes—what his wife called his Geronimo look—showed what he felt. Sintierra leaned forward and spoke softly, almost confidentially, with a worried frown. 'Are you—from the policia?'

Joe handed the canceled check across the desk. Sintierra looked at it thoughtfully, then turned it over to look at the florid, almost calligraphic signature. 'Policia?' he asked again. Joe shook his head. 'Well,' he continued. 'The name confused me. de Rafa. But Rafa is different. It was a long, long time ago.'

'The check is dated three weeks from yesterday.' The innocent look on Sintierra's face became even more pronounced. 'Jose Rafa disappeared three days ago. I'm looking for him.'

'Oh. Is that all?' he said in relief.

'Maybe you can tell me something.'

Then the deluge. A syncopated mixture of English and Spanish reconstructing what Sintierra remembered of the 'Rafa project.'

He was an expert, he explained. A doctor of geneologists. A tracer of the missing histories of persons. A regular family tree climber. A shaker of the limbs of all manner of family trees. Back to antiquity. Where the connections were fragile, delicate, like a spider's web. Where the searching had to be gentle. For if it were too heavy, too fast—poof! The web disappeared.

And of course, one could not worry about the cost. One had to, instead, think of the value. Knowing those threads of relationship to one's noble forebearers. Having the certainty that one sprang from noble stock. Such knowledge was priceless. Something money could not buy.

Not even three hundred dollars, Joe thought.

Sintierra rifled through a pile of papers, then checked through each of several layers of the tray on his desk. 'Here.' He waved a form toward Joe as he continued looking. 'A genealogy chart that I started for your father.'

A coat of arms stared brazenly out from the top of the sheet. Joe glanced past it to the top-heavy geneological tree whose limbs, branches, twigs, and buds showed a complex tangle—a regular bird's nest of kinship. The lines for ancestral names started with Jose Rafa, born in Los Rafas, New Mexico, February 11, 1906. Then Joe's grandparents' and great-grandparents' names—finally trickling down the trunk to more and more blank lines that ended with the words, 'Albuquerque founded 1706.'

When Joe looked up, Sintierra's words pounced to bar him from asking the obvious question: Just this for three hundred dollars? 'I can't find the second sheet,' Sintierra said. 'The one that goes back through Mexico to Spain. But as you can see there,' pointing to the words at the bottom of the sheet, 'Los Rafas, New Mexico. The farm country outside of Albuquerque. 1706. A historical family name.

'You can even see the name scratched on Inscription Rock in Arizona. On the wall about the height of a man on horseback. "Paso por aqui. Passed by here. Jose Rafa." Your great-great-great-something or other. Who knows how many times removed.

'If it hadn't been for the Anglos—if the United States had become Spanish—you'd be one of the first families. Like Adams or Jefferson.'

The flattering son-of-a-bitch, Joe thought. He could see how his father had fallen into this web. He himself couldn't help but be drawn in by Sintierra's enthusiasm. 'But we lost,' Joe said. 'And losers don't get many pages in history books.'

'Here,' Sintierra said, handing a sheet to Joe. 'Those are the names of two men, two experts—one in Mexico City, the other in Madrid—who are my connections in those parts of the Hispanic world. I gave that plus the geneological forms to your father.'

'Did he say what he planned to do with this information?'

'Pues no. No mas paso por aqui,' Sintierra said, smiling at his little joke.

Joe folded the paper and placed it in his pocket. The chimes rang out La Cuchuracha as he left. 'Wait!' Sintierra called. 'I remember one more thing.'

'Yes.'

'He said: "I have to go back. Back to the source. From here through Mexico to Spain. Before I die."'

'Is that all?'

'Is that all? Maybe it is everything.'

4

Jose Rafa followed the first passengers to alight from the airliner. This part of the Mexico City airport seemed like what he remembered of Mexico, piles of rubble from which, Phoenix-like, the new unfinished structure rose. Then, past the concrete throughway they were at the door to Customs. Here, after a cursory glance at his passport and much flourishing and banging of the official stamp, the short, swarthy, uniformed man ushered him with a rapid volley of Spanish toward the baggage area where other passengers were waiting.

He felt calm now that they were on the ground. It was not so much relief from the fear of flight as other things—the cocktail the stewardess had served prior to landing, the sight of other Americans confused in a foreign country while he understood what was happening, the fact of Mexico itself. The dark faces, the men with longer hair and mustaches gave him comfort. It was as if a weight had fallen from his shoulders, the weight of countless light-skinned, clean-shaven Anglos who ran things back in los Estados Unidos. Here he felt unburdened. Somehow this was his place to be what he considered his true self.

A few exchanges in Spanish, and a porter disappeared into the milling crowd to return in a few moments with the gray two-suiter. In another moment, the porter had hailed a taxi and stood smiling on the curb as the taxi pulled away, slipping the five peso note into his pocket. Then it happened again to Jose as it occasionally did. The cab driver complimented him on his excellent Spanish. 'But,' the driver continued, 'the senor doesn't sound like a Mexican. Begging the senor's pardon, are you Cuban?'

Jose smiled and lit a forbidden cigarette. 'Norteamericano,' he answered. 'Of Spanish ancestry.'

'Oh, senor. That explains it.'

It was late afternoon now, dusk starting to ease into the still blue sky as the taxi drove toward the center of the city. The suburbs had grown since Jose had been here fifteen years ago. Yet, in many parts, there were still those same crumbling adobe hovels with fifteen years of added decay. Some of the crumbling buildings with partial adobe walls staggering around them, with thin wiry chickens scratching the hard ground, and pantless infants in dirty shirts laughing at play, reminded him of the Los Rafas of his childhood. But at least there had been open country in that New Mexico of fifty, sixty years ago. Here the openness was fast losing the battle to urban encroachment even this far from the Zocalo.

Yes. Even time did not dim the poverty he had come from. It had been a hard life for his parents. And for their parents before them. Scratching a living from the high desert earth that was luckily blessed by the life-giving waters of the Rio Grande River.

Theirs had been a large family. Not a happy one; he had known few of those in his lifetime. Yet not altogether an unhappy family either. More a group of strong-willed individuals, each wanting his own way, yet kept in line by an autocratic and, by today's standards, cruel father. Of this group, it had been he, Jose, who had been blessed. Somehow lightning had touched him and given him that extra bit of intelligence that the others had noticed from the first. It had made him his mother's favorite until the baby of the family, Dandy, had been born. It had resulted in recognition by his oldest brother, Tomas, who took under his wing this gifted son of farming people.

Yet his first memories of a greater world beyond Los Rafas came not from Tomas but from school, from a teacher whose name he could not even remember. She had not even been the regular teacher, but a substitute. Yet, other than the teacher's name, he could remember as if it had happened yesterday.

A glance out the taxi window toward a group of youngsters playing at the edge of the street brought a smile to his lips. Yes. They had been like that. Third grade it had been. Grouped with the other grades in the one-room adobe schoolhouse. The students he knew. Cousins. Neighbors. Friends. All brown-skinned Hispanos except for the few Anglos who lived on the bigger farms in Los Rafas. The smaller students were seated in the back of the room. His cousin, Armando, a second grader, had been banished to the back with the first graders. Armando had been too shy to raise his hand and too pained to control himself, so that he urinated in his pants. The warm flow had run down his leg onto the floor beneath his desk where it formed a puddle whose aroma permeated the room on that warm spring day. Shamefaced, he had been moved to the back as punishment, near the door where in the future he could rush outside if necessary. But Armando was too shy to rush outside without permission and too shy to thrust a hand up with sufficient boldness that the teacher would notice. Even in later years when they were grown men, Jose would smile and hold his nose when he met Armando.

Their regular teacher, an Anglo, had been talking to them about what it meant to be a citizen of a country. About nationality. Jose had not understood it then. The only world he knew well was Los Rafas. Even the city of Albuquerque, a metropolis of thirty thousand, was almost like a foreign country to him, since he had been those five miles to town but a few times in his eight years.

So to talk of country was difficult. He knew Los Rafas. He knew less of Albuquerque. Still less of New Mexico. Then beyond that it was all hearsay. Even the big map that hung at the front of the class, a new one that showed all forty-eight states including what were recently the territories of New Mexico and Arizona, could have been the figment of someone's imagination. The only sense he had of country was in the song they learned in school, 'My country 'tis of thee—'

The teacher's question about nationality was difficult. One of the Smith twins stood straight and proud and volunteered that his ancestors were from England, looking all around the class with that haughty air which would be his undoing after school.

One of Jose's cousins, Vicente, flushed red when the teacher asked him and stared mutely at the floor. 'Well, Vincent,' she chided.

'Uh. Well. Uh. Mexican?'

She closed her eyes for just an instant while her head nodded and her lips tightened with just a trace of a curl at the edges. The students all knew that look. It spoke plainly to them: 'What would you expect from one of these people?' Her smug glance turned and focused on Jose, who for an instant felt the urge to wet his pants and join Armando in the back of the room. But the clock had moved to three, and the older students stood and left, disregarding the teacher—while Vicente motioned his head to a couple of older Hispanos and set out after the Smith twin who was already in a dead run as he hit the door.

Jose slid behind some taller students in order to hide from view and walked cautiously out. 'Hey,' he whispered, tugging on the sleeve of his older sister, Gregoria, 'what's the answer to the question?'

'Don't you know? I thought you were so smart.' He doubled a fist to give her a good one, but she flounced away, giggling with a girl friend.

The next morning he awoke with a stomach ache. At least it was only his stomach until his oldest sister, Euphemia, propelled him out the kitchen door with a swat to his backside. None of the other students were in sight when he approached the schoolyard. He knew he was tardy. The classroom seemed unusually quiet, and when he peered timidly into the open door, he saw a strange teacher at the front of the class *and she was smiling.*

Jose shook his head in disbelief. The smiling face looked directly at him as he stared around the corner of the door jamb, then spoke a beautiful Spanish. 'You must be Jose. Come in. We were waiting for you.'

'Yes, ma'am.'

The rest of the class sat quietly, watching with uncertainty this strange teacher who spoke better Spanish than their parents. 'Your regular teacher is ill. I'll be your teacher for awhile. Jose, I was just asking the class what you've been studying.'

There it was. The question for which he had no answer. His glance showed the restless stirring of the others in the class. One of the Smith twins had a blue-black bruise just below his left eye. In the stillness it seemed that everyone's gaze turned to Jose standing beside his desk. His whisper reverberated through the room like the screech of hard chalk on a blackboard. 'We were talking about nationality, teacher.' Then the stillness again.

The smile faded from the teacher's face, and her puzzled eyes looked away from Jose. 'I see.'

'She asked us our nationality. Smith number one said his ancestors came from England.'

'I see.'

'My ancestors came from Spain.'

With that, Jose slid behind his desk, his body shaking with the pounding of his heart. All eyes were focused on the front of the classroom. Slowly, the teacher walked down the aisle toward Jose. Necks turned; breathing was suspended in anticipation. Jose cowered to the side of his desk farthest from his approaching fate, and it would have taken nothing at all—the drop of a pencil—to send him into tears. The puzzled look was gone from her face, but so was the smile. As the sound of her footsteps ceased, she softly placed an arm about Jose's shoulder. 'Young man,' she said. 'If anyone ever again asks you your nationality, say AMERI-CAN!' She patted him on the back and strode slowly to the front of the class. 'Students. How many of you know the song, 'America?' Almost all of the hands went up. 'Now let's sing together about our sweet land of liberty. If you don't know all the words, listen to your neighbor and let him help you.'

After that, Jose would have gladly died for her. He stayed after school that first day on some pretext or other—then other days. They talked—or rather, Jose listened—as he cleaned the blackboard or emptied the weatherbeaten wooded box that was used for trash. There appeared a tiny crack in his confined Los Rafas' world. Names of characters he had never heard of, in books he had never read. Places. Ideas. The thought that he, too, might be a teacher if he really wanted to.

School was over all too soon. The autumn saw their regular

teacher return. Yet even she could not dampen the small vision he now had of other worlds. And late that September he received the first of several foreign postcards—each with a photograph of a historic site and a different postage stamp—telling of his substitute teacher's sabbatical in 'merry, old England.' Surely, no one in Los Rafas had ever received mail from England, mother of all Anglos, and he kept them secreted in a cigar box with his few other treasures.

'Hotel San Francisco!' The cab driver's voice startled Jose. The mist of his mind cleared so that modern Mexico came into focus. The hotel was on a side street a half a block from the Avenida Juarez, with the Alameda, the city park, across the heavily trafficked avenue. A porter scampered down the steps of the hotel entrance and opened the cab door. Up the stairs to the crowded check-in counter. Then, key and bag in hand, the porter led Jose past the dining room to the elevator.

The room was of adequate size, yet its low ceiling seemed to close in on him. It was neat and clean, with the kind of furniture you see in the less expensive motels in the western U.S. The porter raised the Venetian blinds, uncovering the window that looked out into the central core of the hotel, with a roof a floor below and the lighted windows of other rooms across the way.

When the door clicked behind the departing porter Jose dropped into the bed with relief. He was here. In this small room in this downtown hotel in a foreign city of eight million people. He felt of it, yet not of it. While his mind blinked on and off like those neon signs that dusk brought to life in any large city, he dozed into a restless sleep.

'Over there. Over there. Send the word. Send the word. Over there. For the Yanks are coming...'

They marched in parade past Jose's eyes, each one snapping a smart salute as they passed the reviewing stand on which he stood in his marshall's uniform. They were all there. His third grade substitute teacher, dressed in the uniform of a Buckingham Palace guard, led a platoon of school-age troops similarly uniformed and armed with slates, chalk, and dusty erasers. His older brothers, Tomas and Carlos, in the doughboy khaki of the American Expeditionary Force.

It was 1918. His brother, Tomas, was home on leave before returning to camp from which he would cross the Atlantic Ocean to France. The parade faded until only Tomas marched in review, clicking to a snappy halt. Then, after a smart left face, Tomas marched up the steps of the reviewing stand and saluted the grown man, Jose.

'We have to make the world safe for democracy. We have to beat the Hun.' Tomas placed a hand on Jose's shoulder. Then Jose was suddenly a boy again, looking up with admiration at his big brother. They were in the back yard, under the cottonwood tree where in winter the wood would be stacked for chopping. They were facing away from the adobe house toward the side orchard of apple trees.

'You'll have to be the man now. Carlos wrote me from his camp in California that they were talking about sending his regiment to France. And I have to take the train tomorrow morning to New Jersey. Then we go. I don't know exactly when. It's a military secret.'

Jose was proud of his older brother, not only a doughboy but also lightweight boxing champion of the camp. He'd show those Huns. 'I'm almost a man,' Jose said. 'I'm already as tall as mama.'

'The chickens will be all yours now. Not just to raise and feed but to sell.'

'Yes, Tomas.'

'Papa is not old, but he's not young either. He'll need your help all the more with Carlos and me away.'

'I know.'

'If something should happen to me and Carlos, there'll just be you and the baby, Dandy, to carry on.' Tomas swept an arm past the apple orchard to the fields beyond the irrigation ditch where their two horses grazed placidly.

Jose's eyes followed the sweep of arm. A hot bitterness rose from his stomach, and he shuffled his bare feet restlessly. He looked deeply into his brother's eyes and decided that it was time to tell him. Papa and Carlos he could never tell, but Tomas

29

would listen. Would understand. Even if he did not agree.

'Tomas,' he said gravely. 'I'll help. You know that. But I can never be a farmer when I grow up.'

Tomas' sly glance was framed by a slight smile, 'I've known that longer than you. You weren't meant to be a farmer. You are special in this family. The world is moving on, and you have to move with it.'

'You won't tell papa?'

Tomas shook his head. 'Stay in school. Go to high school. Don't be like the rest of our Hispano farmers, thinking it's enough to be able to sign their names to a paper selling their land to some sharp Anglo. The time of the Anglo has come, even here on the ranchitos. After two hundred years of isolation, our ways are going. You have to be ready to take your place in the new world. So your helping here is only temporary. I won't tell papa. And I'll help you when I come back.'

Jose's heart felt as if it would burst. If mama had not been looking through the screened back porch, he would have whooped with joy. But a whoop would have brought the questions and possibly papa with his whip if the answers weren't satisfactory.

Tomas stuck out a field-toughened brown hand, and Jose shook it. 'Agreed?' Tomas asked.

'Agreed.'

Tomas snapped to attention and saluted Marshall Jose. Then with a smart about face he marched from the reviewing stand to join the passing parade that faded into the distance.

After the last roll of the snare drums there was silence. A deep, vacuous, overpowering silence that knifed through the years and past his dream to focus on the sleeping figure. He fought his way up and sat in bed, eyes still closed, turning his face toward the silence that seemed to call out to him. Jose's eyes popped open, but there was nothing there. Terrified, he reached out onto the bed beside him. Theresa was not there. He was all alone. Tears started to flow silently down his cheeks.

5

Morning light after a good night's sleep brought more than a new day. Some mornings it seemed to bring the beginning of a new life. As if sleep had let Jose slip through a side door into another world, shedding memory as he stepped over the threshold, breathing promise from the air that was ever young.

So it was that Jose awoke, thinking how strange it was that being on the trail of history made him look forward to a new life. But the morning soon brought frustrations. Three times he had telephoned his Mexico City genealogical contact before getting an answer. The woman—she couldn't have been a trained secretary—was inarticulate, even in Spanish. In the background he heard the barking of dogs and the whining of small children, and the woman's voice had that hollow sound of a telephone in a long hall in a rundown boarding house. Finally she had understood. No. Senor Gomez was not in; he was on an assignment with some rich Norteamericano. Yes. She would have him telephone. Then exasperating minutes while Jose assured himself that she had properly written down his name and telephone number. He suspected that she could not write and would have to memorize the information—incorrectly no doubt—so that Gomez would never phone. But eventually Gomez did, late, like almost everything in Mexico.

Now it was late afternoon as the taxicab moved expertly through the maddening traffic along the Paseo de Reforma. Strange place to meet, Jose thought. But then you never know how these Mexicans work. Some with their office in their hat. Ready to run quickly comes the next revolution.

They turned into Chapultepec Park, open air office of Senor Luis Gomez. Before they caught a glimpse of the building, the sombre, stone shape of Tlaloc, the rain god, loomed into view— as overpowering on a sunny, smoggy day like today as on a day when Tlaloc summoned the sky's tears to succor the parched earth so that corn would grow.

As the taxi drove off, Jose stood and looked up at the stone figure that must have been thirty or forty feet tall and half as wide. The huge head was half the height of the figure, strong jaw with powerful huge teeth. Below the clenched fists were the short, stubby feet. Behind the group of trees that nestled this huge stone presence that needed no nestling, he could see the white marble of the buildings. The carved marble sign below Tlaloc read "Museo Nacional De Antropologia.'

An uneasy fear corroded the edge of Jose's good spirits. The awesome Tlaloc did not match the downtrodden Mexico he knew, and this incongruity made him doubt his own perceptions. Did the Spaniards really conquer Tlaloc's children? Or did this great stone god sire another race that had long since disappeared?

Cautiously he crossed the wide courtyard at the entrance to the museum, moving toward the fountain where Gomez was to meet him. A troop of schoolboys in military uniform crowded around the fountain, chattering the usual schoolboy exuberances. Jose's gaze followed those of the boys down into the water where he saw a rainbow shimmering in the spray that traversed the width of the fountain. A good omen, he thought. After the rain god's outpourings comes the rainbow, symbol of peace, symbol of hope, symbol of the pot of gold. He watched the boys pushing and shoving, laughing, chattering in Spanish, uninhibited by the thought of Anglos about. It had not been so in the Los Rafas of his boyhood. Or in Los Angeles where his son had grown up. Always there would be an undercurrent of Anglo superiority pressing on their natural exuberance. Ay, raza suffrida!

Jose searched the periphery of the fountain. A few tourists loitered about waiting for a friend or a guide. The students from the military academy lined up in single file and followed an officer in Mexican army uniform toward the entrance of the marble building. Among the few others sauntering by there was no one who looked like a Senor Gomez.

Then he saw a man strolling purposefully but slowly toward the fountain. Jose did not know why he knew, but he knew this was Gomez. The man was dressed all wrong—not in business suit but in dark brown cotton trousers and a tieless open-collared white shirt. He was of medium height, thick through the waist with the gentle beginnings of the fat man he would become in later years. And he was dark, mahogany dark, Indian dark, moving across the paved courtyard as if he had come through the ages to today in just that short stroll—in full possession of himself, not quite arrogant, but not fearful nor humble either. As he approached the fountain he turned so that the slanting sun's rays illumined the dark face. Now Jose knew why he had recognized this man from among the crowd passing by. He was the twin of Alfonso de Sintierra—a dark, self-possessed counterpart of the man who had started him on this search.

They were sitting at an outdoor table at the edge of the lagoon across the street from the museum. Solemnly, quietly, Jose watched Senor Gomez, sensing the amused tolerance hidden by the Mexican's stoic expression. The waiter set the bottle of beer in front of Gomez, the coffee in front of Jose.

'So you're not a geneologist,' Jose said.

'No, senor.'

'But I have your name. Right here,' pointing to the creased sheet that he removed from his wallet. 'de Sintierra gave it to me.'

Gomez shrugged. 'He was mistaken.'

'You mean that I flew twenty-five hundred miles on a mistake?'

'Well, senor. I wouldn't exactly call it a mistake.'

'Then what would you call it?'

'A lie.'

'A lie?'

Although Gomez's face did not change expression, Jose could hear the seriousness in his voice. 'Those Sintierras. Cousins of mine—I hate to admit it. Liars. Every last one of them. With the devil in their tongue and money in their pockets. Especially that Alfonso. He makes a good Norteamericano, that one. Shrewd. Very shrewd. Too shrewd to be a Mexican.'

'But I paid—' Jose looked wildly around, as if de Sintierra might appear from behind a tree, offering back the three hundred dollars he had received. '—I paid for services.'

'Si, senor.'

33

'That man— He had a business card. Here.' Gomez took the extended card, looked at it, turned it over as if looking under a rock, and handed it back. 'He traced my family back to Spain. With a few missing pieces here in Mexico. I believed him.'

Gomez reached into his wallet. 'Senor. I have a card too. And I'm only a limousine driver.'

A rage welled up from within Jose. He felt himself puff up like a frog, angry heat radiating from a center deep within to the surface of his skin from which popped a thin film of perspiration. The sharp pain in his chest—an old friend—warned him, and he sat very still, feeling this old friend as if he were a new acquaintance. Let go, he thought to himself. Relax. What will it matter a hundred years from now?

'Senor?' Jose shook his head as if to wake himself. 'Are you all right, senor?'

'It—it must be the altitude.' I left my pills in my suitcase, Jose thought. Damn it!

'Can I drive you to your hotel?'

Jose looked across the table but he did not see. A dizziness came over him, and he felt faint and nauseous, with a light headed feeling that he recognized from previous trips to Mexico. La turista, laughingly referred to as 'Moctezuma's curse.' But it was no laughing matter. He felt like he was going to die.

'Yes,' Jose stammered. 'The hotel—would be—nice.'

Steadied by Gomez, he walked cautiously past Tlaloc and across the street to a special parking area for taxicabs and tourist limousines. 'Here,' Gomez said, helping him into the back seat of a shiny Chevrolet. 'Lie down. You'll feel better.'

Jose closed his eyes, trying to tune out the cacophony of horns as the car drove back down the Paseo de la Reforma. The lobby of the hotel was a blur of people and voices. Then he was lying on the bed in his room.

'The hotel doctor will be here soon.' Gomez's voice was distant, a faint echo coming from far up in a mountain. Minutes later the doctor arrived. A bottle of pills for la turista. Questions and a warning about his high blood pressure. A look at his medication. The last distant sound of Gomez's voice. 'I'll call you again in a day or two, senor. When you're better. We have some unfinished business to discuss.' Then sleep.

Jose slept off and on for two days, waking only to eat something that room service delivered and for a daily visit from the hotel doctor. But mostly it was sleep. Brief and restless. Then long and deep. Far back, reliving the years.

Mexican, the voice in his deep dream kept whispering. Mejicano. Chicano.

Albuquerque High School came into view. Brick. Two storied. On the far end of town toward the heights. He was on the bus that was the thin link from Los Rafas to town. A strange place. Almost a foreign land that he visited every week day with fear and apprehension. Be polite. Smile. Always say yes to the Anglo teachers. Hide what you really feel. Then home again at the end of the day, carrying the verbal passport—the shift to the Spanish language—that was his readmission to Los Rafas.

There were not many raza at the high school. High school was really for Anglos, or for Spanish-Americans who were trying to be like Anglos. Not for sons of farmers who were also going to be farmers. Hadn't Jose's own brothers left school after the eighth grade?

Those had been difficult years for Jose, torn between two worlds. The old world was familiar and comfortable. Poor. Dirty. Where he was something special—a favorite. The new was unknown. Ruled by the enemy who saw him as some kind of inferior being. Yet—out there were all those desirable treasures: shiny new automobiles, houses of wood with flowers instead of dirt and cornfields, radios, new clothes, paved roads leading to *somewhere*, Charlie Chaplin and Douglas Fairbanks, steak instead of frijoles—a magnetic world that, against his will, sucked him up from the beanfields of Los Rafas like iron filings from dirt.

Yet he was torn. In the world he wanted he was a stranger. In the world he rejected he was at home. He felt this pulling, this tension, as a constant weight he became so used to that his awareness of it faded away. Until the outside world reminded him. Like the job he had the summer before his senior year in high school. The summer of the race riot.

One of the high school counsellors had recommended Jose for a job with one of the two drugstores downtown, a pleasant change from working on the farm. Eventually he got to wear a white hat and starched white apron and work behind the luncheon counter, fixing sandwiches and serving ice cream concoctions. Friends would stop by, boys and girls, for a fountain drink or—when Mr. Raymond was out—for a chat. Especially his cousin, Herminio, who was one of the few lucky Hispanos who was fair-haired and light complexioned. Jose envied Herminio. If he would keep his mouth shut, Herminio could pass for an Anglo.

Over the warm, lazy summer weeks, Herminio would come in almost daily. He would buy an ice cream soda, and, when Mr. Raymond was out, Jose would treat him to a sandwich of ham cut thick from the larder in back of the drugstore. 'On the house,' Jose would say. Herminio would smile in appreciation at his lucky cousin who could serve such a welcome change from the tortillas and frijoles at home.

Getting thin, Jose thought one day as he sliced at the ham. Herminio had come to accept these free sandwiches as a matter of course, and now that the ham bone was beginning to show Jose grew increasingly irritated at his cousin's arrogant expectations.

'Jose,' Herminio protested, lifting up a corner of the bread and pointing to the inside of the sandwich.

'Sorry, primo. The boss has been cutting back on little extras lately.'

'But man. There's almost no ham in this bread sandwich.'

'And there's no charge at the cash register.'

'Old man Raymond is some cheapskate.'

'He's the boss, and he says cut back.'

Jose watched every mouthful being chewed, heard every smack of the lips, every slurp through a straw with increasing anxiety. Herminio walked out with a wave of the hand, and Jose thought: Good riddance. But that did not solve his problem. How do you fatten up a carved ham? When Mr. Raymond came back from the bank, he asked for a ham sandwich, and Jose knew that discovery was hovering like a hungry vulture, lean as the once-fat ham in the larder.

The rest of the afternoon was filled with anxiety. Mr. Raymond would fire him. He would diminish in the eyes of the school counsellor who had recommended him for this job. Some of his envious acquaintances, his Hispano 'friends,' would be only too glad to give him the horse laugh.

Jose endured the next morning with anxious desperation, waiting for Mr. Raymond to leave the drugstore on his daily errands. When the store was empty, Jose moved quickly, wrapping the depleted ham in paper and tying it securely. Then he went out the rear door into the alley with its trash barrels behind the row of other shops down the block. He picked a full one, one unlikely to be looked into, and buried the package halfway down into the barrel. Then he hurried back to the drugstore and waited nervously for his boss.

When the bell clanged at the opening of the door, Jose almost jumped. He steeled himself and rushed from behind the counter, wiping his hands on his apron. 'Mr. Raymond! A terrible thing happened.' Mr. Raymond strode quickly toward the cash register. 'These—these... Mexicans came in. Young men. They went through the food locker and took a ham. Then—'

Mr. Raymond unlocked the cash register and quickly began to sort through the bill compartments. 'They didn't touch the register,' Jose continued. 'I locked it right away and slipped the key into the pan of dirty dishes. But they took a ham.'

Mr. Raymond was counting silently to himself, his lips mouthing the numbers. 'It's all here,' he said, still staring into the open register. 'Jose?'

'Yes, sir.'

'Can you shoot a pistol?'

'Yes, sir.'

'I'm bringing one from home. The next time that dirty Mexican gang bullies their way in here, somebody's going to get shot.'

'Yes, sir.'

'And Jose. You did a good job in locking the register. I wish more of your people were like you. You're a credit, a real credit.'

'Thank you, sir.'

The ham was not even mentioned. Only the precious cash register and the pistol that Mr. Raymond brought the very next morning. Two weeks later, as if in answer to Jose's lie, Herminio bolted into the drugstore, a wild, hunted look on his face.

37

'Hide me!' he demanded. 'Jesus Christ. They're after me.'

From the street the scuffled sounds of running feet grew louder. Voices, too, became more distinct, the words amplifying and sorting themselves into Spanish obscenities. Herminio bolted into the storage room and Jose followed, keeping an eye on the door. A swarthy Hispano, someone he had never seen before, stuck his head in the store and spoke to Jose in Spanish.

'Hey, compadre. Did a skinny little bolillo run by here? With blonde hair. He was running real fast.' The dark youth smiled at some private joke and winked.

Jose answered in Spanish, his glance brushing past the drawer below the cash register where the pistol lay to the gang that stood threateningly outside the door. 'Was he wearing a blue shirt?' The dark youth nodded. 'He was running like hell down Central Avenue. Toward the depot.'

'Gracias, compadre. Let me give you a little tip. Watch out for gangs of bolillos out in the street unless you have some friends with you. We've had enough of their mierda. Now we're ganging up on them like they do on us. Viva la raza!'

The door slammed, and the gang broke into a run toward the depot. With a sigh of relief, Jose watched them disappear from view before he went back to the storage room.

'Herminio.'

'Are they gone?'

'Yes.'

'Are you sure?'

'Of course.'

Herminio oozed his way to the edge of the storage room door and peered out. 'Jesus. They would have killed me.'

'What happened?'

'Man, you wouldn't believe it. You wouldn't believe it. I was at the park up in the heights, you know. I heard there had been some trouble about the picnic area. Nothing serious. Just a few flying fists here and there. Bolillos. They said there were too many raza using the tables. That we ought to go back where we belong. Eat in the cornfields. Or in an outhouse.

'Then today for some reason the thing exploded. Who knows why today. It could just as well have been any other day this summer. Maybe because today was extra hot. Or because that gang from Los Martinez came up in a mob. Anyway, one minute it was as peaceful as Sunday mass. The next minute there were rocks and bottles and fists flying all over the park.

'I was just lying there, you know, on the grass. I looked up at the noise and saw somebody point at me and shout. "There's one! Under that tree." You didn't have to say anything more. I was on my feet and running like a starving man after a tortilla.

'The whole gang chased me. I yelled back as I was running, "Soy raza, compadres! Soy raza!" All that got me was a shower of rocks. Two of them hit me right in the back. It still hurts like hell. They followed me all the way here. They'd have killed me! They wouldn't believe I was raza.'

Jose shook his head. 'Loco. Plain loco.'

'Now I don't know what to do. They might be waiting down the street for me.'

The ting-a-ling of the bell silenced them. Mr. Raymond nodded at them as he walked quickly to the cash register and checked the drawer beneath it for the pistol. 'There's a race riot out there,' he said, glancing toward Jose. 'Some of our hot-tempered gringos and the local Mexicans.' His hand slid into the drawer, then slyly tucked the pistol into his belt. 'I'm going to lock up,' he continued. 'The police may not get this in control until tomorrow. Jose. You best be careful going home. There are gringo gangs roaming the streets. And you, young man,' he said to Herminio. 'You watch out for the other side.'

Jose and Herminio exchanged fearful glances. Que loco, Jose thought. It's like I can't be either one. Can't be at home either place. In the middle. Nowhere.

A terrible gloom settled in on him. The gloom weighed heavy astride an aching weakness, as Jose moved from memory to the present. As he ascended from deep sleep, he reached a plateau where he wondered if he were reliving those almost fifty years past. The pain, the emotion seemed transplanted intact with all the intensity of the first experience. Then, like a balloon slowly rising, he passed that point and knew he was dreaming. Only then did he realize that what he thought was Mr. Raymond's voice was speaking in Spanish, and when he opened his eyes he saw the stolid figure of Luis Gomez.

'Que tal, Senor Rafa? You've been asleep for a long time.'

6

'You look much better,' Gomez said. 'La turista es muy malo. Very bad. I once got it when I went to Los Angeles. They say it's the food. Or the water. Whatever, I felt like my life's blood had been drained from me.'

Even the merest nod seemd to require extra effort. 'I think I'll be all right now,' Jose said. 'It's like I've been away on a long trip.'

'Well, senor. I don't like to tire you. But when you're ready, I'm at your service. Just telephone me. Now I'll be on my way.'

Two days later Jose had heard Gomez's proposal. He had nothing to sell but time, Gomez said. By the hour or by the day. And the use of a nice new Chevrolet for passing the time. Day or night. Wherever one wanted. At the bull fights. The opera (he pronounced it 'hopera'). Xochimilco. To the pyramids. Or Taxco. The senor had but to say where. A geneologist, Jose kept repeating. Then back to the litany of sights of interest to tourists. Chapultepec Palace. The Plaza of the Three Cultures. The University. The Shrine of Guadalupe.

'A geneologist,' Jose insisted. 'Like—someone from the museum, where I met you. There must be dozens of men in there who could help me.'

'A professor you want?'

'A professor.'

With a shrug, Gomez acquiesced. 'Hire me by the day, and I'll find you a professor.'

'Tomorrow morning then. Early.'

When Jose replaced the telephone receiver, the absurdity of it stuck its tongue out at him. Here he was twenty-five hundred miles from home. On a wild goose chase prompted by misinformation from a born liar who charged him three hundred dollars for the lies. Now he had hired a tourist guide to find a Mexican geneologist who would help him.

He didn't know whether to laugh or cry. He dropped onto the bed and stared at the ceiling. Madness, he thought, shaking his head. The knife edge of madness. It had been madness to begin with, rushing off to a foreign country to find himself. Who was this other self whom he had lived with for sixty-five years? A counterfeit who could only be redeemed by the coin of the realm found in another country? Leaving home without word, like an inmate absenting himself from jail. Had he been running *from* or running *to*?

Yet the passion, the need to hunt were there. An almost raging compulsion that would surely drive him mad if he did not follow it out. Madness to start. Madness to *not* start. Madness to go on. Madness to give up. Follow the madness of your choice. If one finds—Eureka! If one doesn't find, at least one tried. And one was still mad, all the same.

Jose closed his eyes and conjured the image of his wife. The other half of him that he could not meet on equal terms until he had played out his search and found that missing piece of himself. Her face looked at him questioningly—her mouth uncertain whether to smile or not. Jose smiled, and she smiled back.

The Chevrolet drove through the busy city streets out Insurgentes North. Gomez steered a leisurely pace, following traffic with a stoic calm that contrasted with the frantic honking of horns that they had left behind nearer the central city.

'That's Guadalupe up ahead,' Gomez said. 'Have you seen the shrine?'

'No.'

'Would you like me to stop? Would you like to see it?' No answer. 'Perhaps, senor, you are not a Catholic.' Still no response. Jose stared out the side window, eyes blank, as if he looked but saw nothing. 'It doesn't matter, senor. I'm no Catholic myself. I'm free of all that superstition. Those priests. Robbing us blind. Until the government had to take over. Took everything away from the Church. Made it the property of the state. That was in the 1920's.

'Si, senor. If fear and superstition keep you under their thumb, they can steal your very life and convince you that it's for the glory of God. Look up there.' He pointed up the hill behind the Basilica of Guadalupe. 'Talk about superstition. The story of Juan Diego and the Virgin is just that. See that hill? Tepeyac it's called. Where the supposed miracle took place. The miracle that made Catholics out of so many Indians. Well. Tepeyac used to be an old Aztec worshipping place. A sanctuary for Tonantzin, goddess of fertility. And the Catolicos claimed it for their own. With their humble Indian, Juan Diego, and their dark skinned little Indian Virgin of Guadalupe.

'Well, senor. More Spanish tricks. If we Mexicans had been green, they would have given us a green virgin. They not only raped our bodies, but also our souls. So this poor Indian. This humble, ignorant man. He was their dupe.

'One morning Juan Diego was going to mass. Personally, I think he had just come from a cantina. He passed by the hill—up there. The sounds of music came from the sky. Too much pulque if you ask me. A rainbow shone above a light on the ground. Who could imagine such things on this God forsaken hill? Frightened and curious, he walked toward the light. 'Come closer,' a lady said. 'I am the Virgin Mary. It is my wish that a church be built here.' So there it was. The second chinga. The first was Cortez. When we were betrayed by the Aztec woman, Malinche. Now the second. Betrayed to the church by another woman. Hijos de la chingada. First they take the balls from your body, then they take the balls from your soul.

'The Indian ran to the Bishop. Like all men in power, the Bishop did not believe his ignorant subject. Or pretended not to. "Go back to the hill for proof," he said. And he secretly sent two flunkeys to follow Juan Diego, but he disappeared from their view. Again the Indian saw the lady. She sent him up the hill to pick roses. Roses. In December yet. The man was a monumental drunk. When Juan Diego came back she touched them and then sent him to the Bishop, carrying the flowers in his mantle. When the Bishop opened the mantle, there was a figure of the Virgin painted on it. Or so the story goes. A painting such as an ignorant Indian had never seen, and certainly could not have painted. Like the Madonnas of the best European artists of history. And there were no painters like that in Mexico. Not in 1531. I think the Bishop faked the whole thing; brought the painting from Spain; convinced the dumb Indian that he had really seen something. I don't believe in miracles.

'Anyway, they built a chapel here. Then later the Basilica. And the painting hangs in the church, above the high altar. The Indians who gave up their Aztec gods walk barefoot for hundreds of miles, crawling across the stones to the altar on their knees. As superstitious as ever. Trading one god for another.'

Jose had leaned back, listening distractedly. As the car slowed to park he could see the crowds moving across the plaza about the church—some toward, others away from the entrance, like ants scurrying about their anthill.

Gomez' story puzzled Jose, but he did not have the energy, the focus to question. Where did the roses come from? he thought. Alighting from the car, he mumbled in embarrassment at the non-believing chauffeur, 'I'll just be a minute.' Then he followed the crowd toward the basilica. After a momentary glance at the steps that rose up the hill of Tepeyac, Jose instead turned around the corner of the church to the front entrance. With a surreptitious pat at his wallet, he cautiously moved into the building.

The church was packed—not with gringo tourists, although there were a few—but with the faithful. Wrinkled, mahogany faces. Calloused, dusty feet slipped into crude sandals. Jose dipped his fingers into the holy water font, staring incredulously at the family on their knees in the center aisle. Palms clasped. The whisper of prayer as they moved on their knees to the front altar.

No wonder four hundred Spaniards toppled the empire, he thought.

From behind came the sibilant murmuring of what must have been prayer, though the language may have been ancient Aztec for all Jose could understand. He rose, made another sign of the cross, and walked past the Indian family still inching their way on their knees to the altar. Jose disapproved of their childlike lack of self-awareness, and their hissing lips reminded him painfully of the black-garbed viejitas in New Mexico—like his mother.

Jose moved down the aisle to the altar. High up he could see the golden frame holding the miraculous painting. It was distant and therefore small, so what he poorly saw of the painting was fleshed out by his memory of countless reproductions.

He knelt at the altar rail, made the sign of the cross, and silently whispered a Hail Mary. So different from the little church in Los Rafas. Here a stone monument, almost the size of a cathedral. There a tiny adobe structure. Here the splendor, the pomp, the richness of a monument endowed by the poverty-burdened millions who somehow always found another centavo for the church. There the hand-carved wooden statues, the make-do trappings of a few poor people in a poor land. Here an army of priests and helpers to carry on the business of God and the Virgin of Guadalupe. There an itinerant priest who, in Jose's boyhood, rode on horseback once a month to hear confessions and celebrate mass. From these poor Indians earthly glories to God. From the poor Spanish New Mexicans pride and poverty.

All wrong, Jose thought. All wrong. We Spanish beat them. We were conquerors. Yet look what happened. Our institutions won, but our people lost.

Disconcerted, he brushed quickly past the worshippers in the aisle and through the exit. It was as if the house of God had mocked him. Briskly he aimed himself at the parked Chevrolet, while Gomez peeled himself from a nearby group of drivers casually smoking and talking.

'Are you ready, senor?'

Jose seated himself in the car. 'Senor Gomez.' Uplifted eyes reflected in the rear view mirror. 'You say that you are not a Catholic and that Aztec gods are just superstitions. Tell me. What is your heritage? Isn't it Spanish?'

'No, senor.'

'Indian then?'

'No, senor!'

'Then what?'

'Neither, senor. I am a Mexican!' For emphasis Gomez stomped on the accelerator and the car shot along the highway that led to Teotihuacan with its pyramids.

44

Gomez stood at the edge of the highway beside the automobile whose hood was up as a signal of distress. 'There'll be someone along in a few minutes, senor.'

Jose sank back onto the seat and closed his eyes. Why shouldn't the damned car break down? Everything else in this manana country did. Some morning, he was sure, he would open his eyes and find that the sun had not risen. Manana. He hoped he would not have to wait until manana for a beer. He was thirsty.

A prolonged squeal of brakes. Gomez ambled to the driver's side of the limousine. From the distance their exchange was but a Spanish murmur. Then Gomez ambled back to Jose. 'A tour,' he explained. 'They have room to take us to the next town. I can phone for help from there.'

In the United States the next town would have been an intersection with a gasoline station warily facing a general store. Here there were anonymous adobe hovels, dirt roads, and scrawny chickens. After Gomez had made his telephone call, he stood with polite, apologetic hesitancy while he explained to Jose. 'We could wait outside in the shade of that little store. I don't think you'd want to go to the cantina. It's not for gentlemen like you, senor.'

'I don't care.'

With a shrug, Gomez led the way through the screen door that hung askew, gaping holes leaving large passageways for flies. The single small room looked as if it had once been someone's home. There were a few small tables, no bar, and one of the men at a table rose when they entered. The two men who had stayed seated turned and looked impassively at them. In a corner another man sat on the earthen floor, leaning against the wall, asleep.

Without seeming to, Gomez looked cautiously into all corners of the room. The bartender looked at Jose, then blinked in recognition at Gomez. 'Regulars,' he said in an undertone. 'Old friends.'

The bottles were fished out from a battered metal container, dripping with moisture. Lukewarm, but satisfactory under the

45

circumstances. Gomez sat so that he could watch the door as well as the cantina. He spoke in an undertone. 'We should quietly have our cerveza, senor, and then go. Some very bad hombres frequent places like this.'

'But that one man is asleep, and the other two are regulars.'

'Regular what? See the one on the right? There's a pistola in his belt. There are some places where they would shoot you for the clothes on your back.'

'Mi cabeza!' one of the Mexicans groaned.

'But you're here with me,' Jose said.

Gomez flashed him a grim smile. 'Clothes enough for two.'

The sleeping man snorted, shaking his head at a fly. Jose swallowed his beer more quickly, his eyes constantly moving with nervous fear. The inside of the cantina was familiar. Not so much its appearance. Perhaps a little of the people there. Mostly, though, the mood. A furtive sense of secrecy. Of violence. Of sin. It had been a little cantina like this where his Uncle Pio had been shot. In Los Rafas. An argument about la politica. In a time when most New Mexicans packed a pistol.

But then it wasn't his Uncle Pio that he was really remembering. The Mexican at the table groaned again, an incomprehensible cursing at some affliction of life. The voice, the tone, again the mood—took Jose back. Not the events. The events had been different. But nonetheless he remembered himself at fifteen with his cousin, Herminio. Racing across the fields at night until they had crossed the irrigation ditch and passed across the clearing sheltered by the huge cottonwood trees. The light from the shaded cantina window was dim in this darkest of nights. They were quiet, walking that last hundred yards slowly, wondering who might be there tonight. If there were no one, at least not their fathers or uncles or brothers or cousins, the proprietor would sell them a beer that they could take out into the fields and drink, sitting in the dark against the trunk of a tree.

They sidled against the adobe wall, speaking to each other in whispers. They were by the window now. 'Herminio. Can you see inside?' Herminio doubled over in silent, convulsive laughter. Jose shook by the shoulder. 'Hey, loco. What do you see?'

The words came out in sputtered gasps, like bursts of silent bullets. 'You... better... not... look... man.' After a crazy statement like that, what could Jose do but step to the window to see what was so funny. Herminio leaned against him to push him away. 'No... man. No.' But, caught up by another spasm of laughter, Herminio slid off Jose and pitched over onto the ground, clasping his sides as the laughter grew louder.

'Shut up! They'll hear you.' Then quickly, Jose stepped to the window and stared through the small crack between the curtains. A dark shadow inside lifted a curtain, and Jose found himself staring past the face on the other side of the window at his father slouched at a corner table. Papa's hair was hanging over his eyes which even from this distance looked slightly crossed. One hand grasped a glass as if for support, while the other was out of sight, the work shirt sleeve disappearing up under the skirts of the smiling, over rouged, dark-skinned—she could only have been a puta.

Jose turned in anger at the prostrate Herminio, kicked him hard in the rump, and ran off into the darkness towards the ditch.

'Mi cabeza!' The drunken shout again from the other table. 'Que dolor!' Then the two men lapsed into undertones of pain and consolation.

No, Jose thought sadly. That cantina of his youth hadn't been exactly like this. He had hated his father back then. But with the passage of years his tolerance had blossomed from the hard, bitter seed of hate. Who knows? Maybe papa had had a reason.

Again the groan from the table. Even the man asleep on the floor blinked open his eyes and looked about in surprise. Gomez sighed as the bartender walked over to the two men, offering a small bottle. The conversation was low and rapid so that Jose turned to Gomez with a questioning look.

'Aspirina,' Gomez said. 'But the man says no. He's tried aspirina before. It doesn't work. Neither does whiskey, but whiskey tastes better. He says he has the chingada of all headaches. The grandfather-chingada of all headaches. A real Mexican headache. And nothing can cure it.'

47

The drunk started to cry now, while the bartender went back to the corner and sat on a wooden chair alongside the metal beer container. He nodded toward Gomez who shook his head. The bartender nodded toward Senor Headache, then circled a forefinger alongside his temple. Suddenly Senor Headache's companion began to shout.

'Day after day,' he yelled in Spanish, 'I have to put up with your infernal headache! Your incurable headache! The devil with your headache and all its offspring for a thousand years!' He leaped to his feet, leaned over, and pulled the pistola from Senor Headache's belt. 'I'll cure your headache for you!'

The shot echoed like a cannon in the small room. Jose looked away, but not in time to avoid seeing Senor Headache's headache torn off by the bullet that hit the sleeping man in the leg. Just as Jose started to vomit, he heard Gomez gasp, 'Jesus Christo!' Then Gomez dragged him wretching from the cantina.

'That man—' Jose started to say.

'One man is dead, and the bartender will tend to the wounded one. If he doesn't get shot.'

'But the policia—'

'They can take care of it without us, senor.'

They crossed the dirt road quickly, moving toward the highway, while heads popped out of the adobe hovels. 'That way,' Gomez pointed. 'Maybe we can meet the car that's coming for us.'

'Not so fast,' Jose said. He felt weak, almost to the point of faintness. 'If I make it to a car, I want to be taken back to the hotel.'

A backward glance showed the headache doctor outside of the cantina, the pistol hanging down in his limp hand, while several people from the village surrounded him. 'Ay Mejico,' Gomez sighed. 'Hijos de la chingada.'

7

Death in any language would have been a shock to Jose. But the cantina compounded the shock. It awoke unpleasant memories of his father who had recently passed away. Then that purely Mexican method of curing a headache with a bullet. Every edition of the daily papers was scanned for news about the murder. For two days he acutely sensed the presence of a particular stranger almost everywhere he went. One night he sat up sleepless, waiting for a knock by the undercover policeman who he was certain had been following him. The knock never came. Imagination, he tried to convince himself. But he didn't want another such night, so he changed hotels before breakfast, moving from the downtown area closer toward Chapultepec Park.

The first night, like every night in a new bed, was a restless one. In his dreams he was on an endless search—seeking, asking, but never finding. For the longest time he wandered about the Mexican pyramids. Even though he had not yet seen them, they stood out vividly in his dreams. The Pyramid of the Sun and the Pyramid of the Moon. He was on a treadmill that ran along the courtyard leading from one to the other, when a voice—the wind—whispered to him, 'Climb to the top of the Pyramid of the Sun. You can see everything from there.'

At first Jose thought that there was a mistake. These were the steps leading up the hill of Tepeyec where Juan Diego had seen the Virgin. Then the treadmill lurched into motion like an escalator, moving him closer to the steps which now he could see more clearly. They were high, formed of stone, and he stepped off the escalator and started to climb. It was a long way up, and he stopped every few steps to catch his breath and check his pulse.

The view from the top was spectacular. Before him spread the Valley of Mexico. There, basked in a halo of sunlight, was the jewel-like Shrine of Guadalupe. It shone white in his dream, like a decoration made of confectioner's sugar ready to place on a wedding cake. The bride and groom were a brown-sugared Juan Diego with his white-garbed, brown-faced Virgin.

The adobe village to the left was a reincarnation of the Los Rafas of his boyhood. From behind the village came the intermittent roar of a crowd, like at a bullfight. And slowly along the dirt road marched a procession that at first looked like tiny moving specks approaching. Jose sat on the stone top and watched the specks grow larger and larger. Now, within range of his eyesight, they took form.

They were dressed in loin cloths, with cotton capes tied around their throats and flowing over their shoulders. At the head was an Aztec priest, wearing a mask that was an open-mouthed giant serpent and whose cape was stitched of serpent skin. Six men bore a litter whose rectangular burden was woven with flowers. Following the priest and the litter were torchbearers. They moved in eery silence, and as they came closer, the rustle of their capes was like the wind that had spoken to him earlier. It spoke again, though the words were indistinct, and he knew that he had to climb down and greet the procession.

The procession had turned onto the walkway alongside the Pyramid of the Moon, and as Jose descended, it disappeared from his view. Then, as he walked along the broad path, the Aztec priest emerged from behind a corner, turning towards him. Now that the procession was closer, the flowers on the litter formed a pattern. Jose felt as if he had turned to ice when he saw the multi-colored, miniature skulls grinning at him in the flowered splendor.

It was too late to turn and run. The priest had already seen him, and though the stoic Indian face remained impassive, Jose sensed the flicker of acknowledgement. So Jose continued. Slower. Hoping—as in that silly conundrum, that if he only went half the distance during each successive interval of time, he would never actually get there because he would always be half the distance away. He needn't have worried. The procession stopped, and he found himself staring into the questioning face of the priest.

'What is that?' Jose's ghostly voice was followed by the pointing of his trembling hand.

The bearers lowered the litter to the ground, and the priest nodded his stoic, serpent head for Jose to approach. A group of torchbearers half-circled the litter while two bearers drew back a curtain of flowers and lifted the lid on the box inside. Jose, against every screaming nerve in his body, strained forward and leaned over the litter.

He felt as if his heart had stopped. Until now, Jose had not recognized the box as a coffin. When he leaned forward to peer in, he had a terrifying foreboding of what he would see. He was right. There, decked in Aztec loin cloth with a headdress of tiny wilted flowers forming numerous grinning skulls—was himself.

A soundless scream vibrated through his throat, and he fought himself awake—drenched in perspiration, his heart pounding.

That very morning he cancelled his trip to the pyramids and made hurried arrangements to fly to Spain. Mexico was not for him. This was the wrong place. The hell with the missing links in Mexico. To Spain! To the beginnings of the exploration of the Indies. And of himself.

8

It seemed as if Theresa has always been married—always part of Jose's life as he had always been a part of hers. Had she been born married? Sometimes it seemed so. Through sickness and health. From poorer to poor. Till death do us part.

They had met at a baille in Old Town Social Hall. How many years ago? Too many. Theresa had been sixteen. Her education completed—eighth grade. And working as a domestic for the Harold Johnsons. At least she had been until that Friday. Until she had been fired. She remembered that too well. It had been because of those cats, Bootsy and Felix. Fat, sleek, shiny furred, pink tongued felines whose yellow eyes watched her slyly as she helped in the kitchen.

Theresa had hated those cats. Sassy, spoiled things who purred like racing engines when Mrs. Johnson was around, then spat like tigers when the patrona left.

For weeks she had watched those furry ogres dine—not gobble, or even eat—but dine like feline caricatures of millionaires she saw in the movies or in newspaper cartoons. Fat cats, indeed! With bits of liver and fresh fish served in China bowls fit for a Mandarin prince. No frijoles in those bowls. Nor bits of dry, two-day old tortilla. Not for Bootsy and Felix.

What upset her most, though, was not the liver or beef or trout, but the tuna. Bright tin cans whose opened lids yielded the flaky, almost white fish soaking in oil. She loved tuna, yet her family could seldom afford it. So when she saw the greedy Bootsy and Felix sharing an entire can between them, she was furious.

That Friday Theresa had been eating a late lunch of Johnson leftovers while the cats sat on the kitchen counter watching her with disdain. An unopened tin of tuna for tonight's dinner lay beside them. Theresa's glance went from the pink tongues barely protruding from whisker-bordered mouths to the shiny tin. Why not? she thought. She took her half-finished plate and scraped portions into the two cats' dishes. Then she dropped the can of tuna into the pocket of her apron.

'There gatitos,' she mewed sarcastically. 'Some frijolitos so you can learn to fart in Spanish.'

It was not until late in the afternoon, when Theresa was finishing the laundry, that Mrs. Johnson sashayed in. 'Bootsey. Felix. How are my pussies? Did Theresa feed you your dinnies already?'

'Yes, Mrs. Johnson,' Theresa answered.

'How nice.' Mrs. Johnson continued to speak to the cats in her baby-talk falsetto. 'Did all the shirts get ironed, Felix?'

'Yes, Mrs. Johnson.'

'And the towels and tablecloths. We mustn't forget the towels and the tablecloths, must we, Bootsy?'

'No, Mrs. Johnson.'

On it went. Mrs. Johnson fussing and pampering her cats while Theresa was the voice for three: Bootsy, Felix, and herself. Finally, with an exasperated sigh, Theresa took off her apron and tossed it at a kitchen chair. She had forgotten the tin in the pocket; the apron hit the back of the chair with a klunk and dropped heavily onto the floor. Mrs. Johnson, Bootsy, and Felix turned, startled, and three pairs of eyes stared as the can of tuna lit on its side and rolled out of the apron pocket across the kitchen floor.

It was not necessary for anyone to say, 'You're fired!' Perhaps it had been Felix who had mewed it. Certainly Mrs. Johnson never spoke directly to Theresa. At any rate, humiliated, Theresa had fled, not needing the superfluous words to send her forever from the Johnson household.

She had been crying quietly in the room she shared when her sister, Cecilia, rushed in. 'What's the matter?' she asked. 'Did the old man smack you again?'

Theresa shook her head and hissed the story out. 'I'll help you go strangle those cats,' Cecilia said. 'You'll find a better job. That old Mrs. Johnson can't talk to anything but animals anyway.'

'But mama and papa. They'll really be angry when they find out.'

'Don't tell them.'

'Until payday when they put their hands out and get nothing but the feel of a moist palm.'

'Maybe you'll find another job by then. A better job.'

'Yes,' Theresa said. 'Another job.' But then she thought about it some more while Cecilia was changing into her good dress, and the tears started again.

'Oh, come on,' Cecilia said. 'Crying won't help now. Why don't you come to the dance with us? Over at Old Town. You've never been to a dance at Old Town.'

'Mama won't let me.'

'She doesn't have to know.'

'Are Priscilla and Angie going?' These were her other two sisters.

'No. And I won't tell them.'

Quickly, Theresa borrowed two pillows from Priscilla's and Angie's beds and stuffed them under the covers of her own bed, patting them into shape. She went into the kitchen to say good-night to her mama and papa, then came back into the room and quickly changed into her good dress, and climbed out the window. She could hear the loud good night as Cecilia left through the front door. Theresa waited for her in the alley.

After they had arrived at the Hall, Cecilia had gone off to gossip with some friends, leaving Theresa alone. Shy, she withdrew into herself as she watched. Many of them seemed so much older. The aroma of bootleg hootch tainted the air, and here and there she saw a 'fast' girl puffing at a cigarette.

A few young men, as shy as herself, asked her to dance, then turned away almost in relief as she shook her head. Another young man kept walking past her, progressing from interested glance to smile to wink, his manner more free as he walked from wherever he nipped at his hip flask to where she stood demurely against the wall.

Finally he staggered up to her, and Theresa turned her face from his breath as he spoke. 'How about it?' he asked, motioning toward the dance floor.

'No thank you.'

'Don't think I'm good enough for you, eh? Just because you look like an Anglo. I'm too dark for you, isn't that it? A New Mexico farmer isn't good enough for you? Goddamn it—'

'No,' she said, trying to break through the avalanche of words that seemed to feed on itself. 'That isn't what I said.'

'—from Los Martinez. Good people. As good as you. Better. I got my pride. We're just as good as you. Who the hell are you anyway?'

'Please—'

By this time a small crowd had gathered, several other young men smelling of alcohol flanking the angry young man from Los Martinez.

'Leave her alone!' Theresa turned with relief toward the voice just behind her. He was a short young man, handsome in a dark, strange way with a large Spanish face and piercing dark eyebrows. He was better dressed than most of the others, a cap perched stylishly on his head and a buttoned jacket that was almost formal in this place.

The young man from Los Martinez turned in mid-sentence at this new outrage. 'Leave her alone? What do you mean leave her alone? What business is that of yours? I'll do whatever I Goddamn well please, and no sonofabitch from Los Rafas is going to tell me a thing!'

54

Theresa did not see who threw the first punch. It seemed that half the dance floor had emptied to crowd around them when that blow landed. 'Pelea!' someone shouted. 'Fight!' A girl's scream punctuated the hubbub. Then bedlam. Someone shoved her so she hit the wall hard. The sound of blows was lubricated by curses.

A strong hand gripped Theresa's shoulder and pushed her down. She resisted with the uncommon strength of fear. 'It's me.' She felt the moist breath of the words on her ear. It was her defender from Los Rafas, who carefully removed his cap, tipping it in a brief, short, gallant way, then folding it and pushing it into the rear pocket of his trousers. 'If we duck down,' he whispered, 'we can crawl out from this mob.'

Down they went until hands and knees were on the dance floor. He motioned toward her with his head, then led the way through the tangle of legs and bodies while the fight raged on above them. When they were clear of the crowd, he took her hand and dragged her running through the exit, not stopping until they had passed San Felipe church and were out of sight of the Hall.

'Whew,' he said, 'that was close.' Then he started to laugh as if it had all been a big joke.

Theresa could not bring herself to laugh nor even smile. 'Thank God,' she said. 'He was really terrible.'

'What's your name?'

'Theresa. Theresa Maria Mathilda Trujillo.'

'Jose Hernando Rafa. At your service.' The upper part of his body leaned toward her ever so slightly, with a formality at which she might have laughed at another time. Under the circumstances the austere politeness was ingratiating. 'May I take you home? I have a car.' He nodded down the dark country road, where, in the darkness, she could barely see the outline of a little roadster under the protecting branches of a huge cottonwood tree.

'My sister—' she had started to say. But then again that strong hand, this time just above her elbow, propelled her toward the roadster. Jose had not heard her, and she thought: My sister can take care of herself.

'There. Over at the next crossroad will be fine.' She was not going to let him take her all the way home. He, with his nice clothes and car and fine manners. Not to the little mud barrio by the river. Los Rafas was farm country. Families that owned their own land. Here the little adobe houses were clustered close together, with small corrals for a few chickens and a goat—but no land. Here men worked on other men's land.

'I'd be glad to take you right to your door. A gentleman could do no less.'

'No,' she said, shaking her head. She alighted from the car and headed down the dark country road. 'Goodnight, Jose.'

Theresa started to run as soon as she was out of sight. 'Goodnight, Cinderella.' The auto horn a-oo-gahed at her. 'When will I see you again?' came the shout.

'Saturday?' she shouted back.

'After supper. Eight o'clock. I'll be here.'

'Eight o'clock.'

'Adios, Cinderella.'

She ran quickly, before the prince could see her adobe castle where the unemployed housemaid took off her shoes before she climbed silently through the window into the room she shared with her three sisters.

9

Sneaking out the bedroom window to meet Jose had been exciting. Theresa would look for the parked roadster under the trees. If Jose were late, she drew back in the shadows until she saw the approaching automobile. It was summer and still light late into the evening, so she waited in hiding, watching carefully all who passed. Perhaps her mother on the way to the store. Or her father weaving home from a cantina. Or any of her three sisters or three brothers, off to liaisons of their own.

Even as the summer drew to a close, she still did not let Jose take her home. Her mother would not let her date boys. Her father was mean and drank and picked fights with her older sisters' boy friends. It had taken her weeks to find another job, and to be doing anything as frivolous as dating while not bringing home her share of money was a sin of the most grievous kind.

'Then come home with me,' Jose said one evening. 'Meet my family. Summer is almost gone and soon it will be too late.'

The significance of what 'too late' might mean passed by her. What she did know was that he wanted to introduce her to his parents. While the replacement of the horse by the automobile sounded the death knell of many of the old ways, too much custom had been entrenched over some three centuries for some changes to come any way but grudgingly. It was the custom for a Hispano young man and his parents to pay a call on the girl's family as a preliminary to engagement. Theresa visiting Jose's family might not be the custom, but it was close enough that she saw it as significant.

The next Sunday she told her mother that she had been invited to dinner at a girl friend's house. Mama had looked quietly, thoughtfully, before she nodded—perhaps not wanting to know more than that. Theresa had been too concerned with her own desires to sense that mama knew something.

She had run to the crossroad where Jose would pick her up. He loves me, she thought to herself. He wants me more than anything in the world. He's so handsome and so smart. Already he and his brother own a car, and he dresses so nice. I'm going to be happy.

Even the few minutes that Jose had been late did not bother her tonight. Her excitement overrode her natural impatience. In her exuberance, her sureness, she stood boldly on the side of the road, not caring who saw her.

When she saw the little roadster approaching, she felt as if she could fly to meet it. She could fly to Los Rafas propelled by sheer joy. The jaunty horn signalled her, and behind the wheel, his cap pulled straight above his brows, sat the serious looking Jose.

Oh, joy, she thought. Tonight he'll be mine. And I'll be his. Forever.

Jose reached across the seat and opened the door. She barely sensed his serious manner. Brushed it aside with the quick thought that this was an important occasion and therefore serious. Theresa kissed him lightly on the cheek, and he rubbed it in alarm.

The car wheeled around and headed back north along the paved street. Past the center of town toward stretches of open country. Left at the dirt Los Rafas Road, past the fields whose growing corn you could smell with their barb wired fences that divided road from field. Then they bumped over the rise above the main irrigation ditch to park under the shelter of trees in front of the adobe house.

Theresa stared hard at the house, hoping to see what secrets it must hold that would foretell her future. It was a typical New Mexico house, flat, dirt, few windows, but larger than her own house and those of her neighbors. West of the house was an apple orchard. Behind, to the north, were fields that ran far, far back. With closer, the corral with its animals.

'How much land you have,' she said.

'We owned more once. Most of Los Rafas.'

'You must be rich.'

Jose smiled and led her to the door. There were three brothers and three sisters, Theresa already knew that. Of Tomas, the oldest brother, she had heard much. Tomas was Jose's favorite, his counsellor and champion, who had been gassed in the war. A government pension had helped the ambitious Tomas set himself up in business as a carpenter and contractor. Then, in order of age, Eufemia, Carlos, Gregoria, the eighteen-year old Juana, and the youngest Rafa, the eight-year old Dandy.

With the oldest brothers and sisters married, only Juana and Dandy would be home with Senor y Senora Rafa.

There was no living room in the adobe house. They stepped into a room that once served as a bedroom, with a small bed pushed into one corner and a rocking chair in the middle. Then they passed into another similar room, then one more before they came into the large kitchen.

The house was silent, and Theresa's nervous laughter seemed to echo monstrously through the adobe interior. She was still laughing when they turned into the kitchen. Her laughter ceased abruptly, the silence hanging wretchedly as she blinked in dismay at the full room. They must have all been there. The two older brothers with their wives. The two older sisters with their husbands. The young Juana and the boy, Daniel. Senor y Senora Rafa. And another older couple. No doubt Jose's madrina y padrino, his Godparents.

'Well,' Senora Rafa said. 'So this is the girl.'

Somehow Theresa had endured through dinner. She could not recall seeing anyone else eat, and somehow each bite seemed like a monument chiseled in stone. It was as if they all sat around the theatre where tonight's performance was Theresa eating. She was intimidated by the first passing of the plate piled high with flour tortillas. The roasted ears of corn stared at her with malice from the platter. Then Juana set a huge platter with a beefsteak in front of her. It was a monstrous piece of meat. Big enough for several Theresas.

'Go ahead,' Jose whispered.

All eyes were on her. Oh, Lord, she thought. Do I have to eat all of that by myself? The Lord did not answer. Only fifteen pairs of non-committal eyes as she looked around the huge, crowded table. Self-consciously Theresa cut a small piece from a corner of the steak. She was about to lift the piece to her mouth when she looked up. They were still watching. Only now in a different way. The jaws of a few moved ever so slightly followed by silent swallows. Senor Rafa stared impatiently across the table and grasped his plate as if to pass it.

'Isn't she going to give us any?' Dandy whispered.

'Shut your mouth,' Senora Rafa whispered back.

Theresa turned the fork and inspected the cut side of the small piece of steak. 'It looks cooked just right,' she said. Her voice faltered, and her hand trembled as she thought of how close she had come. 'Do you have a bigger knife?'

'Juana! You forgot the carving knife. Stupid girl,' Senora Rafa said.

Still trembling, Theresa carved and served. After that it could get no worse. She ate in silence while the talk whirled about her like a tornado. She answered their questions with a timid yes or no or a weak smile. By dessert she had sufficiently regained her composure to notice that the empanadas were fresh baked. Then came coffee. And finally the men left, out the screened porch to the back where they perched under a tall cottonwood tree. Light was fading slowly, and the murmur of their voices drifted to the kitchen where the women remained.

'Tell me, honey,' Euphemia asked, 'how old are you?'

Before Theresa could answer, Senora Rafa stared through her, saying, 'So this is the girl.'

'Sixteen,' Theresa said to Euphemia.

'She's younger than me,' Juana said. 'Marriage? The idea!'

'So you're the girl.' Senora Rafa spoke directly to her now.

One of the sisters-in-law smiled, the only smile in that kitchen of frozen faces. 'You're very pretty,' she said. 'Such nice fair skin. Like real Spanish.'

'Do you know,' Senora Rafa said, 'that your mother is your best friend?' The way she said the words and the resulting silence were ominous. Theresa knew that the gauntlet had been hurled. 'I am Jose's best friend. Isn't that right, girls?'

Gabble. Gabble. Gabble. Si, mama. Si. Si. Like a gaggle of geese agreeing with a fox.

'When your mother is your best friend, the wisest thing you can do is listen to your mother.'

'You listen, honey,' Eufemia said.

Theresa felt the anger swell up in her. These frozen faced old hens blazed their eyes at her like a circle of searchlights. If your mother is your best friend, she thought, she should be talking to her own mother—not to her boyfriend's.

'Jose will be going back to school in two weeks,' the Senora continued. 'To the teacher's school.' Her voice trailed off. The other words need not be said: He won't have time for you. 'He is a bright boy. A very smart boy. Senor Rafa has his two older sons. One of them will be a farmer. But Jose will not be a farmer. There isn't enough land for more than one farmer. And the world is changing. Jose will be something different. A teacher. Everyone respects a teacher. So he has to go back to school.'

'I see.'

'He has finished the high school. Nobody else from our family ever finished the high school.' The daughters nodded quickly, listening with respect to their best friend. 'Now he goes to the Normal school, to learn to be a teacher. He will have to work hard in the Anglo college. He will only have time for work.'

'I see.'

'Tell me, young lady. What school do you go to?'

If Theresa hadn't already been half frightened out of her underpants, that question would have done it. Her voice was soft and barely louder than a whisper. 'I don't.'

The women looked at each other, turning like hens rustling. 'Then you've finished the high school already? At sixteen? How smart.'

Theresa wanted to cry. But then she saw the expressions on their faces and would not give them the satisfaction. Look at them. Not one of them had probably gone beyond the third grade—if they had gone to school at all. 'No,' she said. 'I quit.'

'You quit?'

'I had to work.'

'I see. And what work do you do?'

'I clean house. For a rich Anglo lady.'

Well, their smug expressions seemed to say. Do you see? This brazen child has her eye on our Jose. Well.

Yes, Theresa thought in response. At least I get money for my housework. That's better than a beating once a week with a screwing once a year for your birthday.

Theresa looked desperately through the screened porch, but the men were still talking and occasionally a phrase would drift into hearing range. Corn. Chili. Melons. Horses. The same old topics.

'And where do you live, young lady?' She told them, and once again there was that wordless rustling like the settling of hens as they exchanged glances. 'Your people are not farmers then,' continued Senora Rafa.

'My father works in the Santa Fe shops. Repairing the trains.' There was more she could have told them about her father. That he was mean. And drank too much. And that he would gladly have been a farmer if he'd had a piece of land to farm.

There was a long silence—a shifting of mood. Whatever it was that they had wanted from her they had received. Or no longer wanted. 'Would you like a cup of coffee?' Senora Rafa finally asked. Theresa shook her head. 'Thank you for coming to visit,' the Senora continued. 'I don't understand the ways of young people nowadays. In my time it would have been unthinkable for a young man to bring a girl to meet his family. It was the other way around. But then, we couldn't do that. That would mean a proposal—a marriage. And as you can see, we are not ready for that. So, daring as it is, it is better that you came here.'

I intend to marry him, Theresa said in her thoughts. And best friend though you may be, there's something even more powerful than friendship. 'Thank you for dinner,' Theresa said.

'Call your papa,' the Senora said to Juana. When the men came the women fell silent. They seemed to recede into the adobe walls, part of the fixtures, like the recessed niche for the statue of a saint, or the small basin used for washing one's hands and face. The all powerful men had entered.

'Well,' Senor Rafa said to his wife. Even that one word was enough to tell Theresa to keep her place. There was a tone of voice, the set of face—especially the hard eyes—that stamped him of the same breed as her father.

'We talked,' the Senora said.

'You told about the teachers' school?' It was as if Theresa were not even there.

'Yes.'

'Good. Then it's settled.'

Tomas turned seriously toward Theresa. 'I'm glad you understand,' he said. 'Jose is going to be a teacher, and he has to work hard.'

'Bah!' Senor Rafa spat.

'You're an intelligent young woman,' Tomas continued. 'I think you will see how right it is for you and Jose to not see each other.'

Theresa smiled, but not in acquiescence. She looked around the room at them—stern faced, lean, hard farmers—with that remnant of their Spanish forebearers' cruelty in the men and in the women that docility that came from the Indian ancestors that they would deny. 'Jose,' she said. 'Would you take me home?'

They sat quiet on the bumpy trip along the country road. Once past Los Rafas with its oppressive atmosphere, Theresa slid across the seat of the roadster and leaned into Jose. She would have him, she thought. There was no way that they could prevent her from having him. She put her arm around him and felt his body stiffen. Yes, she thought. It would be easy.

'Jose. Why don't you park somewhere so we can talk.' Easy, she thought to herself. So easy.

10

At sixteen life had been almost all illusion. Especially when it came to love—and marriage. The first illusion to go was the honeymoon. What Theresa hadn't realized until much later was that the honeymoon had been over before the wedding. On that brief passionate night that had catalyzed it all.

What had obscured it was the immense relief at how easy the seduction and the subsequent wedding had been. There probably wasn't a man in a million who wasn't seduceable once a woman made up her mind. And her family—especially her father—had surprised her. He had not beat her, which was his usual answer to everything, because of the baby she was carrying and of her good catch.

As for Jose's family, they were strangely silent. Whatever they felt and said was filtered through Jose, whose strain Theresa had overlooked in her euphoria. Only later did she realize that he had told them nothing, although her abdomen felt the blazing scrutiny of their eyes.

After the wedding at the little adobe church there had been the fiestas with the food and the crowds and the dancing and the music. At the appropriate time the bride and groom 'escaped' to their little honeymoon adobe house, with the jeering and teasing following them. It was an anticlimax. Monday morning they both arose to the reality of their lives. Theresa as a domestic for an Anglo lady. Jose to the Santa Fe shops. The honeymoon was truly over.

They had been married two months when it happened. It had been fun for two months in many ways. After a day at work she and Jose could do whatever they wanted—no parents to nag at them. They could go to the dances. Or to the movies. Or stop by the bootlegger's on the way to visit friends. Make their own home brew, which, while cheap, tasted poisonous until you had drunk enough that the taste didn't matter. Leave the beds unmade and the unwashed dishes stacked on the kitchen counter. Even stay up all night if they wanted to.

It happened one day at work. Theresa had been scrubbing the kitchen floor when a pain knifed through her, clutching her tenaciously for what seemed like minutes. Then she sensed the flow and she knew she was bleeding. Pale, frightened, Theresa told the Senora that she didn't feel well and struggled to her mother's—Jose was at the shops.

I'm going to lose the baby, Theresa thought. I'm being punished.

Her mother put her to bed and sent for the doctor. All she could remember was the pain, feeling icy cold, while her teeth chattered more from fear than from cold.

'I think she's waking now.' It was a stranger's voice, an Anglo voice.

When she opened her eyes, Theresa saw Jose standing beside the bed, his forehead and brows pinched in a worried expression. 'Cinderella,' he sighed in relief. When he leaned over to kiss her, she could see the tears in his eyes.

Behind Jose the nurse quietly moved to the other end of the ward. The adjacent bed was empty. 'How come you're not at work?' He shook his head mutely. 'How long have I been here?'

'Since yesterday.'

'I lost the baby.' In contrast to her matter of fact statement, tears flowed down Jose's cheeks. 'How long will they keep me here?'

'Just until tomorrow.'

'But the hospital? It costs money.'

'You don't have to worry about the money.'

'And my baby—' Now her tears came, the pain not physical but from loss. 'God is punishing me,' she said. 'For what I did.'

'What are you talking about?' Jose's manner was stiff, a frown furrowing his brow, but she did not notice.

'It—the baby—rejected me. It didn't want to be born through me. God took my baby away.'

'Don't be silly.' Jose's tears had stopped, and the frown on his face gave way to a look of puzzlement.

But Theresa was not even aware of him. She was trying to sort out what had happened to her. She had become pregnant because she had wanted to marry Jose Rafa. The baby had only been the means to an end. Now, with no baby, would he leave her? Would he go back to school, back to learning to be a teacher?

Her trembling hand reached out for reassurance. 'Do you hate me?' she cried.

Her fingers clutched at Jose's hand as he let go, rearing back in his chair. 'What are you talking about?' Theresa could almost hear the unspoken words: Are you crazy?

'About the baby.' She could not stem the flood of words now. 'About you not going to school. About you having to marry me. *Having* to. Not wanting to.'

'Don't be silly,' Jose said. But she could tell he was angry. Like her father. Like *his* father. Like all the men who became angry when someone—especially a woman—spoke about that which they did not want to hear.

'I want to know. Oh, Jose. I feel so bad.' Then the tears came so strong that she could speak no longer. She would try, and the words would come out a blubbering nonsense.

Through the sounds of her own tears she heard the stern voice of the Anglo nurse. 'We can't have any of that. Young man, you'll have to leave. We can't be upsetting the patient.'

After a moment it was quiet, and she fell asleep. It had hardly seemed a minute when she heard voices again—a man's and a woman's. Jose and her mother. Talking softly and intensely.

65

'I don't know what to do,' Jose was saying. 'She wasn't herself this morning. Like she was out of her head. Crazy or something.'

'It's just the sickness talking.'

'She wanted to know—if I hated her. If I really had wanted to marry her. She was out of her head. And crying. I didn't know what to do.'

'She needs to be taken care of.'

'Well, it worries me. I have to be at work at the shops. I can't miss anymore, or they'll fire me. And I can't afford a nurse. I have to go in debt for the hospital as it is.'

'If I didn't have to work, I'd help,' Theresa's mother said. 'A son is a son till he takes a wife, but a daughter's a daughter all of her life.'

'One of my sisters can come,' Jose said. 'Only they're not nurses.'

'Shhh. I think she's waking up.'

As Theresa slowly opened her eyes, she could see the shadows of afternoon through the window behind her visitors. They sat conspiratorially close, forcing smiles.

'See how nice she looks,' her mother said.

'Much better than this morning,' Jose said.

'When am I going home?'

'Tomorrow morning,' Jose said. Theresa could see the look on his face as he turned toward her mother.

While they chatted, Theresa thought of how nice it would be to be far away where it was quiet and peaceful. At her grandmother's—her Nana's—up in the mountains away from hospitals and the city and people. It was so pleasant thinking about her Nana that she closed her eyes and drifted off to sleep as her visitors continued their bright, chirpy conversation.

Early the next morning Jose took Theresa home, where her youngest sister-in-law, Juana, interrupted a flurry of house cleaning to help her to bed. But then day by day the visitors multiplied. It was like the plague descending on the little house. Why had she and Jose moved way across town from Los Rafas? There was land in Los Rafas. Didn't Jose himself own a lot adjacent to his parents' house? That would be the ideal place. Close to father. Close to mother. Close to their best friend. Where

Theresa could be looked after properly.

As if I weren't half mad already about the baby, Theresa thought. I'll go even more mad. Can you be crazier than crazy?

Yet the constant insistence continued with the almost daily stream of visitors. Brothers. Sisters. In-laws. Cousins. Messengers from Mama Rafa. If it was like this now, Theresa thought, how would it be if the family lived next door? God is not easy on me. First He took away my baby. Then He gave me a family of Rafas.

While the Rafas assaulted her life with a swirling trail of words and commotion, the baby softly touched her life in quiet moments. Would it have been a boy or a girl? A girl, she decided. With outstretched little hands like the dolls you see in store windows at Christmas time. She would cry, thinking about wanting a doll for Christmas all through her childhood and never being able to afford one. Poor little Theresa. She had been too poor to receive a visit from Santa Claus. Too poor or too wicked.

Jose would gently touch a forefinger across her tear stained cheek and ask her what was wrong. 'Nothing. I'm just thinking how happy I am.' But then she would burst into louder crying while awkwardly he tried to comfort her.

At mass one Sunday morning she looked at the statue of the Virgin holding the doll-like infant, Jesus, in her arms. Again the tears came—softly, in the midst of prayer. Blindly she wept, not seeing the glances of the little old ladies in black who raised the level of their whispered prayers to drown out her snifflings. She did not feel Jose's hand grip her arm and lead her out from the church in the middle of mass.

'I can't stand it!' she shouted at Jose as they walked into the dusty church yard. 'I don't want to go back home. I don't want Juana there. I don't want anybody. I want my Nana!'

A hurried consultation at home that morning as Theresa lay in bed crying without let up. Then the door opened cautiously, and she looked up to see Jose and her mother. 'I'll take you to your grandmother's,' he said. 'This afternoon.'

11

It was a long drive along the road that paralleled the Rio Grande River northeast toward Santa Fe. Then through Santa Fe, still going east toward the Pecos River until their car turned up the dirt road past the tiny village and a few miles north into the less inhabited part of the valley. There beside a clear stream stood the small adobe house, her Grandmother and Grandfather Baca's house. It stood isolated, yet not lonely. Man-made, yet made from the earth so that it took its rightful place among the beans, chili, and corn in the small field, and green herbs in the cared for garden.

When Theresa had been small a trip to Nana's had been a long journey. Not a few hours in an automobile but much longer in a horse drawn wagon. She did not remember when she had first come here. Perhaps when her father had been so sick and had not been able to work for many months. When all the children, she being the youngest, were sent to aunts and uncles and grandparents for temporary keeping. Whenever it had been, this uncrowded place in the foothills of the Sangre de Cristo Mountains had become as much home to her as her parents' house. It had a nesting quality of comfort and refuge; it was a retreat uncluttered by people and things, a place in which to be fed and kept warm.

Nana was not surprised to see her. Pleased, yes. But not surprised. As if it had only been yesterday that they had parted, not the more than a year since Theresa's last visit. After the initial flood of exchanging news, it settled into the peaceful quiet that she so well remembered.

Daily, Theresa would join her grandparents for breakfast—early, by kerosene lamp, before the rising sun had shone over the mountains down into the protected valley.

Then, while Tatu went into the fields by first light, or down stream where the trout were hungriest, or down the road to help a neighbor or to work at the Christian brothers retreat, Theresa would help Nana wash the dishes and sweep the house. Midmorning, when the sun was climbing and warming the valley, she would take the unpainted wooden bench outdoors and place it against the adobe wall, facing the sun.

Outdoors they would alternately sit and work in the garden. At rest, Nana would pull a sack of Bull Durham from her pocket and roll a cigarette which she would smoke distractedly while staring into space. On the third day, Theresa finally realized that they had barely spoken a word and that instead of staring toward the mountains, Nana had been quietly looking at her.

'What are you thinking, child?'

'Of how every day I know what is going to happen here. And wondering how many years you've lived like that.'

Nana laughed. 'I'm seventy-six years old, child. I was forty when your mother was born here. My mother was born here thirty years before me. And her parents before that. Back to when the Spanish first came from Mexico, following the Rio Grande north.'

Nana leaned back against the adobe wall and savored a puff from her cigarette. The wisps of smoke were like memories stirred and set free from where they had been entrapped for a long time. Theresa knew she was going to hear about the old days.

'That's how long we've lived this life,' Nana continued. 'Here, in this place. Farmers. With our corn and our beans and our chili. A cow or two. With our mother, the earth—the land the good Lord lets us use. The river. The stream. We plant. We hoe. We weed. We harvest. In between we rest, we laugh. We thank God. It seems like every day we know what is going to happen. Yes. I can see how one could say that. But it all depends on the eyes one sees with. We have more than one pair of eyes, did you know that? Our body has one pair. Our minds another. Our hearts still another. And the bigger your soul, the more of your eyes you can see with.'

Nana's eyes sparkled alertly. 'By that little plant there? See.' Carefully she pointed a gnarled finger, and Theresa watched, not seeing until a bird hopped through the foliage out into the open. 'I did not know I was going to see you today,' she said to the bird.

'Oh, Nana.'

But Nana did not seem to hear her. She reached into the pocket of her apron for a piece of flour tortilla that she crumbled into bits and tossed into the garden. 'Watch,' Nana said.

The bird hopped toward them, following the trail of crumbs. 'But it's just a bird, Nana. And not a very pretty one either.'

'Look. His left foot.'

Theresa turned her gaze downward. 'But—but he has no left foot. It's just a stump.'

'Yes. But see how he hops. How he walks. He doesn't know he doesn't have a foot. Or if he knows, he doesn't care. He goes on living the best way he can. Not like people. They *know* they don't have a foot. Or, if they have one, they imagine they don't have one.'

'Nana, I don't understand.'

'Oh, I'm just an old lady talking too much. Sometimes your grandfather and I go for days without hardly a word. Then sometimes I talk to the birds or the trees. This bird, One Foot, is an old friend whom I haven't seen for weeks. I was surprised to see him today.'

'So you don't know what's going to happen every day, is that it, Nana?'

'Child, I'm boring you.'

'No, Nana.'

Nana patted Theresa's hand and smiled. 'I'll be quick. Isn't that what young people want today? Yes,' she said. 'I really don't know what's going to happen each day. Although for generations our family has lived right here, in the valley, things have changed. Not everyday things. Like the farming and the animals. Other things.

'The first of us who came were Spanish. Farmers. It was that way for a long time. Until the Mexicans revolted from the Spanish. Then we became Mexican. That was in my grandparents' time. When my mother was a baby.

'It was about then, too, that we started to see the first Anglos. The traders and trappers. Coming across the Santa Fe Trail. But Anglos were rare even then. In all of New Mexico there was but a handful. It was mostly us. Hispanos. Speaking only Spanish like we had for generations. Farming the same farms. Living the same old ways.

'Then, when my mother was a young woman, the war. It wasn't much of a war. The Anglo came with his army and his promises and his talk of money and suddenly we were Americans. The same farm. The same ways.

'And even then things changed slow. Until the railroad. It bypassed Santa Fe. Chose Albuquerque instead. As a young woman I saw some of the changes start. Young men, whose fathers were farmers, moving to Albuquerque to work for the railroad. And now the automobile. Young people leaving their home for California. Leaving the farms. Becoming like Anglos. Grasping for money. All Anglos think about is money.

'Still, some of us stay. Nothing good can become of trying to be something you are not. God put us here for a reason. We have to be still and listen. Hear the reason and act on it.'

Theresa felt a blush warm her face. One-Foot had flown away, his belly full of tortilla crumbs. Perhaps the farm had been enough in the old days for the old people. It was not enough for her. Yet it was peaceful here, restful. And for now she needed the rest.

Nana clasped Theresa on the shoulder and kissed her cheek.

'Enough talk. The garden waits.' She stood on her old legs, shushed her apron at the chickens, and took the hoe from against the adobe wall.

The next morning as they were resting in the garden, Theresa spoke. 'Nana. Do you believe that your mother is your best friend?'

Nana removed the cigarette from her lips and held it cupped in her hand. She turned toward the girl, her lips on the verge of a smile.

'Who told you that, child?'

'Do you believe it, Nana?'

Silence. Still and warm like the rising sun, but with an edge of morning chill to it. Finally. 'No. Your mother is a good friend. The Virgin Mother is a good friend. Our mother, the earth, is a good friend. But none of them is your best friend.'

'But, Nana. A son is a son till he gets a wife. But a daughter's a daughter all of her life. Isn't that what they say?'

Nana shook her head. 'No. A mother loves her children—son or

71

daughter equally—always. But they are not really hers. They belong to themselves. Like the birds. Or the trees. Or the river. Even when they are born they are not yours. Certainly not when they grow older.'

'I don't understand,' Theresa said. 'Who is your best friend if it's not your mother?'

'God.'

'Oh, Nana.'

'And of one's human friends—well, a woman's husband is her best friend. She must obey him.'

Theresa looked away from the bright, piercing eyes set in the wrinkled skin. Theresa had seldom thought of Jose the days she had been here—only of herself. Her own pain. Her own guilt. Her own disappointment. Nana had probably never spent a day away from her husband in her entire married life. And here Theresa was, while Jose worked in the railroad shops to pay her doctor bills, to let her run away to her Nana to be taken care of like a little girl. Yes. Because of her Jose was working at a job that he found degrading, not like being the teacher that he had hoped to be. Like being a boy again and working in the hot fields while his father watched from under the shade of a tree. His father, who like the fathers of la raza back for generations was to be obeyed by his children without question—who had prodded Jose to work harder with the threat of the whip. At the shops the prod was the much needed weekly paycheck. Jose had traded one cruel master for another—the feudal Spanish 'lord' for the Anglo's money—because of her. Her best human friend. Yes. Nana was right.

'How is he, Theresa? Your husband.'

The words would not come because of her tears. Theresa could only nod her head.

'Are you here because of your young husband?'

This time a slow shaking of the head. The tears came faster now, a regular flood, but her drowned voice fought its way through. 'Oh, Nana. I'm so unhappy!'

The frail arms embraced her softly, like thin child's arms. The shrunken breast was warm, emanating a faint aroma of human sweat and moist earth tinged with tobacco smoke. It reminded

Theresa of the comforting warmth of the childhood pallet in Nana's room—where she had been shielded from the night sounds by a heavy quilt that smelled faintly of perspiration and urine.

'I've been so bad, Nana. That's why God took my baby away from me.'

'You're not bad. No one is really bad. It's just that sometimes we're ignorant.'

'No, Nana. Bad. To my husband. My best friend. To the baby I lost. To God.'

'I cannot be your confessor. There are some things one only speaks of to her priest. Or to her doctor. Or to her husband.'

'But, Nana. I want you to forgive me.'

'There's nothing to forgive. If I don't blame, how can I forgive?'

'Oh, Nana. I want to talk, and you won't listen! Why don't you listen to me?'

'All right. I'm sorry I put you off.'

So Theresa told her. Haltingly at first, because she was ashamed. Then quicker, with strength and anger. Finally slower, when her feelings had all gushed out leaving a weakness, an emptiness in their wake.

'So you see,' she said, 'You have to forgive me.'

'My dear. Like I said before. There is nothing for me to forgive. I've lived so long and seen so much that I cannot judge anymore. I cannot advise anyone about their lives. I can only tell them about me, about what I would do.'

'But what can I do?'

'If it were me, I would make a confession. Only God has the power to forgive—through his priests.' Nana took from around her neck a small bag on a string necklace. 'Here. I carry this to help me when I need help. It's earth from the Sanctuario at Chimayo. Holy dirt that heals. When I was younger and could still ride a horse, we went on a pilgrimage to the Sanctuario. Your grandfather's leg had been bothering him for so long. The horseback ride was hard on him. When we got there we said a rosary in front of the statue of the infant Jesus—the statue whose shoes wear out because the infant walks at night. Then we went into the back, into the earthen room, a hole really, where the earth is sacred. Your grandfather rolled up his trouser leg and bathed his leg in the earth. I filled this little sack for myself to wear around my neck. When we rode back it was as if his leg had grown young again, like the legs of that little statue. And this sack has stayed with me for almost twenty years.'

Theresa took the soiled string of the necklace and pulled it slowly over her head. The sack had taken the color of earth, and it smelled moist and fresh like the earth in the fields that one turned with a spade after a spring rain.

'The priest will be here Sunday,' Nana continued. 'At the church in the little village. We can walk. Early. While he's hearing confessions.'

'Yes, Nana.'

During the slow walk to the church, Theresa thought fearfully of what she would have to confess. At least she would be talking to a strange priest, one who would not recognize her voice as Father Martinez would at home.

The confession came easy to her. It was as if someone else were talking, telling of the sins they had committed. Her remorse was deeply felt, and somehow the penance did not seem adequate. Throughout the mass that followed, Theresa felt an irritation, an unrest, as if atonement required still more of her. Even the communion wafer did not still this feeling, and she watched with wonder the unperturbable faith of her grandmother and the quiet strength of her grandfather.

After mass the three of them paid their respects to neighbors before heading up the canyon toward home. It was uphill, the short cut a path that veered off from the dirt road. At the top of a rise Theresa stopped to wait for Nana and Tatu who had slowly fallen behind. A bird lit on the low branch of a tree downhill from her, the quiet fluttering of its wings drawing her eye. As it hopped onto the path, Theresa saw that one of its feet was missing—One Foot. Startled, she looked down the path at her advancing grandparents.

Beyond the two old people the clear vista ended in the little valley where the adobe church stood, hills rising behind it, fields surrounding it. Though she had trod this path a hundred times before, it was as if she were seeing it for the first time. The bird, her grandmother's friend. The two old people gently helping each other move slowly up the path. The church and its fields.

Then One Foot glided onto a low branch on the opposite side of the path. Facing her, his throat and chest swelled as his birdsong rose, its winged sweetness touching every part of the silent valley.

Theresa reached for the little sack of earth that hung around her neck. Transfixed, she stared at the view down the hill and into the valley. It seemed to leap at her as if it had a physical presence of its own apart from the surroundings. As if the surroundings were but a cardboard setting for the vivid stereoscope of the church, her grandparents, and One Foot.

A pang of fear struck her. She felt as if she might faint if she continued to stare, but the feeling of wonder was so compelling that she did not want to close her eyes. It was as if she were a light bulb that was being switched on and off by an invisible finger, a bulb pulsing with whatever gave that more than lifelike vividness to what her eyes saw. It was as if they were all one—the adobe church, the path, the two old people, the singing bird, the valley itself. As if they all throbbed with that same vibrant energy, that same vibrant life. All part of the vivid, giant bulb that shone its light bright and unyielding in response to that finger on the switch. God's finger.

Finally Theresa looked away and closed her eyes. When she opened them again the vividness had decreased, the vista had receded back into its place in the natural surroundings, and a great feeling of calm and peace came over her.

Her grandparents, puffing, had climbed those last few steps up the path alongside her. 'What is it?' Nana asked. 'Are you all right?'

Theresa nodded, still staring down the path toward the church. From behind the concealing tree-covered hill an automobile rounded the curve of the dirt road heading up the canyon. Jose!

Nana and Tatu turned as if they had heard her thoughts, then Nana turned back smiling. Silently, the three moved forward on

75

the path, faster now that they had passed the summit of the hill.

I believe, Theresa thought. And because I believe, everything will be all right.

12

Belief became the guiding word for Theresa, and it made the difficult early years of marriage more bearable. When, one by one, her married girl friends swelled up as if party balloons had been inflated at the waists of their dresses, she believed. Through three miscarriages, she believed. During the difficult times when Jose's job depressed him unbearably, Theresa believed. Throughout the interferences and maddening irritations of her in-laws, she believed. Especially the time her father-in-law and Carlos brought them plans for a house on the family property in Los Rafas as a fait accompli. Until that sudden summer when two miracles, like twin blessings, changed their lives. Jose's oldest brother, Tomas, bought the plot of land on which the family had hoped that Jose would build his house, paying generously for it, a disguised gift. With it, Tomas gave an even more generous gift— the encouragement that Jose needed to move to California. At first Theresa thought that the excitement of the move had caused her to miss her menstrual period, but as the weeks of preparation went by, she knew she was pregnant again and that this time it would come to fruition. She dared not speak to Jose. Let them make the trip to California first. There was ample time. Yet her spirits soared. It was time to strike out, to seek more. More than her parents. More than her Nana and her little mountain home. More for what she would be carrying inside for the next few months. It was time to leave home and claim a new life. California, here we come.

13

All life, Joe Rafa believed, is an education for death—for that ultimate merging with the infinite that the believer calls 'joining God.' One subspecies of believer even states that if one does not merge joyfully, consciously, truthfully, one must be born again in another form to try once more for the celestial brass ring. For immortality begins in a truthful, joyful, conscious life—resulting in the only kind of immortality mere humans can aspire to—the leaving behind with those our lives have touched, with those we have loved, a bit more of truth and joy and consciousness that thereafter can transmit itself from one generation to the next. Much like brown eyes, or straight hair, or a bulbous nose. Until every human on earth is brown-eyed, straight haired, with a beak like a cherry tomato.

The worst sin is to be born, yet not to live at all. To be unreal. And the only real thing that his father ever did, Joe thought, was to run away. The rest was shadow boxing. Throwing angry, ineffectual punches at phantasmagoria.

Ay, raza suffrida. Suffering race. The spectral shadow is but a monstrous magnification of our own selves.

Mexicanness, Joe knew, was at the root of his father's flight from life. He learned that early. During one of their annual summer trips to Albuquerque. To visit the family. Joe must have been quite young, still a small boy. Because he remembered that he had to use the outhouse in back; indoor plumbing had not been installed until World War II.

The uncles were all there at his grandmother's little adobe house. The aunts too. The women in the kitchen while the men stood or squatted under the huge cottonwood tree out by the chicken coops.

'Just let some sonofabitch call me a Mexican,' Dandy had said. 'Anglo bastard. I'll give him what for.'

'Hush,' Jose said. 'The boy.'

Dandy laughed. 'You didn't hear me, did you?' Joe shook his

head quickly.

'We always get into this,' Tomas said. 'It's tiresome. What difference does it make what someone calls you. Mexican. Spanish. American. Indian for that matter. Does it put any more beans on your plate? Or a new pair of shoes on your feet? Senseless talk.'

'Well tell me,' Dandy said. 'Are you a Mexican or aren't you?'

Tomas' face reddened, and he shifted the wad of tobacco from one cheek to the other slowly before he spat toward the tree stump where the axe was imbedded.

'Did he come from Mexico?' Jose asked.

'Hell no,' Dandy said. 'And that's exactly what I mean. How can you be a Mexican if you don't come from there?'

'Who cares?' Carlos said. He was squatting, picking up a handful of earth and letting it sift through his fingers, then picking up another handful. Of all the brothers he was the farmer; he knew the value of earth.

'Joey.' Joe had looked up to his father. 'Go play with your cousins.'

All of the uncles were looking at him now, so Joe stared at the hand-marked ground in front of his Uncle Carlos. 'They went across the fields to the ditch, and mama said I wasn't to get my clothes dirty.' Besides, he had thought, they always want to fight, and it's me who usually gets hit.

'Go,' his father said. The voice was not angry like it often was, not here in front of the uncles. But Joe knew it wasn't far from anger. Fathers did not like to be disobeyed in front of family or friends.

Reluctantly Joe walked off, turning the adobe corner of the house. He stopped, knowing he would not be seen.

'You can say who cares,' Dandy said to Carlos. 'But tell me. Who bought the fields across from you when Old Gutierrez died. Tell me that. Some rich Anglo who calls you a Mexican. Before you know it all of Los Rafas will be owned by Anglos.'

'What does that have to do with anything?' Jose asked.

'They're taking over!' Dandy's voice was almost a shout. 'And one of their weapons is what they call you. So they can steal from you and not feel guilty about it.'

'It doesn't matter what they call you. What counts is how they treat you,' Jose said.

'Bullshit! You can talk like that because you've got a job. In a Goddamned bank for all that. But that's in California. I'm talking about here. New Mexico. Do you see any of us working in a bank? Yeah. Sweeping floors. If I had a good job working in a bank they could call me anything they wanted to.'

'You ought to go back to school,' Jose said. 'A kid of seventeen's got no business bumming around doing nothing.'

'All right,' Tomas said. 'In a minute we're going to have a fight.'

'Sonofabitch!' Dandy said. 'Don't talk to me about bumming around. I'm waiting to go into the CCC.'

'Who are you calling a sonofabitch?' Jose challenged.

'All right!' Tomas interposed himself between them. Dandy leaned toward the wood pile and grasped the handle of the imbedded axe. 'Don't be a fool, Dandy,' Tomas said.

'I'm no unemployed Mexican,' Dandy said.

'If you went back to school and studied history, you'd know that,' Jose said.

'And I'm no uneducated Mexican. High school a la chingada.'

'If people were content to be farmers—like their fathers—there wouldn't be all this nonsense about high school.' Carlos did not look up as he spoke. Did not look at any of them. Still sifting dirt through his fingers into a little pile in front of where he squatted, rolling a toothpick around between his teeth.

'The world changes,' Tomas said. 'We change with it. A carpenter is a good profession. Jesus was a carpenter.'

'And a bank is a good place to work, too,' Jose said.

'Break your back in the sun,' Dandy said to Carlos. 'Only animals were meant to do that. And if our old man hadn't been out there prodding you in the ass, you wouldn't have done it either. It's just your greed for owning more land. It's nothing to do with being a farmer.'

'Some day your mouth's going to get you in bad trouble,' Carlos said. 'Anyway. What does all this have to do with being a Mexican?'

'New Mexican!' Dandy said. 'We're a new race. Not Mexican.

Not Spanish anymore. More than just American. We're New Mexicans.'

'Well. For once I agree with you,' Jose said.

'You're Goddamned right!'

Around the corner, Joe had listened, sitting against the adobe wall. What had once been shade was now sun, and the warmth made him almost as drowsy as the talk. He was confused. What was he? His father and uncles did not seem to know. Except perhaps Dandy, who everybody knew was the black sheep of the family. At seventeen. So if these grownups did not know, how could he know? For whatever they were, he was the same. And as he grew older, this same conversation seemed to repeat and repeat. Endlessly. Never resolved.

Flushed and drowsy, Joe circled the house and crept through the fields so he would not be seen. He could hear the voices of his cousins by the ditch. Laughing and talking a mixture of Spanish and English. Joe felt drawn to them. As if somehow they might give him the answer that the men could not.

'There he is,' one of them shouted. 'Junior.' They turned and watched Joe approach. There were five of them, all about the same age— some a year younger, some a year older.

'Es verdad que no puedes hablar espanol?' the oldest boy asked.

Joe flushed. Here it came. The outsider. The one who was different. When Joe did not answer, the boys elbowed one another in the ribs and smiled knowingly. The anger was hot in Joe's chest.

'Es verdad?' another continued. 'No puedes?'

'I thought you were going swimming,' he finally said. They all laughed and jeered. It was the wrong answer.

'No puedes. No puedes,' came the singsong taunt.

'Some kind of Mexican you are,' his oldest cousin said. 'Can't even speak the language.'

'It's Spanish,' Joe said. 'Not Mexican.'

'And listen to your English,' another said. 'You speak with an accent. A California Anglo accent.' The way he pronounced it it sounded like Een-gleesh.

'Whatever I am, I'm the same as you!' Joe said.

'Oh, no you're not,' they taunted. 'You're from California, and you can't speak Spanish. No puedes.'

If I don't do something soon, I'm going to cry, Joe thought. The thought of tears made him more furious. His oldest cousin, their leader, stood on the mound of dirt that rose to the ditch, where the muddy water flowed past the closed sluice gates that led to the fields. His cousin was laughing, hands on hips, rocking his head from side to side as he hurled the malicious sound of his voice down at Joe.

Joe hurled himself up the mound, lowering his head just before he hit his cousin with full force in the pit of the stomach. Together they toppled into the muddy waters, Joe grasping onto his cousin to force him down into the oozy bottom. When his head came out of the water he could hear the shouts. 'Uncle! Uncle! Junior's trying to drown Damacio.' Then down again, giving Damacio a few good licks while he still had the chance.

Strong, wiry arms pulled him from the water. When he looked up his father was frowning at his wet, muddy clothes.

'We went swimming,' Joe said.

'Wait until your mother sees you,' Jose said. He pointed toward the house, and Joe walked off, his shoes squishing, while behind he could hear Damacio blubbering. Then he heard his father's footsteps walking briskly behind. Then in undertones, 'You're going to get it now.'

I don't care, Joe thought. Damacio deserved it. And you too, he thought at his father. Because if it wasn't for you, I wouldn't have those damned Mexican cousins.

That had been one side of being in-between. Back home, in Los Angeles, was the other side. It had been a few years later. Someone in the neighborhood whom he had seen around but did not know.

One Saturday that autumn everyone else had either gone to the football game in the Coliseum to see USC play Notre Dame, or else had some other reason not to be around. Joe had wandered aimlessly to the playground, then back toward home when he hadn't seen anyone he knew.

This boy, about his own age, approached from down the block, and as he came nearer Joe could see that he was smiling at him. Joe looked away from him. 'Hey. Your name is Joe, isn't it?'

Grunt.

'I hear you got fired from your newspaper job at the Coliseum. Last week. You didn't come out to sell more papers after the third quarter.That was a dumb thing to do. It wasn't even a good game.'

Grunt. Underneath Joe could feel the heat rising.

'I could've gone today. But I couldn't have got a job.'

Mumble. Grunt.

'They got quotas. You know that? Yeah. It's not just government jobs or going to medical school and stuff like that. It's even a lousy job selling newspapers at the Coliseum.'

'Bull!' Joe moved aside to pass the boy who had stopped in front of him, but he felt the warm breath at his shoulder following.

'What's the matter? Don't you like me?'

'I don't even know you.'

'I bet you're just like the rest.'

Joe started to walk faster, but the pad of alien tennis shoes sped up to keep pace, almost as if he were a motorcycle pulling a sidecar. 'Just because I'm a Jew,' Sidecar said, 'that's why you're trying to get away from me.' Joe stopped abruptly, while the sidecar zoomed past—but only a few steps before the boy turned to face him. 'Who do you think you are to look down on me? You're nothing but a Mexican anyway.'

Joe was stunned into impotence, his fists dangling at his sides. Sensing that he had crossed some threshold, Sidecar flickered a smile. 'Tell me,' he asked confidentially, 'how does it feel to be a Mexican?'

Bam! Joe's fist went out and caught him full in the nose. 'Like that!' Joe hissed. 'And that!' The second blow again on the nose. Like the bursting of a dam, the blood gushed mercilessly, its brilliant red dripping onto Sidecar's shirt front. The boy's eyes saw, then filled with terror before he turned and started to run shouting back, 'You dirty Mexican!'

'Now you know how it feels!' Joe shouted back. 'Now you know.'

That had been during Joe's fighting years. But in school like in his neighborhood, he had many friends. It was not all angry words and flying fists. There were Catholics of many backgrounds, mostly Irish, who attended the same church. Jews— especially the Sephardics, who were his favorites; they spoke their own language, Ladino, which was a Spanish somewhat like that spoken by Joe's aunts and uncles in New Mexico. With exotic names like Mizrahi and Alhadeff. There was a Negro or two. Then the others—he hesitated to call them Anglos. That was old country talk that he'd expect from his cousins in New Mexico.

Besides, Joe wasn't sure what an Anglo was. It didn't seem right that Catholics were Anglos; he had too many Catholic friends who shared with him this common religion. And a Jew? He supposed that in New Mexico a Jew might be considered an Anglo, but somehow it didn't make sense to him. As for calling a Negro an Anglo? Come on. The same for orientals, of which there were a few Japanese-Americans in school until they had been sent to internment camps during the war. So who did that leave to be an Anglo? Those others. The 'enemy.' Who were Protestants. Non-minority. And some of whom were unaccepting.

Among these there was always someone who asked for a bloody nose. More than among the 'non-Anglos.' Until one day in school Joe was summoned from class to the principal's office.

What now? he thought, as he slowly walked down the hall, resisting every step. Eventually, even the slowest of steps brought him to Mrs. Wilson's door. As he walked in, he was surprised to see his mother there, grim faced with tense eyes.

'Come in, Joseph,' Mrs. Wilson said. 'Your mother and I have been having a nice talk.' His mother bobbed her head in a quick, short nod, and he nodded back. He could tell from the look on his mother's face that it hadn't been a nice talk.

'I haven't done anything,' Joe said. 'Not even when Bill Hall called me—'

'Your mother and I have been reviewing your school record, Joseph.'

'My report card is OK, and I'm not behind in any homework.'

'Be quiet, Joe. Let Mrs. Wilson speak.'

'Thank you, Mrs. Rafa.' Then to Joe. 'It's not your school work. That's certainly satisfactory. But school is more than book lessons. There's the problem of deportment, too. Of getting along with your fellow students.'

'Mrs. Wilson says you've been fighting, Joe.'

'I never start it,' Joe said. 'Only when somebody calls me a name. And I never fight in class.'

'You've been involved in some fracas at least twice a week the entire semester,' Mrs. Wilson said.

'They call me names!'

'Sticks and stones, young man. Sticks and stones.'

'What kind of names, Joe?'

His face flushed, and he looked uneasily toward Mrs. Wilson. Then he walked over to his mother and whispered in her ear.

'We can't have any secrets,' Mrs. Wilson said.

Joe clamped his mouth shut even tighter and shook his head. He blinked his eyelashes to hold back the quiet surge of tears, but the feeling was from anger and frustration, not from fear.

'They were names no boy ought to put up with,' Mrs. Rafa said. 'What happens to the boys who call names?'

'There have been no reports of name calling,' Mrs. Wilson said. 'We've had reports of fighting, and most of them seem to involve Joseph.'

'What about the others?' Joe asked. 'Some of them fight as much as me. What about Denver Harris? Or Harry Kramer? Did their mothers have to come to school?'

'We're talking about Joseph Rafa. I've had no reports of other boys fighting or of name-calling.'

'Everytime I got into a fight it was because someone called me something.'

'What did they call you?'

Again the tightly clamped mouth, the curt shaking of the head. Joe's mother sighed in capitulation. 'He said they called him "Dirty Mexican"—'

'I'm not!' Joe protested. 'I take as many baths as they do.'

'Greaser,' his mother continued. 'Senor Enchilada.'

'I'm shocked,' Mrs. Wilson said. 'I'm sure none of our boys would do anything like that.'

'Well they did,' Joe said, 'and I'm the one that gets sent to the principal.'

'What happens to the boys who call names?' Mrs. Rafa asked.

'I'm sure there must be a mistake. I know our boys wouldn't behave like that.'

'Only my son!'

'Mrs. Rafa—'

'It's all right for boys to call my son names, but he can't fight back. Is that what you're saying?'

Mrs. Wilson drew back in her chair, sitting even straighter and more stiffly. The matter was over, Joe knew. He had seen that posture before—many times.

'We have a school to maintain here. We have rules about student behavior. Fighting is not allowed. Whether one is called names or not.'

'But name calling is all right,' Mrs. Rafa said stiffly. 'I don't like your rules.'

'There have been no reports. Only reports of Joseph's fighting.'

'It takes two to fight. Even though just one gets reported.'

'As we discussed before, Mrs. Rafa, something has to be done.'

Joe's mother was leaning forward in her chair, her voice soft but firm, while Mrs. Wilson sat stiffly resistant. There would be no give from either one.

'I think,' his mother said, 'that Joey needs to go to another school.'

'If you wish.'

'He is not being treated fairly here.'

'I'll sign a transfer. "For personal reasons." They'll need a reason.'

His mother rose quietly. 'Let's go, Joey.'

He followed her out of the office, whispering as they hurried down the hall. 'But school isn't over yet, mom. And call me Joe, not Joey.' He took her silence as agreement. Secretly delighted that he would have a free day, he strode happily down the hall.

14

I start out thinking about my father and his Mexicanness, Joe thought. And end up thinking about myself. I guess it's the same thing.

That change of school was the beginning of other changes. Joe's parents had somehow scraped together the money to send him to parochial school. 'For the discipline,' he had overheard them saying to each other in guarded tones. 'The Sisters will put an end to that fighting.'

But Joe hadn't noticed the discipline—or needed it. The reasons to fight simply dropped away, like snow sliding off a steep roof when the sun comes out. He was here, in his own parish, with students he knew and who accepted him as a fellow Catholic. When his urge to fight stilled, he had time to think. He didn't like to fight. He couldn't possibly fight everyone who called him a name. He would have to deal with Anglos another way—win with something other than fists.

The fifth grade teacher was Sister Marie Cecilia. Hidden in the recesses of her cowl Joe made out a strikingly pretty face—young, with piercing blue eyes that shifted from warm understanding to imperious chastisement. Oh, unholy thought. She was beautiful. Joe felt awkward and self-conscious in her presence. A kind word—praise for a lesson well done—were enough to bless his entire day. Oh, unholy blessedness. He wanted to be the smartest student in the class to win her greatest praises.

One day Joe realized that doing well in school had other values. It was where he could beat Anglos without the trauma and pain of fisticuffs—although, in a puzzled way, he didn't consider his fellow Catholics Anglos.

Be still, he learned. Be quiet. But be smart. Smarter than

anybody. Lay back. Let them fool themselves. Let them laugh and scratch and call names. Knowledge was the real power. Intelligence and hard work. They won't even know they're losing, and by the time they find out, it will be too late.

His school career blossomed. From the fifth to the eighth grade at Nativity School to the public junior high school for a year and then on to Washington High School. There were awards along the way. The honor roll. California Scholarship Federation. Recognition.

But there was more than honors. There were friends. An unconscious evolution—a broadening of his circle of friends, of his knowledge of people different than himself. Catholic classmates—Irish and Italian mostly, with a few Polish or French or German. An occasional Hispano like himself. Joe found the non-Hispanos not much different than himself in spite of what he had heard at home and from his relatives.

In public school there were others. Jews, of which the Sephardics seemed almost like himself. But others, too. German, Russian. There were even some Anglo friends. Wasps, his father would call them. White Anglo-Saxon Protestants. The privileged of America. But here, too, they were like himself. Some great pals. Others snobs. But then, he knew snobs among his own Hispanos. Vices and virtues had no ethnic exclusiveness. By the time Joe had gone to college, he had moved a long way from his father's ethnic outlook.

'There are two burning questions every college man has to ask himself,' Levy said. 'One. Would you marry a girl who wasn't a virgin? And two. Are fraternities and sororities a thing of the past?'

'There are three burning questions?' Joe countered.

'Whether a Jew should marry a goyim?'

'No, you dummy. Whether the war should end before we get drafted and get our asses shot off in Korea.'

'Fuck the Communists! Fucking's too good for them. Kill the bastards. And feed their balls to the lions in Griffith Park zoo.'

'I don't see you volunteering to rid the world of the Red menace.'

'I don't want to get my ass shot off. All I want to do is join a non-sectarian fraternity. Marry a virgin. And earn ten thousand dollars a year before I'm thirty. With a little house in—not Bel Aire or Beverly Hills, mind you—just West L.A.'

'Levy, you're impossible.'

'And a wet enchilada to you.'

'Come on. About burning question number two. What's this meeting about tonight?'

'A new fraternity.'

'I know that. Who's going to be there?'

'A surprise. We're going to set the interfraternity council on its tail. Nothing like it ever before. Watch out Betas. Watch out SAE's. Watch out Sammies. There's a new age a-coming.'

'Bullshit!'

'Our new fraternity secret handshake will be an extended middle finger. Our pin will be three balls—pearls really—from the traditional pawn shop symbol. But with a new meaning. Because we'll reinforce it with a shiny gold penis—circumsized yet. The new age for three-balled fraternity men like us.'

'You're crazy. What time? Where?'

'Eight. At Lipsky's. His old man's out of town, and he's got the key to the liquor cabinet.'

'Hasta la vista.'

'Shalom.'

Joe descended the library steps and walked down the slope toward the student union. He answered the casual wave of hands from a group in front of the coffee shop and veered sharply to the right toward the men's gymnasium away from them. They were the politicos. The angry yellow-brown-black group with their petitions and picket lines.

Joe stopped at the corner of the gym and looked back up the slope, a puzzled expression on his face. AYD. American Youth for Democracy. A young Communist group. Chicanos from East Los Angeles—Boyle Heights—with the accent of the Mexican ghetto still on their tongues. The pretty Eurasian girl who smiled at him in the main library Mondays, Wednesdays, and Fridays from ten to eleven AM. Was she seeking another recruit? Blacks. Young men and women with a kind of fearless thrust that bristled with assertiveness unlike many overly solicitous blacks he knew.

And yet, to see them only in their political aspects was to miss the most important things. After he had looked long and calmly at their anger—after he had dismissed their rhetoric as the kind of childish sing-song he himself had cried out ('My old man's a garbage man. What the hell is your old man?')—after he had depersonalized the angry words enough to realize that he was not the target—after all that—Joe saw their pain.

It was no different from his own pain. More intense, no doubt. More like his father's. And like his father's—and his own—it was a curious mixture. Family trauma (Weren't we all Oedipal, anal, generation-gap neurotics?) Social stigma (Ay, raza suffrida! Black! Jew! Scum of the earth!). Belief in false gods (A new political system—or money—or a college degree—will save us!). Yet, unlike Joe, these others seemed catalyzed by an unusual sensitivity, directing their personal compasses to the false north labeled 'outcast.' And, once outcast, one could destroy. As Joe looked at the world around him, at the 'WASP controlled system,' he knew that he could not destroy. That his stability or greed or whatever, made him want to join in and get his share. That any destruction destroyed what he wanted.

As he started to turn away, the Eurasian girl turned in his direction and smiled. For an instant he was tempted, but all he could do was nod his head unsmiling and walk away.

There were six of them at Lipsky's. They gathered in the living room, a lighted island in the otherwise dark, two-storied colonial house. A bottle of Canadian Club stood open alongside a huge bowl of ice cubes on the massive coffee table.

Lipsky lifted the unlit cigar from his mouth and flicked an imaginary ash onto the carpet. 'All right, Levy. Nobody else is going to show up. Let's get this show on the road.'

'Just a little bit longer. There were supposed to be an even dozen of us.'

'Where are your folks?' Joe asked. He wasn't used to being in a house where adults were not in evidence.

Lipsky sounded bored. 'You don't have to worry about them. They're in Palm Springs.'

'Come on,' someone else said. 'If we don't get to the evening's business, Zuckerman is going to get drunk and fall asleep.'

'Bullshhhh—' Zuckerman said.

'Let's do it,' Joe said. 'If someone comes in late, they can pick up wherever we're at.'

'Five more minutes,' Levy said.

'Bullshhhh—.' Zuckerman peered out through narrow-slitted eyes.

'Yeah. Let's go.' Lipsky said. 'Levy. You called this meeting.'

Levy sighed. 'All right. You've each been asked here because of the common bonds we share.' Joe surveyed the others cautiously. His friend, Levy. The other acquaintances. Lipsky. Zuckerman. Moskowitz. Scherr. 'We all have enlightened liberal attitudes. None of us want any truck with the bigots on fraternity row on the one hand, or the weirdos in the young Commie group on the other hand. We need a bigger brotherhood. A non-sectarian fraternity that will appeal to those not normally attracted to Greek organizations.'

'I Felta Thigh,' Zuckerman mumbled.

'I talked to each of you individually, and I thought it was time we got together and talked.'

'Six people?' Lipsky said. 'That's one hell of a fraternity?'

'Even Jesus started with just twelve Apostles—my apologies, Joe—and we're already halfway there.'

'Well. Who else did you ask that didn't show up? We don't want to foul up the organization with a bunch of schmucks.'

'Yeah. Schmucks,' Zuckerman echoed.

'To begin with, there's Willie Jefferson.'

'That's all right,' Joe said. 'He's a good guy.'

'Jefferson? Do I know Jefferson?' Lipsky asked.

'That's Levy's Negro friend,' Scherr said. 'Third string basketball team. Et cetera.'

'Oh. The guy who looks like a Hawaiian?'

'What do you mean Hawaiian?' Levy countered. 'He's a Negro. Isn't he, Joe?'

'Yeah.'

'Well, he looks like a Hawaiian.'

'So what?'

'He's not black enough. Can't you get somebody black? Really black. Like that Harry Towne.'

'Harry Towne's a fag. A ballet dancer.'

'Well, then. Somebody—'

Joe turned off his attention, watching Zuckerman slowly ooze off the sofa onto the floor. Zuckerman's eyes had finally closed and his mouth hung loosely open, so his lips quivered with each expiration of breath. The slight snore served as counterpoint to the drone of voices.

It went on like that for a long time, reviewing the six who did not show up, and arguing about possible substitutions. Joe nursed a weak Canadian Club and Seven-Up, interjecting an occasional comment, but he did not feel a part of the proceedings. Detached —insulated—he watched Zuckerman snore and stared alternately at the feet of the others because he could not bring himself to look at their faces. Rather, he did not want to risk meeting their eyes. They would see what he was thinking.

When the meeting broke up, Joe was the first to leave. Levy walked with him to the door while the others quietly and carefully prepared to wake the sleeping Zuckerman with a hotfoot.

'What do you think?' Levy asked. Joe shrugged. 'You were awfully quiet tonight. Is something wrong? You want to be in the fraternity don't you?'

'I don't know.'

'You don't know?'

Joe looked away. How could he tell him—his friend? The whole thing was a farce. The all-American, non-sectarian crew. 'It's—it's just not for me. I've been thinking about the whole bit. I just don't want to belong to a fraternity.'

'But we need you.'

And Willie Jefferson, Joe thought. Token goyim. 'I'm sorry.'

'Eeee-ooow! You dumb schmucks!' The scream was drowned out by a roar of laughter. Zuckerman was awake.

'I've got to go,' Joe said.

'We'll talk some more.'

'Sure,' Joe said. But he didn't mean it.

91

Monday morning at ten o'clock, Joe, as usual, climbed the library steps on his way for an hour of study. He exchanged a few words with several students. Politely refused an invitation to join a bridge game.

Halfway up he sensed a short, dark figure cutting rapidly across from the top steps toward him. It was one of the Chicanos from East Los Angeles, a young man that he had seen before among the politicos talking in undertones about whatever it was they talked about. El Chicano was headed right at him, head down, eyes peering up through unkempt hair.

Joe tried to avoid him, but El Chicano stopped immediately in front of him and looked up furtively. 'Eres Mejicano?' Are you a Mexican?

Joe drew back in surprise. He almost blurted out, 'Hell no! I'm an American!' when he saw a nervous brown hand clasping and unclasping around a textbook. 'Si,' he said instead.

With a quick smile of relief, El Chicano raced down the remaining steps. Joe turned and watched him in amazement. He wanted to laugh. Not at the absurdity of the situation. Nor at El Chicano—he felt a strange sadness that the question even had to be asked. But at his own response. His own freedom to answer. As if the bogeyman that had hung over his father for his entire life, and over Joe for so many years, had disappeared with that simple word: yes.

Yes, he thought. American. Mexican. Human. Ape descendent son of God. Yes. Yes. Yes.

15

One always comes back to the father. One can ignore or evade only so long. Then one must come back and face it. The truth was: young Joe had hated his father. At some level he could not acknowledge that this man with all his shortcomings was his sire. It must have been some magnificent prince who had stolen into his mother's bedroom—But then he couldn't think about that. That wasn't true either. Not *his* virginal mother. What then? A foundling? Certainly not. His mother was *his* mother. The child of a previous marriage then? His strict Catholic upbringing gave the lie to that.

'Little Indian boy,' his father used to tease. 'Found on the doorstep wrapped in a Navajo blanket.'

Joe could not abide his father's teasing. In memory, his boyhood seemed to be concerned mainly with tears—hiding tears, fighting back tears—such that the sound of his father's loud voice automatically brought on the flicker of eyelids.

To Joe's mother. 'Crybaby. I don't know what's wrong with that boy. He's no Rafa. I'll have to make a man out of him.'

With no siblings, Joe could have led the indulged life of an only child. However, what nature had not given Joe Rafa he adopted for himself. Joe remembered it from his early years, from that spring they were in Albuquerque before he was old enough to go to school.

It had been Easter week in Old Town. There had been church the previous Sunday, of course. There would be church again the coming Sunday. Not as much fun as hunting Easter eggs with his cousins. And Joe was more concerned about seeing the Easter bunny than the resurrection of Christ. He had not even made his first communion yet; that would be next year around Easter time. So his view of church was that crowded, stuffy place where you had to stay impossibly quiet and still.

It was during that week that his father had taken him to the little store in Los Rafas. Just the two of them. While mama visited with her mother. Joe felt timid and at the same time grown up. A bell tinkled, announcing their entry into the tienda. Father peered cautiously around, taking an unduly long time to survey the tiny store. A male voice boomed out from a back room. 'Un momento!'

'Herminio?'

'Si. Si.' The tiny man came out briskly, wiping his hands on a butcher's smock. He glanced quickly as he strode toward the counter, not really seeing them.

Father was smiling. 'Primo. You haven't changed.'

The narrowed eyes, the quizzical look expanded into a smile. 'Jose!' They rushed toward each other, a quick shake of hands, then clasping each other with an abrazzo.

'Here,' Jose said, gently propelling Joe toward this stranger. 'I want you to meet Senor Padilla. He's your second cousin. Mi hijo,' he said to Herminio. 'No habla espanol. Es agringado.' An Americanized Mexican. There was a touch of pride in his father's voice, tinged with a sense of apology. Look at this new generation that can't speak the mother language, he seemed to say. But what can one do?

Senor Padilla extended a firm hand. 'Hello, boy. What's your name?'

'Joe. Joe Rafa, Junior.'

Another boy, a miniature of Herminio, eased quietly beside his father who put an arm around his shoulder. 'Eddie,' Herminio said. 'Say hello to your padrino, your Godfather, Senor Rafa. And Junior.'

Eddie looked up at Joe's father who smiled and shook his hand. 'You want a jawbreaker?' Eddie said to Joe. He nodded and followed him to the glass candy case.

'He's the image of you,' Jose said. 'Just the way I remember you when we were boys. A true Padilla.' Joe could hear his father laugh in approval. A true Padilla. While he, crybaby, was no Rafa. Hadn't he heard his father say that? And didn't his aunts tell him what a sweet boy he was—no temper like the Rafas—just like his mother. Even looking like her. Like a Trujillo.

'Tell me,' Eddie said shyly, handing a black jawbreaker to Joe. 'Are you going to the play?' What play? Joe thought as he shook his head, his jawbreaker-mouth incapable of speech. 'You have to. My papa's in it. It's about Easter. He's Judas.'

They went to the play. In Old Town Social Hall. The event of Easter week. They sat with Senora Padilla and Eddie and Eddie's little sister, Eva; the baby had been left home with a cousin. Joe did not understand the play, but at least it wasn't as boring as church. Eddie, who sat next to him, would slip him a piece of candy and smile secretly every once in a while.

The play was in Spanish so Joe understood a few words now and then—not like the Latin mumbo-jumbo of the priests. They moved around in sort of a story, with different people talking so it wouldn't be so dull. There was the Virgin Mary. Joe could tell by the blue gown she wore, like that on the statues in church except that all the statues were covered during Lent. She was sweet and pure and worried about her son. That was Jesus, the son of God, strong and manly—but gentle too. Washing the feet of his Apostles as they sat around the table for the Last Supper. And Judas. Some in the audience hissed when He came to Judas' feet, and Judas turned and made a terrible face at the audience so that they hissed even more.

Joe turned toward Eddie and saw that he was hissing too, so he knew it was all right. Hiss! Joe went. Hissss, Judas! Hissssss!

Then that terrible scene when Judas went up to Jesus and kissed him. Not terrible for a man to kiss a man. Fathers kissed their sons—at least some fathers did. And all his male relatives hugged each other as greeting—abrazzo, they called it. What was terrible was that Judas used the sign of love as a betrayal, because right after the kiss the Roman soldiers looked at each other knowingly and came and seized Jesus. Then Judas took his sack of money, his dirty pieces of silver, and shook the sack at the audience. The audience hissed even louder, drowning out the jingle of the traitor's reward so that even those in the first row could not hear it.

But later retribution. Even Judas had a conscience—knew when he had done an awful thing. He came running onto the stage, berating himself, wringing his hands, falling to his knees, pleading with the audience that hissed and booed. Until Judas reached under his robes and pulled out a short length of stout rope looped into a hangman's noose. Then everybody cheered. When Judas placed the noose over his head and tightened it around his neck until his tongue stuck out and his eyes bugged, the audience grew silent. Could one cheer even when a Judas killed himself? With a final scream, Judas stiffened and fell to the floor, kicking his legs with his Jesus-washed feet a few times before he grew still, and the soldiers came and dragged him off the stage. There was not a sound in the hall.

Then later, after the crucifixion and the resurrection, the actors came out. There was the Virgin Mary. Jesus. The Apostles. Mary Magdalene. All bowing and acknowledging the applause. But the greatest applause, the wildest cheering, was for Judas. He had stolen the show. And when after the third bow, he pulled the hangman's rope from beneath his gown and draped it around his neck, the audience roared and some even stood to applaud some more.

Judas, Joe thought. In his memory ever after, Senor Padilla became Judas, and Eddie became Judas' son.

As Joe grew older he became aware of other aspects of being a Judas. His cousins must have thought him one with his city ways and unaccented English and pidgeon Spanish—a betrayer of la raza. An Anglicized Chicano—which was almost nothing at all. On their annual trips to Albuquerque Joe preferred the company of Eddie Padilla, Judas' son, because for some reason Eddie liked him and he in turn liked Eddie. Until much later. But then that had not been Eddie's fault. The Judas at that time had been his own father, Jose, who had betrayed his own son.

'Do you want to read Herminio's letter?' Jose called out to Theresa.

'What does he say?'

'That Eddie. He's a real Padilla. He's been working on a farm this summer. Plans to sell some of the crop. He pencilled a note. Says hello to Junior. Sorry we won't be in Albuquerque this year. Working on the farm already. What a man!'

'Did they say anything else?'

Jose shifted into Spanish, but Joe understood anyway. Senora Padilla had problems. She drank. It was getting worse. Even when Herminio joined her so she wouldn't drink it all herself, she'd sneak wine from the store. He'd find the empty bottles under the bed. If he could cash them in for two cents each, he'd be rich.

'Maybe I'll send Eddie a little something. Poor kid. Do you want to read the letter?'

'What more do they say?'

'That's all.'

'Then no need for me to read it.'

Joe didn't remember what his father sent Eddie that time. Whatever it was that twelve-year old boys liked that year. At any rate, it was only the beginning. After while the occasional letters contained more and more from Eddie and less and less from Herminio. Uncle Joe, they were addressed. A package would follow or an envelope with some money. While at home there seemed to be little of such for Joe.

In time Joe would look through the mail on the desk first thing after school. When he saw the familiar handwriting, a gloom would settle over him and more than once he was tempted to rip that envelope to shreds and throw the pieces into the incinerator.

The crop came in, and Eddie made some money. Eddie learned to work the new cash register at the store. He clerked after school now. His father was not feeling well—not as bad as his wife though. Eddie was going to high school next year. High school already? Then out for track. He was small, but he could run. And run. And run. The mile. The two mile. A newspaper clipping from the Albuquerque Journal. E. Padilla. Third. One mile run. A snapshot in his track suit.

You, Joe? Didn't you ever get interested in sports? I used to be pretty good in my day. Maybe you'll take after the old man.

No athletics. I like chemistry.

A true Rafa would like sports. Did you see this clipping? Eddie took a second in the mile. Going to be another Glenn Cunningham.

True Rafas, Joe thought. Probably running from the sheriff. I got straight A's. But nobody appreciates that.

Then the letter about the scholarship. Three schools wanted Eddie to run for them. The Lobos at the University of New Mexico. A college in Texas. Another one in Colorado.

By this time Joe was already a freshman at UCLA: he had finished high school a year early. His mother had gone to work in a defense plant to help out while his father still talked about

Judas' son. Well, Joe thought. Forget it. It's too late now. I will do what I must whether he likes it or not. Screw it!

Then the letter one day. Not from Eddie. Or his father. A time-bomb. Jose read it after dinner. His eyes filled as he silently handed it to Theresa. He left the house for a walk.

'What's the matter?' Joe asked. 'Bad news?'

She handed him the letter. It was in a handwriting he did not recognize. 'They took him to jail last week,' he read. 'Drugs they say. Heroin. He'd been selling it as well as using it himself. With so much to look forward to. To college if he wanted to. To all the things—" Joe could read no further. He handed it back.

'Your father is very upset.'

'Yes.'

'You know Herminio's wife was killed in an auto accident two years ago. Drinking.'

'I didn't know.'

'Your father always felt something special about Eddie.'

'Almost like a son,' Joe said bitterly. 'What does it take for him to have some feeling for me? You to jump off a bridge?'

If she had been closer she would have slapped him. 'Herminio was not just a cousin but your father's closest friend when they were boys. He felt a special loyalty. Eddie was his Godson. And when he saw the problems there, he wanted to help Eddie.'

'The shoemaker's children,' Joe said.

'You have to understand your father. He's a very good person. Loyal. He has old ties that are very strong.'

'I'm sorry. It's just that I can't even talk to him. About anything. Without it turning into a fight.'

'You're very much like him in many ways.'

Joe felt an icy chill squeeze through his body. He looked at his mother incredulously. 'No,' he said. 'I don't think that at all. Or we'd get along better. It's that he wants me to kowtow to him. Like my cousins in the country. Like Eddie. Tell him how great he is when it isn't true. He wants to be like grandpa. To rule the roost. The patriarch—whose sons tremble when he wiggles his bushy eyebrows. Well, it's not like that anymore. This isn't the little ranchito in Adobe Flats. He even wants me to quit school and go to work to make money. Probably to turn my paycheck over to him the way my cousins do to their parents. But, no! I won't! I'm going to finish college no matter what. I want more. I want to be better than him!'

Joe looked away in anger and fear, wondering if he had gone too far. Silence answered him. Finally he turned toward his mother. She was looking at him, deep in thought, a solemn expression on her face.

'I'm sorry,' he said.

'You're a son of your mother, too,' she said. 'Not a real Rafa like your father thinks he wants.'

The front door opened, and his father walked solemnly in, his large face set stoicly like the paintings Joe had seen of American Indians. Carefully he carried a paper sack under his arm. 'You want a beer?' Jose asked Theresa. She shook her head, and he went slowly into the kitchen, closing the door behind him.

Never again did Joe hear his father mention Eddie or Judas.

16

Worst of all, though, had been the girl—Joe's first love. Isabel Calderon. It had led to an open rupture with his father.

Only now could he think back on it with any objectivity. He had been a junior in college then. He must have had an erection twenty-four hours a day for the year and a half that he went with Isabel. And he had behaved himself the whole time—half insane, wearing his baggy pants to hide his condition. Having insufferable dreams. Conditioned like Pavlov's dogs to salivate at the mere thought of her.

Isabel. Isabel. Tus nalgas. Tus pechos. But pedestals were not for humping on, gutters were. And Joe had been brought up on the pedestal theory of womanhood. As for gutters, that was something to avoid at all costs. Not like young people today. New freedom? Who was kidding whom? It was just the same old lust.

99

Joe had met her at the time that young people still danced and he still attended church. The Cinderella Ball. At St. Ann's parish hall. With a live orchestra, the Mello-tones. She had been elected Cinderella and sat on stage with a paper mache crown painted with gold glitter. Her smile seemed forced, and for a long while Joe looked around the hall, puzzled that none of the young men were rushing to ask her to dance. Perhaps they were afraid. He had seen that before with pretty girls. Everyone always assumed that they already had a boyfriend or that there was too much competition, while the poor girl stood alone unasked with a forced smile on her face, getting more and more tired.

Joe could tell she was a Latin when he got close to the stage. There were not many in the parishes in this part of Los Angeles. 'Isabella,' he said when he stood in front of her, 'my name is Ferdinand. May I have this dance?' Her smile faded as she looked at him, puzzled. 'Isabella and Ferdinand,' he said. 'The king and queen of Spain during Columbus' time.'

She took his hand and walked alongside him to the dance floor. 'Ferdinand,' she said. 'That's the name of a bull, isn't it? Is that really your name?'

Touche.

Such was the beginning. Inauspicious enough. There was another girl he had been smitten with at the time. Mary Margaret Sweeney. He really had no room in his affections for anyone other than Mary Margaret. But it was going badly. She had just finished high school and was working at the telephone company. She was in awe of going with a college man and acted it. Prim. Proper. As if college men were above a little rassling in a parked car. The guys he knew around the neighborhood would elbow him and wink, smiling lecherously.

'I hear she's the hottest neck in three parishes,' one said.

'If she likes you, she'll let you hold more than her hand,' another leered. 'Bare tit and all.'

But for a college man—Miss Prim and Proper. With a goodnight kiss like your old Aunt Matilda. When he had asked her to the football game of the year, USC versus UCLA, she had said no. Who were they? She didn't know anything about football. She had something else to do on Saturday.

That was it! He telephoned Cinderella who had been delighted at the invitation. They sat in the rooters' section. Joe in a white shirt; Isabel in a white blouse. Like all the others. A white background for the card tricks at half time. Colored cards to spell out words, draw pictures. On a field a hundred students wide by a hundred rows of students high.

When Joe saw the other young men look at her, he took another look himself. But there was still Mary Margaret. It was ego. He realized it much later. At the time he thought it was unrequited love. So the shift of his affections was gradual. Until one day Mary Margaret had faded from his thoughts, and the vacuum had been filled by Isabel.

Those had been busy times. Joe was seldom home. He commuted to UCLA on the bus, or shared rides with those few friends fortunate enough to have cars. He worked part-time on campus, so his days were long. Free time was occupied with studying and Isabel. With dances. Parties. Movies. Football games. The beach. All the amusements of young people.

The weeks were too busy for Joe to read the signs. There was the strange atmosphere when he called on Isabel at home. The house normal enough. Old frame. In a borderline part of the city, the moving edge of poor into lower middle class. But the house uninviting. Stand-offish. Strangely quiet. With many rooms. Like a boarding house whose tenants scurried away at the first sound of the turning doorknob—with their presence still lingering in the rooms and the air moving in the direction they had fled.

There seemed to be many people in the house. Quiet. Furtive. Like one of those grade B horror movies with dark settings and parted curtains quickly closed. He half expected to see someone named Igor come loping through the entry hall, crippled body tilting up so that the heavy browed face would twist a smile up at him and give greetings in Spanish. Joe didn't care. So what if Isabel were Igor's little sister. She was beautiful and nothing else mattered.

But then there were signs of Igor in Isabel's actions toward him. Her hesitations to commit herself to dates after a long period

of almost taking each other for granted. The sudden changes—
the moodiness—when they were together. Until finally it tore
itself from her. An old love. Attachments she couldn't forget. A
clinging—a holding on to what was already past.

But it wasn't just an old love that she clung to. There were
those invisible strangers in the empty rooms of her house. He met
them one by one. First the grandmother. In her black garments
sitting in a rocking chair in an unlighted room at the back of the
house. It could have been his grandmother Rafa. All that was
needed was rosary in her hands, a tailor-made cigarette clutched
in her lips, and a pint bottle of wine poorly hidden under the
chair where the metal cap peeped out from under the long skirt.
There had been a hasty exchange of a few words in Spanish, then
the click of the door, sealing off the empty hall from the one
palpable sign of life in the house.

On subsequent visits the others showed themselves. The uncle
who was a musician—between engagements. The aunt with
three small and very quiet children. Too quiet. Isabel's mother—
but no father. No one ever said it, but somehow Joe knew there
had been a divorce, an unmentionable subject in many a Catholic household. Occasionally other aunts, uncles, cousins came and
went. A married older brother. The younger brother and sister
that Isabel talked about often, but who never seemed to be at
home. Perhaps they were at their father's.

It came together in pieces, like a puzzle. With her moodiness.
Her affection. Countered almost abruptly by her desire not to see
him again. An old love—but even that not enough to cause such
torment. The physical invisibility of her family contrasting stark-
ly with the powerful presence they seemed to have in Isabel's
mind. To the exclusion, at times, of what Joe thought should
have been her prime concern—himself.

But a few passionate kisses on a night-darkened porch. The
fumbling hands resistant, but not too resistant. His passion held
in check by his code of behavior on the one hand and the strange-
ness of Isabel's behavior on the other. Turmoil. Confusion. Until
that evening his mother asked him to bring his girl friend to
dinner.

'What's the matter, Isabel?' She had been sullen and withdrawn as Joe drove his father's car toward home. Her head shook in answer. 'Oh, come on,' he said in exasperation. 'What is eating you?'

'Nothing.' The whisper was almost inaudible, the expression on her face stony with unseeing eyes that told him she was not really present.

'Well try to cheer up. We'll be there in a few minutes.'

The sobs that burst from her shocked Joe. Her face contorted in tears and the level of her voice rose to an intensity that was in startling contrast to the previous silence. He steered the car to the curb and parked, taking her hand in his and patting it comfortingly.

'I'll... be... all right,' she gasped through the tears. 'I will.'

'There's nothing to be afraid of. You've met them both already. They don't bite.'

'I'll... be... all right.' She took his handkerchief and blew her nose and wiped her eyes. Her breathing calmed, and after a few moments she began to look in the mirror at her make-up.

'There. I'm glad you're feeling better.'

'I'm a sight. Look at my eyes.'

Joe started to say: They'll love you even if you're a sight. But he knew better. One outburst a night was enough. 'Here.' He turned the rear view mirror toward her. 'Now you can see better.'

But silence the rest of the drive. Followed by an artificial, almost manic talkativeness once they entered the house.

Theresa was alert. Aware. Trying in her quiet way to calm the tension. Asking a question here. Commenting there. Filling the disjointed leaps of conversation so that they seemed of a piece rather than the embarrassing thrashing of an uncomfortable guest. Then there was his father. Theresa was like a conductor who inherited half a string quartet and half a Dixieland band and was trying to orchestrate some music from it.

It almost worked. The dessert plates were being cleared when Joe made the mistake of going to the kitchen. On his return, although less than a minute had passed, he saw something had

103

gone wrong. There was the look on Isabel's face. A different expression on Jose's face. Relaxed, almost limp, like a cat eyeing its prey.

'Where did you say your father was born?'

The wild look of terror in Isabel's eyes sought out Joe. Her lips moved but no sound came out. 'Guadalajara,' Joe said.

Jose continued to watch the girl. 'Mexican!' His voice was low enough, but he said the word viciously, twisting it cruelly as if stabbing were not enough.

A little choked cry peeped out of Isabel, and she turned and rushed for the front door, but not before Joe could see the tears streaming down her face. He turned with a look of outrage toward his father, then followed her.

'He hates me!' she whined. She was heading for the car.

'No,' Joe answered. Thinking: He hates Mexicans, and that includes himself.

'It's all off,' she said. 'Everything is off!'

They were backing out of the driveway now, then down the street heading toward Normandie Avenue. 'What do you mean?'

"Getting engaged. Getting married. You couldn't have bought me a half-carat diamond anyway.'

'What the hell does that have to do with anything?' Madmen, Joe thought. Isabel and his father both.

'He hates me.'

'So what? Who are you going to marry? Him or me?'

'I wanted him to like me.'

'He'll like you all right.'

'He won't. I can just tell.'

'So tough shit. As I said before, you're not marrying my father.'

Then she started to wail, and all Joe could do was shake his head and press harder on the accelerator. Was this what marriage was going to be like? Jesus Christ. The family—the whole spooky houseful of them. The vacillations—yes, no, maybe, tomorrow. The ultra sensitivity. Christ. His father's family was like that already. His parents had left New Mexico to get away from that maddening entanglement. Now was he going to marry into the same sort of thing? Bullshit!

But then there had been the provocative behavior of his father. Talk about madness. *'And where was your father born?'* In the same kind of adobe hut mine was. So what? *'Oh? Guadalajara. What kind of Indian does that make you?'* A kindred tribe to the pueblo where some of our ancestors sneaked in to propagate—or sneaked out to pass as 'Spanish.'

Christ! Christ! Christ! Joe bounced from anger at his father to anger/sorrow for Isabel. But his feelings did not light and take a permanent stance. They vacillated like Isabel's. It was contagious. The vacillation would drive him mad. NO! Something had to be settled. One way or the other. He was not a ping-pong ball to be battered from paddle to paddle.

When they reached her house, Isabel leaped out of the car and rushed to the door. The key was already fumbling in the lock when Joe walked up the steps onto the porch. 'Are you all right now?' he whispered.

'No.'

'Let's talk.' He tried to follow her through the partially opened door, but she closed it on him.

'No,' she said. 'Your father doesn't like me and that means it's all off.'

'Let me come in.'

'No.'

'I'll call you tomorrow.'

Click. There was a finality to the closing door that caused Joe to hesitate a moment in the darkness. Inside was silence. The ghosts floating from room to room never touching—neither floor nor door nor another person.

Joe walked thoughtfully to the car and drove home, his anger rising now that he could focus on the cause of it all, his father. When he walked into the house he knew that words had already been exchanged. He could feel their presence still in the charged, silent air. Theresa was sitting stonily on the sofa, an apron untied, her arms folded angrily across her chest. Jose's tie was loose and he sat slumped in the easy chair, the 'papa' chair.

'Bullshit!' Jose said to Theresa.

'What did you say to Isabel?' Joe angrily asked his father.

'Your mother and I are talking.'

'You drove the girl away,' Joe said. 'She cried all the way home.'

'She's not good enough for you,' Jose said.

'Whaa—'

'She was a guest in our house,' Theresa said. 'There was no cause to chase her away.'

'I didn't chase her away.'

'Well, Goddamn it! she left,' Joe said. Jose leaned forward as if to rise to his feet.

Theresa stood and placed herself in the middle of the room between them. 'What did you say, Jose?'

'I said: "Hablas espanol?" When she nodded, I told her we were Spanish. Real Spanish. Descendants of conquistadors. Not that so-called Spanish from south of the border. Indians with Spanish names.'

'Oh, my God,' Joe said.

'Then I asked her where her father was born. That was when Joe came in.'

'Oh, Jose. That poor child.'

'Why didn't you tell me you were going with a Mexican girl?'

Joe shook his head in bewilderment. 'I don't go around broadcasting the ancestry of every girl I date. What does it matter?'

It was just the two of them talking now. Theresa hovered there like a referee, watching for illegal blows.

'I won't have you marrying a Mexican!'

'I'll marry who I want.'

'No respect. You have no respect for your father. If I had talked like that to my father—'

'Oh, go to hell, will you. This is ridiculous.'

Joe could see his father flinch, but unlike the angry times of his boyhood there were no blows. Just the flinch, a kind of instinctual call to arms that was not followed through.

'Stop it!' Theresa said.

Joe turned for the door. 'I have to get out of here,' he shouted. 'A nuthouse. A crazy nuthouse.'

Outside the cool air swept clean some of his anger and frustration. He walked. For blocks. Miles. When he returned home late, the house was dark and quiet, the silence unrelieved except for his father's snores. The sleep of the innocent, Joe thought ironically. Sleep came uneasily to him. He felt betrayed—both by Isabel and by his father.

The next day he telephoned her, but a voice that he did not recognize answered. Then he realized. It was her mother whom he had seen but a few times the year and a half they had gone together. 'She's not at home, young man. What do you want?' The words came cold, distant. A mother protecting her daughter from an unwanted suitor.

Joe rode the streetcar to her house the next night. The door finally opened a crack. The same voice, almost tinny, like it was still over the telephone. 'She's not here, young man. Why don't you go away?'

He did. Trying to telephone three nights before he gave up. Why was he trying to reach her? She had said it: It's all off. And he was truly relieved, because deep down he had known it was finished. It was just that he hadn't known how to tell her or he would have finished it first.

Later, when the cinders of his passion had disintegrated into dust, he saw something he had completely missed. His anger at his father—he could have killed him—had somehow been defused by his father's refusal to rise to the bait. Jose must have known what Joe was feeling. Had not felt pity nor anger, but had let it go like the passing storm he knew it was. In his own way—for the wrong reason—his father had been right about the girl. And in his own way—instinctively—had done the right thing by Joe. Let him alone to face his own emotions. To do his own growing up.

17

Well, where was he? Theresa thought as she knelt in church. It was almost two weeks now and not a word. Only the report from her son that Jose had probably gone to Spain. With a three-hundred dollar geneology chart in one hand and fist full of travellers' checks in the other.

The interior of St. Agnes was ablaze with the candles that she had lighted this past week. It was as if all the neon in Las Vegas had been converted into candles. There was no sense in lighting another one.

Spain! What was this madness that drove Jose to Spain? At least it was a Catholic country. If something happened, there would always be a priest nearby. Especially now. For age had brought Jose closer to God. Not like when he had been a young man. He and all the rest. Catolicos? Si. Somos Catolicos. Of course. We're Catholics. Catholics who never went to church except for weddings, baptisms, and funerals. Church was for women. Like the home and kitchen. Praying was women's work. Until you got old. Then, the fear of God—of the coming reckoning—made women out of old men. They went to church then. Prayed. Came back to the fold.

It must be in the nature of the male to not seek God. Although the priests were male, with many it was because they wanted to run things, to tell people what to do, rather than to seek God. It was as if they were trying to *be* God, not seek him. While with women, the nature of things automatically brought you closer. The mystery of life was incarnate in your womb, and the only answer to that mystery was the Almighty. Men seek power to be God. Women create life and thereby see God.

Once upon a time, Theresa thought, men were closer to God. Not like her son, Joe. A scientist. An agnostic—or whatever the word was. Back in her grandfather's time, when men were of the soil—farmers—they too participated in the creation of life in a way that they could see. Not like now with a forceful thrust of their organ and a subsequent indifference, but with the nurturing hand that planted seed in soil, that watered and cared for the fruit of that seed, that patiently held still to let time and nature grow a new life while one could only wonder in awe at the mystery. A row of corn. The hot, delicious red chilis. Squash. Beans. Vegetable children of God to nourish God's animal children.

There was a faint stir in the vestibule of the church. Theresa sat back on the bench and turned her head. A small group hovered about the holy water font and a mumble of prayers was punctuated by the tiny crying of a baby.

'I baptize thee in the name of the Father, and of the Son, and of the Holy Ghost.'

Theresa smiled. The words brought back memories of her grandchildren. All three of them. She had said the very same words over them. Sprinkled the few drops of holy water that she had collected surrepticiously at church in a small vial—it wasn't really stealing. It was there in the font for all to use. Then, just as surrepticiously she had baptized her baby grandchildren one by one when she was babysitting them. Just because Joe no longer went to church was no reason to deny heaven to those beautiful babies. Theresa never told Joe. Nor Margaret either. Joe was a free spirit who didn't believe in all that mumbo jumbo. While Margaret, God love her, might not have understood. Well, she might have understood, but it would have placed her in a peculiar situation. Though she was a free spirit like Joe, Margaret's parents were Congregationalists. So one might have to balance a baptism with whatever it was Congregationalists did to children.

As it was, the tiny souls had been saved. The threat of limbo had been removed. If something terrible had happened to one of them, they would go straight to heaven. Baptized in the true church. But thankfully nothing had happened. And now they were growing up. With Joey, the oldest, already having his driver's license and probably smoking pot or drinking beer with his high school friends. They go through such terrible things trying to grow up. Acting so old and making mistake after mistake in their ignorance. With mistakes being like bowling pins. One topples over, knocking into another and another until it seems like the world is falling apart. Then you set the pieces back up again and try to do better. It takes so long for wisdom to set in. Forever.

From the back of the church came the tiny cry again, and again Theresa smiled. Now she thought not only of her grandchildren but of her grandmother. Her Nana. What a beautiful old lady she had been. If I could only have been like that, she thought. Well, I tried. I tried. A sadness softly enveloped her, and tears ran down her cheeks. She thought of what her Nana had once told her: 'Your husband is your best friend.' A friend she still did not understand after more than forty years. Where are you? she asked the silent air. Jose. Where are you?

The day Theresa had come home from the hospital with Baby Rafa seemed like yesterday. She remembered the Anglo nurse—she had been a nun—with a grim, celibate's face handing over the brown-faced little monkey wrapped in a cotton blanket.

'You're barely a child yourself,' the nun said in accusation. 'Do you remember what I told you about feeding him ?'

'Yes.'

'As soon as your husband pays the bill and gets the release you'll have to leave. There's another one waiting to come into the ward right now.'

Theresa had stared at the waxen face bound tight in the head-dress. The flat voice verged on anger. The lips were tight and thin with the furrows between her brows like two exclamation points. Did she crab at Jesus like that when she prayed?

'You haven't named the child yet, have you. I can tell you haven't. Do that right away. With a proper baptism. Limbo is too full. There isn't room for any more. Only heaven has ample room—if you're good enough.'

Tears overflowed Theresa's eyes. For a moment she felt a panic like that time she had fallen from grace and gone to her Nana's to be cured. Then she secured her arms around her baby, and a surge of anger flowed through her.

'I'll name him when I'm good and ready,' Theresa said. 'And who are you to talk about limbo—have you been there and counted?' She opened her robe and freed a breast to offer it to the searching little lips. 'Now leave me alone. I want to feed my baby.'

The nun's face turned scarlet. For a moment she seemed suspended, undecided whether to leave or to give in to the impulse to slap Theresa. Just then the doctor breezed in, and the nun turned on her heel and stomped from the ward.

'You all packed? Your husband is waiting for you in the lobby.

Shall I send him in to help you?'

Theresa nodded. When the doctor left, the tears came freely. The patient next to her who had just had her fifth child—another girl—rolled over. 'Don't let that bitch upset you. What she needs is to go through labor just once. Then she'd forget all those dreams about being raped by a handsome priest.' Theresa tried to smile. 'Babies are supposed to get easier,' the woman went on. 'But I swear. Each one comes harder than the last. The next time my husband says he wants to try for a boy I'm going to cross my legs.'

Then Jose was at the door to the ward, standing shyly as if he were waiting to be asked in. 'Are you ready?' He came forward, carefully taking the wrapped baby in his arms, watching it make the sucking movements with its tiny mouth as it nuzzled into his chest.

'Well, look at him,' Jose said. 'He already knows how to eat and everything.' Cautiously he wiped a moist hand on his thigh. 'He's our hope. Did you know that? Our hope for things to be better.'

'Take care of her,' Theresa's neighbor said. 'You've got a sweet little wife there.'

Theresa took the baby from Jose, while he closed the small suitcase. 'Goodbye,' she called to her neighbor. 'And thank you.' Then, as they entered the corridor, she whispered to Jose, 'Is everything taken care of?'

'Tomas sent me the money. Everything's OK.'

They passed through the reception area where waiting eyes turned away in disappointment. They were poor, most of those waiting. Clothed in old work clothes that even a recent washing could not help. On charity, many of them. Not so lucky as Jose who had a job.

'Cootchy-cootchy-coo. You little rascal. He's our hope, Theresa. Our hope.'

'Have you thought of a name?'

'Junior. Jose Tomas Rafa, Junior.'

'Are you sure?'

'What do you mean?'

'What will your father think?'

A curtain seemed to fall behind Jose's eyes and the sparkle had flattened out into a dullness. 'Tomas was the one who sent the money,' he said stiffly. 'If it weren't for Tomas we wouldn't be here in California.'

'All right,' Her answer was a whisper. She could tell when she reached that barrier against which she should not push any harder. She wasn't certain what would happen. But whatever it would be, Theresa was certain it would be terrible. She shivered as they crossed the sunny parking area to the car.

'Our hope,' Jose said somberly. The words weren't spoken to her but to something else, something inside of him. 'The first Rafa not to be born in the beanfields. To be born in a city. In California.'

'Joey,' Theresa said, 'Joey, Junior. I like that. Do you like that, Joey?'

18

There was no real home those first few years, Theresa remembered. She had been a fool to think that physical distance would have severed the family ties. It was as if Los Rafas were a giant, powerful magnet that constantly asserted its pull on Jose even in California.

'What now?' Theresa had asked in irritation that one time she remembered most, when they had finally decided where home was to be.

The expression on Jose's face froze into counter irritation, the look Theresa remembered from Jose's father when there was even a hint of questioning his authority. He handed the airmail letter to her. 'My mother. She's sick, and they're worried. It's serious.'

The letter was from Euphemia. Her usual wheedling, accusing letter to her little brother who had deserted them by running away to California. 'What do you think?'

'I've got to go.'

'Don't you think all your sisters and brothers can take care of her?'

'Mama would want me there.'

'We were just there on vacation three months ago.' That look again. Cold. Silent. 'How are you going to get off work?'

'Goddamn it! Are you trying to tell me I can't go. When my poor old mother is probably dying. Goddamn it! You just don't seem to understand who's boss around here.'

'What happens if they won't let you off work?'

'The hell with the Goddamn job. I'm going—job or no job. Whether you like it or not!'

Her answering words remained unspoken as he turned and stomped into the kitchen. She could hear the icebox door open and close and knew Jose would be at the kitchen table, sullen, drinking from a quart bottle of beer. Bastard! she thought. But she did not follow him. When he drank or when the subject of his father came up, she had learned to bite her tongue, to avoid him.

A tiny cry from the bedroom. Joey was awake. 'Hello, Joey, baby. Did oo havum a good sleepy byes?' Joey smiled and stretched out his arms to be lifted from the crib.

'I bet you're confused, Joey. You don't know if you were born in Los Angeles or Los Rafas.' A playful gurgle ended in a tiny bead of saliva yo-yoing from Joey's lower lip. 'Let me tell you, Joey. No matter how your father acts, you were born in Los Angeles. You've been placed here to start a new life. And even your father says you're his hope. Well. You're not his hope. You're your own hope. It's just you. Remember that. Not your father nor your mother nor whomever. Just you.'

'Ga-ga. Goo-goo. Mama.'

'Ga-ga, goo-goo yourself. It's a good thing you don't understand or you'd be worried too. How many times can you leave your job in a year before they decide to hire someone else? This is 1932. People are lucky to have jobs. Ga-ga, goo—' But she couldn't go on. Theresa held Joey close to her so he couldn't see her tears.

I'm losing my mind, she thought. Talking to this poor little baby like he was a person, an adult. What can he do? He doesn't even understand what I'm saying. Joey can't help. Jose won't. So I'll just have to do it myself.

Early the next Saturday morning they were on the road—Joey bundled up and sleeping in Theresa's arms as she sat beside Jose driving toward Albuquerque. Years later she would remember all the towns the old Ford chugged through when someone finally wrote a song about it. Gallup, New Mexico. Flagstaff, Arizona. Winona. Kingman. Barstow. San Bernadino. Only the song was about driving back from Los Rafas. And every time they went, she was not sure if they would return.

Theresa sat in the rocking chair beside the bed. She had finally chased the others out. Their constant agitation which they believed was concern could make a well person sick. Now the late afternoon slowly faded into darkness, bringing with it the quiet that she needed almost as much as the sick old lady in the bed. Senora Rafa's breathing was deeper now, slower—with a rasp that bordered on snoring. Only whispers could be heard in the rest of the adobe house; Theresa's outburst had shocked them into silence. From the kitchen came the quiet sounds of dinner being prepared. The occasional clump of a piece of wood into the big stove. The soft pat of hand on dough being shaped into tortillas.

Slowly, quietly, Theresa started lulling herself with an abbreviated motion of the rocking chair, knowing that if she rocked too far the chair would squeak. After a few moments she reached into the pocket of her apron and pulled out a cigarette.

It had been a trying few days. The rest of the family had been in the house most of the time. The comings and goings made it resemble less a place of convalescence than a raucous party. With loud talking. Arguments. The banging of chairs and doors in a fierce competition to be seen and heard. Theresa had seen little of Jose. He had been with his brother or sitting sullenly with his father. Joey had been taken over by one of Jose's aunts whose tasks in the kitchen had been usurped by another member of the family.

Lost in thought now that it was quiet, Theresa did not hear the faint snoring fade away. The soft Spanish words in the semi-dark startled her. 'Let me have a cigarette.'

Theresa froze for an instant before she realized that it was Senora Rafa. Then she continued her rocking while she reached into her pocket for another cigarette and match. 'How are you, mama?' she asked.

Senora Rafa rose to a sitting position and drew on the cigarette whose red tip glowed momentarily. 'I'd be fine if it weren't so noisy around here. They're hovering around like they think I'm going to die.'

'No, mama.'

'Then why are you and Jose here?'

'They sent—' Theresa stopped short.

Once again the red glow from the inhaled cigarette. 'Yes. They sent for Jose. Simpletons. A little pain in the chest. A little cough. And they have me buried. I'm still a young woman. Not yet sixty years. Reach under the left side of the bureau. You'll find something there. Bring it to me.'

Theresa's hand fumbled beneath the bureau, searching. She felt it. Cold and hard. Startled, she fished it out. 'My tonic,' Senora Rafa said. Theresa handed over the half full bottle of wine. 'It helps keep out the noise.'

Theresa sat still, not knowing what to say. She realized that this was the first time she had ever been alone with Jose's mother. The first time they had exchanged more than polite hellos and how are yous? She could hear the wine slosh in the bottle, hear the soft exhalation of cigarette smoke. The eyes were looking toward her. Could her mother-in-law see in the dark like a cat? Finally, Theresa could no longer tolerate the silence, and she spoke. 'I'm glad you're feeling better.'

'Thank you, honey.' Then silence again except for the soft exhalation of cigarette smoke. 'Here.' Theresa could barely make out the wine bottle extended toward her. 'Put it away. And don't tell them about it. Or that you gave me a cigarette. I'll tell them you lied.'

Theresa folded her arms across her body to ward off the chill she felt from Senora Rafa's words. A soft chuckle came from the bed. 'Don't be afraid of me, honey. Remember. Your mother is your best friend, and I'm one of your mothers now.' Theresa did not know what to say.

'Is Jose happy?' Senora Rafa asked.

'Yes,' Theresa lied.

'He doesn't miss going to the Normal school? Being a teacher?'

'No.' But her answer was less sure, more hesitant.

'I understand Jose works in a fish factory. What kind of work is that for him?' The words were accusatory.

'Jobs are hard to find.'

'What does Jose do in this fish factory?'

'I—I don't know. They put fish in cans. They bring in the fish from the boats and do whatever they have to do to it before they use the machines to put it in cans. Sometimes he brings home cans of tuna.'

'And this place you live—is it near the ocean?'

'Yes. San Pedro.'

'Where they had that big earthquake?'

'Near there. Near Long Beach.'

'I cried for two days when I heard. They said California was going to fall off into the ocean. We didn't hear from Jose. He always used to tell me everything. Now nothing. Don't you let him write to his old mother? His best friend?'

Theresa started to rock from nervousness, the chair squeaking with the strong back and forth motion. For an answer she lit another cigarette.

'You shouldn't smoke so much,' Senora Rafa said. 'Young women shouldn't smoke at all.' Theresa blew smoke in the direction of the voice. Then the scratch of a wooden match and the coal oil lamp beside the bed dimly lit the room.

'Jose was always my favorite,' Senora Rafa said. 'I love all of my children, God bless them. But there is always one who is the favorite. You'll see when you have more. Jose was the one who was different. He was smarter than the rest. And he always thought about his mother. Considered her. Helped her. Not like the others. Constant bickering. Constant arguing. Like Navajoes on the warpath. No. Jose seemed to understand about other people. Especially his mother. And Jose's son. Jose, Junior. How is my grandson?'

Like his father, Theresa could have said. That's what grandma wanted to hear. 'He's smart, and he has a mind of his own.'

'Like Jose.' The old lady smiled. 'Bring him to me.'

Theresa started to say that he was asleep, but then she thought: No. Let Joey see grandma so he can start to learn what he is up against.

Tia Maralena sat exhausted on a bench in the kitchen. Joey scrambled on the wooden floor after a handful of cooked frijoles. 'Mama.' He toddled to her, dropping the three squashed beans he had held tight in his little fist.

'Your grandma's awake,' she said. 'She wants to see you.' Theresa lifted him up and kissed him on the cheek. A Rafa who was not going to be a Rafa, she promised herself. Grandma, who was a tough old lady, didn't know what a tough daughter-in-law she had.

The voices from the front room grew louder. The women in the kitchen turned, listened briefly, then looked at each other with wide eyes. Theresa could hear the angry voice of her father-in-law, then the evasive answer from Jose.

'Papa wants him to come back to Los Rafas,' Juana whispered.

Theresa turned and went back to the bedroom. She kissed Joey on the cheek again. 'Never,' she whispered. 'Never.'

The noisy, confusing day dissipated into a dark, quiet country night. Everyone else had gone home, leaving Theresa and Jose with his parents. As Theresa lay in bed she could hear through the still, black night the frogs in the distance. She snuggled down under the blankets and smiled, feeling a peace that only came to her in the country. The silence was unassailed by the engines or horns of passing motor cars. The darkness was undiminished by lights from house or street lamp. Silence and darkness brought her back to the earth, to a sense of being a part of the fields and the trees and the not too distant river—as well as being an innocent, one of God's children under the great expanse of sky whose stars pierced the dark. Even thoughts of her mother-in-law did not upset her.

Theresa turned toward her husband. She put a hand on his tight, tense shoulder and knew that he was still awake. 'What is it, Jose?' she whispered.

'Nothing.'

'Is it your father?' No answer. 'Are you worried about your mother?'

The long sigh seemed to rise up slowly from deep inside. 'She told Eufemia to send for me,' Jose said.

'Oh?'

'She didn't want to die without me here.'

'She was that sick?'

Again the long sigh. 'No,' he finally said. 'They didn't even send for the doctor.'

'Maybe they don't have the money.'

'No. They were afraid that the doctor would find something really wrong with her.'

'That's crazy.'

Jose lapsed into silence, and Theresa could hear his breathing as a counterpoint to the distant frogs. 'Honey,' he finally said. 'I've hardly seen you these past three days. We could be in different countries, different worlds.' Theresa felt the bed shift as Jose turned and put an arm around her. 'This place drives me crazy,' he said. 'When I'm not here, I keep being pulled back. I worry about my mother. I feel homesick. Then when I'm here, I can't stand it. The noise. The confusion. People pulling in different directions. I never know who to believe. Who's telling the truth; who's telling lies. And why.'

'We don't have to stay here,' Theresa said. 'We can go back home tomorrow.'

His arm unfurled and Jose rolled onto his back, not touching her. 'My father wants us to move back here. He and my brother will build us a house. Over in the next field. Where we'd be near the rest of the family.'

'So that's what you were arguing about?'

'I don't argue with my father. I learned that as a small boy. One day I sassed back at him during dinner. It was the last time my mother was able to talk him out of beating me. He took me out in the yard behind the big cottonwood tree and used a switch on me. A switching was never more painful than that first time. I ate my meals standing up for three days. My mother cried and tried to comfort me afterwards; she knew well enough not to interfere during the switching. My father said: "Leave him alone. He's not a baby anymore. When he's disrespectful, he will have to take the consequences like anyone else." I didn't argue with him much after that.'

'But he was angry with you today.'

'But I didn't argue. If he tried to beat me now—.' Jose's voice trailed off. 'You are supposed to honor your father and your mother. He's the boss. But if he tried to beat me now, I don't know if I could control myself. So I don't argue.'

Theresa thought of her own father, dead now from a barroom brawl. It was still hard for her to feel sorry. The whippings he had administered in the name of discipline and respect had merely forced her into more rebellion and disrespect. She put her arm around Jose, wishing there was some way she could help him. 'What will we do?' she asked.

'Go home tomorrow.'

'What about your mother?'

'A son is a son till he takes a wife—'

And a daughter is a daughter all of her life, Theresa thought. She had not been to see her own mother this time. Your mother is your best friend, Senora Rafa had told her. But her Nana had said that your husband was your best human friend. And Nana was right.

'I'll pack in the morning,' Theresa said.

'I saw Junior eating beans off the floor,' Jose said with disgust. 'And the flies. Every time someone opens a door a swarm of flies follows them in. It will be nice to go home.'

19

Theresa had forgotten, but there had been another time when Jose had disappeared from home. Just shortly after they had

119

returned from Los Rafas, both finally knowing that their home was forever in California.

She had cooked posole that day. The smell of oregano would bring the memory back to her. The deep pan had been full of posole, what Anglos called hominy, with squares of tripe and a sprinkling of dried red chili in it. A pan full of heated grease was on the other burner of the little stove, waiting for Jose's entry before she would drop in the squares of flat dough that would puff up into crisp browned sopaipillas, little pillows of fried bread.

When six o'clock passed and she had not heard the usual sound of the automobile out back in the alley, Theresa felt a slight irritation. The sopaipilla dough was laid carefully into the hot grease so that dinner would be ready when Jose walked in the door. Surely he would be here any minute. He was not one of those husbands who would stop at some bar on the way home to have a few drinks with his friends.

Six o'clock marched relentlessly into seven o'clock. The cooked sopaipillas lay flat and cold on a plate on top of the stove. Theresa had passed from irritation through anger to concern. It was really unlike Jose. We should have put in a telephone, she thought. What if we couldn't afford it? We need one at times like this.

Then she thought of their next door neighbors—the blonde couple with the funny name and accent. They had a telephone. When she hurried next door, the house was dark, but she knocked anyway, with the futile hope that someone would be there. No one was. It was too dark to make that long walk to the nearest pay telephone. In this neighborhood even short walks could be dangerous. So she ran back home, filled with anxiety that some-thing might also happen to Joey. He was asleep, peacefully oblivious to his father's absence and to his mother's concern.

Be sensible, Theresa said to herself. So sensibly she ate her dinner, a tasteless, alternately soft and chewy mixture that made even less impression on her stomach. Then sensibly she cleaned up the kitchen and mended clothes while she listened to the radio. Then, still sensibly, only a little later than usual, she went to bed. But she could not sleep. She did not believe her own argu-ments about how everything was really all right. It seemed that she had barely dropped into a fitful sleep when a pounding on the door woke her. She bolted upright, heart racing, and reached for Jose. He was not there, and then the fearful knocking came again.

Oh, God, she thought. What is it? Someone from the hospital? A man from the morgue?

Theresa flung her cotton robe around her as she flicked on the light and hurried the few steps across the tiny hall. Opening the door with chain still in place, she peered through the crack out onto the lighted porch. 'Yes? What is it?'

'Police Department, m'am.' The dark uniformed man with a bright silver badge on his chest came into view. 'Are you Mrs. Jose Rafa?'

'Yes.' She could barely utter the word. All her fears encircled her, trapping her in old prejudices. Police. Trouble. 'Them.' What are they trying to do to us now? She had seen enough growing up in a Spanish-speaking barrio of Albuquerque to think of policia, los chotas, as the enemy.

The officer shifted awkwardly from one foot to the other, but Theresa could not see through her circle of fear and recognize his concern. 'It's about your husband.'

She started to say, 'He's dead,' but the words did not come out. All she could do was stare with her silent mouth working like a fish drowning in air.

'He was taken into custody this afternoon. We didn't have a telephone number to call. That's why they sent me. To tell you he's in jail.'

Theresa slid the latch on the chain and walked onto the porch toward the walk. 'I'm sorry, m'am,' the officer said. 'There's nothing you can do now. You'll have to wait until morning.'

Theresa turned and looked unseeing at him. She felt dazed, confused. In no way could she imagine what had happened that Jose would be in jail. She blinked, thinking hard on whether or not she had heard the words properly. She wanted to sit down, but for some strange reason the chairs had disappeared; she was on the porch and did not know how she got there.

'Are you all right, m'am?'

Theresa nodded. 'What— What happened?'

'I don't know, m'am. You'll have to find out at the jail tomorrow.' The officer had turned slowly, shepherding her so that she walked unknowingly into the house. 'Are you sure you're all right?'

'Yes.' Theresa closed the door behind her and dropped onto the nearest chair.

It had been a futile, frustrating day. Waiting anxiously for the neighbors to be up so she could use the telephone to locate Jose. Dialing one number after another—from the Police Department at San Pedro to the one at Long Beach, the Los Angeles County Sheriff's Office—without success. Theresa began to disbelieve that a policeman visited; it was her imagination playing tricks.

'All right, honey,' her neighbor, Mrs. Vanovich said. 'I'll watch the kid for you if you wanna take the bus to the police station. What's one more kid for a day?' Theresa tried not to look at the circle of small sleepy faces hovering over bowls of cornflakes— hair uncombed, a few noses dripping. 'If it was me—good riddance. A few days in jail would give him and me both a rest.'

'Jose couldn't do anything wrong,' Theresa said. 'That's not like him.'

'Drunk,' Mrs. Vanovich said. 'That's what they all do. Then they start looking around for a fight. Or a woman.'

'If you could watch Joey, it would be a real help.'

'Sure.' Then to her own five breakfasting children. 'All right you kids. Let's start shaking your asses off to school!'

As she rode the bus, Theresa berated herself for not getting the officer's name. That would have made the search easier. She felt inadequate as she approached the desk at the police station, her usual self assurance dissolving into fear and confusion over her husband's whereabouts.

'What did you say the prisoner's name was, m'am?' the uniformed officer at the desk asked.

'Jose Rafa.'

'How do you spell that?' Theresa spelled it out while the officer looked down a typed list. 'When was the prisoner booked?'

'I don't know. He didn't come home from work last night. So it must have been around five or six o'clock.'

The officer turned to another officer behind him. 'Anything on a prisoner named Rafa?'

Theresa was getting irritated. Why did that chota have to say 'Prisoner'? Jose was no prisoner. Whatever it was, she was sure it was a mistake. And the official's attitude. He was civil enough. Yet there was an undercurrent of something. 'Prisoner's wife.' Maybe that's what he was thinking.

'Sorry, m'am. We have no record of any Rafa being booked. Could it have been Long Beach? Or the Sheriff's office?'

'I telephoned. They told me there was no such—' She caught herself before she said prisoner. 'A policeman came to our house early this morning. In uniform. In a police car.'

'Hey, Anderson!' The officer turned around toward the voice. 'What about that group of Mexicans that was brought in last night?'

When Anderson turned back, a stony rigidness had set into the expression on Theresa's face. She cursed the flush that heated her face almost as much as she cursed the way the other officer had used the word 'Mexicans.' It was not even true, she thought. She and Jose were Americans. But more than that, there was a cruel twist to the word so that it meant more than it said. Literally yes, there were people who were Mexicans, people born in Mexico. But that was not what was meant. The officer meant poor. Uneducated. Dark complexioned. Dirty. Don't enter here. Go back where you came from. I'm better than you.

Her eyes challenged Anderson's until he looked away. His voice was harsher now, yet he no longer looked at her. 'Where was your husband born, lady?' She was longer m'am, but lady. And lady, too, had a twist to it that bordered on insolence.

'Los Rafas, New Mexico.'

The officer caught himself before his face broke into a knowing smile. The edges of his mouth twitched and settled into a pleasant expression, but his eyes betrayed him. 'Well, then. If he was born in Mexico—'

'New Mexico! A state in the United States!'

'Now that's too bad. We had a bunch from old Mexico last night. He couldn't have been one of those!'

He couldn't have been one of those. A chill pulsed through her body, and she looked up at that pleasant expression with a sense of foreboding. 'What bunch was that?'

'Immigration people rounded them up.'

'It couldn't have been my husband.' But the sureness had gone from her voice. What had Jose told her? About some of the workers in the cannery? Surumatos, rowdies from south of the border. Taking some of the jobs that should have gone to unemployed Americans. Mejicanos who took the dirtiest jobs of all and worked for almost nothing.

'Not if he was born in the United States.'

'What if there was a mix-up? A mistake? Maybe they took my husband by mistake.'

'I don't think so, lady.'

She could no longer hold back the tears. They flooded her eyes and flowed down her cheeks; she turned away so they wouldn't be seen. But Theresa could no longer hold back the sob that had gathered deep in the pit of her stomach and finally burst upwards.

'Are you all right, lady?'

Through sheer force of will, Theresa's pride dammed up the flow. She could not answer for a moment. She would not answer until she was in control again. Then she looked up, face blank, but not crying. 'They could have made a mistake,' she said. 'If they did, where would they take him?'

The two officers looked at each other. 'That would be a Federal case,' Officer Anderson said. 'Maybe they'd take them to Terminal Island. Or maybe they drove them to San Diego to take them back across the border.'

Terminal Island. That was where the cannery was. But would they have taken an innocent man? And San Diego. How could they just take someone from work and drive them to another country without telling their families? But Theresa did not ask. She would find Terminal Island by herself.

As she turned and left, she heard one officer speak to the other in undertones. 'Some of these spics really get touchy, don't they?'

'They're never Mexican,' Anderson answered. 'It's Spanish. Hah!'

Chingados! Theresa said to herself. Then she walked quickly

to the nearest bus stop, sat on the empty bench, and had her cry.

It was night when Theresa finally returned home, the time she would normally be preparing dinner. She was not hungry even though she had missed lunch. With Joey beside her, she sat staring, oblivious to him, oblivious to the passing time. Even the sound of an automobile did not pierce that wall she had placed around herself. The slow footsteps on the porch were remote like in a dream, and she did not hear the door open.

'Hello, corazon.'

Theresa looked up, thinking it a mirage like the policeman last night. When the mirage leaned over and kissed her, she burst into tears.

'Papa come,' Joey said. 'Papa come.'

'Oh, God, Jose. I've been so worried.'

'That makes two of us. I could see myself being shipped off to Mexico, never to come back. Jesus, I was scared.'

'They can't do that! They've got no right to do that.'

'Tell that to the police.'

'It's outrageous,' she said. 'How dare they?'

Jose sat down gently beside her. 'I'm just glad to be home. But those other poor bastards—' She took his hand and they sat quietly until Jose began to talk. His voice was tired, and she could tell from his eyes that he had slept little.

'The police picked us up after work,' he said. 'The more I thought about it, the more strange it seemed. We had finished the shift. Everything was put up. And payday was two days away. There were rumors that they were going to lay some people off at the end of the week. Now they won't have to lay anybody off; they just shipped the poor bastards down to Tijuana. Without their pay, too.'

'You mean somebody from the cannery turned them in to the police?'

Jose shook his head slowly. 'I don't know,' he said. 'All I know is that they made me the leadman because I could speak Spanish. I would think they would check them out before they hired them. It isn't as if workers were hard to find. God knows there are plenty around looking for jobs. When I was helping the time-keeper a few weeks ago I found out some of those poor Mexicans were getting paid half of what I get. And I get damned little enough.'

He reached into the pocket of his work pants and pulled a soiled piece of paper that he unfolded. 'Names and addresses. Some of them had families here. Wives. Children. Or sweethearts. They wouldn't even let them notify their families. I told them I would let their families know. Hinojosa and I talked all night. We couldn't sleep.

'They picked us up right after work like I said. Then down to jail, herded into the damned wagon like a bunch of sheep. The immigration people couldn't come for us, so they put us in the drunk tank. It was like a madhouse. Crying and groaning all night. Screaming. I really began to believe there were bugs crawling all over us. One of them threw up on my back and another pissed all over my shoes.'

His voice broke. Theresa looked down at the stained trouser cuffs and smelled the faint aroma of vomit. There were tears in Jose's eyes. 'Poor Jose. My poor baby.' She placed an arm around him, and nestled his head on her shoulder.

'We couldn't sleep,' Jose went on. 'So Hinojosa and I talked. We got the names, and I wrote them down. Pobres. They were nice for Mexicans. They got screwed when they came into this country—paying much too much money to whoever smuggled them in. Then they get screwed trying to get papers so they could get a job. Then those crooked lawyers have them in their clutches, knowing they're illegal so they can put the bite on them for more money. Finally that damned job. I'm glad I'm not a Mexican.'

'You mean all the rest were taken back across the border? As far as their families know they just disappeared?'

'They shouldn't have come in the first place. Once they break the law, they're going to get what's coming to them.'

'Oh, Jose. What if it had been you? Us?'

'I'm not a Mexican. I don't have to worry about that.'

'But they're people just like us. Children of God just like us.'

'No!' That rock-like expression set onto his face, and Theresa

126

knew that she had reached the boundary line on that subject. 'They're Mexicans,' he said, dismissing them.

'What about your job? You can't continue to work in a place like that.'

'Are you out of your mind? Do you know how many unemployed people there are walking the streets? The foreman was the one who came and got me out of that mess. If he hadn't come, I might be across the border in Tijuana now.'

'You mean you'd work for a place that uses people the way they used those poor Mexicans.'

She felt his body stiffen, and she backed away from him, fearful that he might strike her. 'I'm an American,' he protested. 'An American. Those people came from another country. They were here illegally. Lawbreakers. I can have feeling for them, but I also have feeling for myself. For us. I'm not a Mexican! I don't want to be used like those poor bastards who got shipped over the border. Those damned police, treating me like a Mexican. It's time these Anglos dropped this Mexican crap about us. We're Americans. The same as every Goddamned Anglo who looks down his snotty nose at brown skin.'

'I was just saying that they were people too,' but Theresa's voice was weak, flickering in his gale of emotion.

'I'm people too. You don't see the shit I have to eat just to keep a dirty job nobody else wants. But I eat it. And the worst thing is that I know it. "Delicious. Serve me another helping." And they shovel it to you in bigger shovelsfull.

'You know why? For you, Goddamn it. And for Junior, too. For him most of all. So maybe he won't have to eat the same shit I have to. So he can get himself some kind of education so he can be somebody.

'I come home after a rotten night in jail and what do I get? More shit. From you. Wringing your hands over those poor deported Mexicans. Well, I feel for them. I'm human. But what the hell can I do about it?'

'You're not even hearing me, Jose. You don't even listen.'

'I hear. I hear. But it isn't what I hear or what you say. It's what I feel. I feel rotten. I've been through a degrading experience. I want some sympathy, some understanding. And what do

I get—'

'Jose—'

But the only answer was the slam of the front door. Oh, Christ, Theresa thought. What have I done now? He was right. Everything he had said was right.

She was still awake in bed, eyes open and staring in the darkness up toward the ceiling, when she heard the door quietly open and close. The toilet flushed, then the smell of whiskey grew stronger before she felt the edge of the mattress sink. 'I'm sorry,' Theresa said. 'It was wrong of me to pick on you. Will you forgive me?'

'Yes,' Jose sighed. And almost with the next breath came his snores.

20

The police may be servants of the people to those who can afford servants, but to many of the poor they are more like guards of the invisible jail in which the poor live. Thus her attitude about the police, Theresa thought. The dreadful apprehension lurked quietly hidden until Joe grew older.

There had been Jose's brush with the immigration people. That would never be a problem for Joe, she thought. If you heard but did not see Joe, you could not tell the unaccented voice from American boys named Smith or Jones. Even looking at his bright eyed, brown face there would be but little question that he belonged here.

There were other kinds of police problems though. Close ones. Ones she did not like to think about, even though the news—or rather, gossip—filtered back in letters. The son of a friend. A nephew. Burglary. Dope. Gang fights. Like Jose's boyhood friend, Herminio, whose son turned out bad. Like others in the family that she could name, both her family and Jose's—but she did not even want to think about them. Only about Joe. About what he should not do.

What is it about our people? she asked herself. Was it some kind of heredity like the college professors talked about? Was there a gene linked to brown skin, contaminating the behavior of their young men? But no. Theresa could not believe that. There were brown-skinned priests, too. Even a few brown-skinned policemen. If there was a gene anywhere, it was linked to hunger and unemployment. If you were unemployed long enough and were hungry long enough this gene triggered the desire to get some food—even if it meant stealing. That's what silly creatures of habit genes were. They love food. But then again, everyone has genes and everyone loves food, so she could not claim heredity just for Chicanos.

But whatever the source and for whatever reason the anxiety, there was her concern about Joe. To teach him, to punish him if need be, so that he would learn from her this same anxious concern about his behavior and the police.

What she remembered most was the summer Joe was fifteen. Herminio's son, Eddie, had come from Los Rafas to visit an aunt in East Los Angeles. He had telephoned one day, asking for his Uncle Jose and been invited for dinner.

Theresa had felt a premonition when she had answered the doorbell. 'I'm Eddie Padilla,' the young man had said. His voice was soft, painfully shy, yet there was a furious restlessness about his eyes, a sense of suppressed motion that was barely under control.

'Come in, Eddie. We're glad to see you.' She glanced toward the curb, then up and down the block for a short distance. But no car. 'How did you get here?'

A quick laugh exploded from Eddie. He motioned with a fist, thumb extended, a hitchhiker's motion. 'Is Uncle Jose here?'

'He's not home from work yet. Come in. Joe's here. Joe!' A strange smile animated Eddie's face as Joe entered. Theresa returned to the kitchen with a feeling of uneasiness. It's just my imagination, she thought. He's just a child. A boy. Like Joe.

It was a pleasant dinner. A quiet exchange about things in Los Angeles and things in Los Rafas. Yes, Eddie's father was just fine. Mother was just fine. Sisters were just fine, too. Everything was just fine.

After dinner, Joe came into the kitchen where Theresa was washing dishes. 'Mom,' he said in a quiet voice. 'Can Eddie stay here tonight?'

So that was it, Theresa thought. The strange look on Eddie's face. His curious manner. 'I guess so,' she said. 'Is it all right with his aunt?'

'Oh, sure. Eddie told me it was all right. He can sleep in my room, and I can sleep on the sofa.'

'He can stay tonight.'

It pleased Theresa to see Joe enjoying their visitor. Usually their guests were adults. An older aunt. An older cousin. In-laws. A young man was rare but pleasant company for Joe. A change from his friends from school and neighborhood.

The boys went out for awhile, then came in, talking in quiet, serious tones. The sounds of their voices carried down the hall, the drop in volume alerting Theresa.

'Your parents are rich, aren't they?' Eddie asked.

'Why—no.'

'Yeah. But you have this nice house. Do you own it?'

'Yes.'

'Did you pay cash?'

'Uh—I don't think so.'

'And your car. I bet you have a new car.'

'It's a two-year old Ford.'

'That's a new car. Did you pay cash?'

A tone of annoyance. 'How do I know? Come on. Let's go listen to "Inner Sanctum".'

'What's that?'

Exasperation. 'On the radio. It's a neat program.'

'Does your radio play records, too?'

'Yeah. And we paid cash for it.'

The bedroom door closed and the indistinguishable sound of the radio droned on. Next morning after Jose had gone to work, Joe came to her again.

130

'Can Eddie stay another couple of days?'

'I'll have to talk to your father. I ought to talk with his aunt, too.'

'Oh, mom. Don't be such a pill. Eddie already talked to his aunt. Everything's OK.'

'He doesn't even have a suitcase. His aunt needs to know that he's staying. And he'll need a change of clothes.'

'Oh, mom. I tell you, it's all right.'

Theresa walked to the bedroom and knocked on the door. 'Eddie.'

'Mom. I tell you, everything's all right!' Joe's voice rose in anger.

Theresa knocked again. 'Eddie.' The door opened, and the puffy, red-eyed Eddie peered out at them, wrapped in a blanket. A pungent odor came from the room, an odor somewhat like a cigarette but not quite. 'Breakfast is ready. I'd also like to talk to you.'

'Not hungry,' Eddie said. 'Still sleepy.' His speech was slightly slurred, as if he were not quite awake.

'Have you been smoking?'

Eddie smiled, a distorted grimace through his sleepiness. 'Cigarettes.' Then he slowly, quietly closed the door.

Theresa stood looking at the closed door. In her house. The door of her son's room. Feeling the heat of anger, she flashed a look at her son who shook his head. 'I don't know,' Joe said.

Well, we'll find out, Theresa thought.

Later that morning she told Eddie to telephone his aunt. Still in the kitchen, she heard the telephone dial from the front room, heard the low murmur of a conversation.

'It's all right, auntie,' Eddie reported. 'I can stay as long as I want.'

'What about your clothes?'

'Joe said he'd lend me some of his.'

'Sure,' Joe said. 'We're going to take the bus to the beach today. All he'll need is a bathing suit.'

When they were gone, Theresa moved determinedly toward the bedroom. The heavy odor clung to the room, a reminder of the early morning. She picked the blanket from the floor and made the bed. Sniffing around, she found a pile of burnt matches and ashes on top of the chest of drawers. No, the aroma was definitely not cigarettes. There was a weed-like scent to it. Loco weed, she thought, confirming the strange expression on Eddie's face.

Theresa marched to the telephone with grim determination. A telephone number was scrawled on the writing pad in a hand she did not recognize. Eddie's she thought. It would save looking up his aunt's number.

Impatiently she dialed, not certain what she would say, knowing she would have to say something. The phone rang for what seemed an interminably long time before being answered. Then a woman's voice said, 'When you hear the tone, the time will be—'

Click. Theresa reached for the telephone directory. After the conversation she felt in a state of impatient suspension, waiting for the boys' return from the beach. She almost telephoned Jose at the bank, but no, she thought. Why drag him into this? It was Herminio's son, and Herminio was Jose's cousin and close friend. Eddie was something special to Jose. His Godson. There was no need to taint that relationship.

The sounds of the boys' voices on the porch in late afternoon. Should she confront Eddie alone or in Joe's presence? They dragged through the front door.

'Whew, I'm fried to a crisp,' Joe said. 'Got to take a shower.'

'Yeah,' Eddie said.

'You go first,' Joe said.

Theresa waited until Eddie had showered, then called him. 'You were smoking marijuana in the room this morning, weren't you?' The look of surprise flickered across his face, then settled into the bland, impassive look that betrayed no feeling. Only his eyes gave any sign, radiating turbulence in their inability to be still and focus. 'I can't have that in this house,' she said.

A curt nod of the head and Eddie started to turn. 'I talked to your aunt on the telephone,' Theresa continued. Eddie whirled back; his mouth fell open. Then quickly the mask again. 'She was relieved to know where you were.'

'Wha— What else did she say?'

'That she wanted you back.' No need to say more, Theresa

132

thought. 'They sent him away for the summer,' the aunt had said. 'He got into trouble with the police. Marijuana. Stealing. God knows what else. Herminio thought a change might do some good. At least it will keep Herminio from going crazy, but it all falls on me. He's been here less than a week and already I'm about to go out of my mind. Que demonio!'

'She didn't say anything else?'

'What would she have to say?'

'Nothing.'

'But you have to go back. I'll have Jose drive you after dinner.'

Eddie nodded, then disappeared into the bedroom. A short while later Joe came into the living room wrapped in a towel. 'Hey, where's Eddie?'

'In the bedroom.'

'I just looked. He's not there.'

Together they hurried to the room. Empty. A window open, the screen unhooked. 'Well. Good riddance,' Theresa said.

'Mom!'

'He didn't... ask you to... try anything, did he?'

'What do you mean?' Her answer was a stern look, eyebrows raised. 'Well—he talked a lot about his "Aunt Juana." He had this Bull Durham sack that he carried it in. He rolled one up at the beach, and I told him he'd better not smoke it. The police. He kind of laughed.'

'What about you?'

'I didn't try it. Do you think I'm crazy?'

'Well, he's gone,' Theresa said.

'Maybe it's better.'

'You ought to check your things. Make sure everything is here.'

'Oh, Mom.'

Everything had been there, Theresa remembered. And something more that Eddie had left behind. Suspicion. For awhile Joe felt himself watched by Theresa. A cleavage set in between them. He was no longer her little boy; he had joined that rude, crude world of men, albeit a novice. A world she found hard to understand. Joe could go where she could not follow, do what she would not see.

I have to give it up, she finally decided. I have to let him go.

This other way is madness. Watching. Worrying. I have to let him alone. Let him grow up.

When she let it go, things got better. Yes, there was that cleavage, that separation, but that was natural. She did not worry, and the reasons for possible worry disappeared. She could tell just by looking at Joe. Left alone he would be his own good self. She was glad she had never told Jose about Eddie.

21

'Come Holy Ghost, creator blest.' It was a hymn whose words took Theresa back through the years. Come Holy Ghost. The Father, the Son, and the Holy Ghost. And if Jose was the father and Joe the son, then she must be the holy spirit. That was her family role.

Theresa had sung those words a thousand times. In making a novena. During a rosary. In services during Lent when it seemed she would be in church as much as she was at home. She smiled, thinking of the little boy who used to sit beside her singing those words. Joe would come with her to evening services. Jose was not interested in attending. 'Bull!' Jose would say to her. 'I don't need any of that bull!'

That's the way it had been at first. The son attending church with her while the father did not. They had walked, mother and son, down the three long, darkened blocks past the junior high school. Then along the main boulevard past the men's store owned by the Jew with curly hair who was always standing in front waiting for a customer. Past the Bargain Barbershop where none of the boys wanted to go because the barber always smelled of whiskey, pulled on their hair with his scissors, and usually gave them an uneven cut that took two weeks to grow and look decent—on top of which the other barber shop gave lollipops. Then the bargain movie theatre, the Rathouse. The shoe store.

And on and on past Woolworth's, the drug store, and the Bank of America. From there it was a short two blocks to the church.

They would talk. 'How come dad isn't coming tonight?'

'Your father worked hard all day, and he's tired.'

'But to church. I didn't think were supposed to be too tired to go to church. Isn't it a sin?'

'Only on Sundays and holy days of obligation. Night services are for people who want to do a little extra.'

'Yeah,' he said in a whisper, 'but dad doesn't even go on Sundays all the time.'

'Hush, please. Mind your P's and Q's.'

'What are P's and Q's, mom?'

'I don't know.'

'How can I mind them if I don't know what they are?'

Theresa almost said hush again. If Jose had been with them, he would have exploded in anger. 'I don't know exactly what the letters P and Q stand for,' she finally said, 'but it means don't ask so many silly questions.'

Then they would walk in silence for a while, but it would not last long. 'Sister Mary Frances told me at Catechism Sunday that I ought to go to parochial school.'

'Yes. Wouldn't it be nice?'

'Not really. They'd try to recruit you to be an altar boy or maybe even a priest when you get older. Billy Thomas is going to be priest—that goody-goody.'

'Haven't you ever thought of being a priest?'

'Dad says I ought to be a teacher like he wanted to be. Or a doctor; there's always money in sick people.'

'But not a priest?'

Joe would look at her with wide, secret eyes. 'I'd be scared to be a priest,' he said. 'They have to be so good.'

Theresa would smile. She knew the feeling, the unsaid words: 'They have to be so good... and sometimes I'm so bad.' By now they would be at the church, walking up the steps. There would be a sparse crowd—older women mostly, a few old men, the faithful who sang in the choir or who decorated the church or ushered at Sunday mass, plus a few youngsters—some like Billy Thomas and others dragged to services by the ear for their own

135

good.

Their tall, heavyset pastor would lead the services, Father Ryan. He still spoke with a brogue, had visited his little white haired mother in Ireland last year. Father Ryan lumbered when he moved, a rolling gait like a sailor. When the gait was like a ship that was pitching violently in a storm, Father Ryan had probably had too much wine before services. You could tell for sure during the Friday stations of the cross, because he would lumber along the aisles among the pews, stopping at the plaster depictions of the way of the cross, bellowing the words at the parishioners in his wine smelling brogue. 'Weep not for me,' Jesus' words would come out at one of the stations, 'but weep for yourselves and for your children!' With the faint aroma of—no, Theresa thought, with all the good Father's tirades about the Jews killing Christ could it be Maneschewitz?

Then at some time during services they would rise and sing one of the familiar hymns. Theresa would hear the intense, off-key little voice beside her. 'Holy God, we praise Thy name...' Maybe, she would think, maybe he will become a priest. Wouldn't it be grand to have such a son. To have him save souls, comfort the sick, help the spiritually downfallen.

But as the years went by, she found herself going alone to evening services, or with a neighbor lady from around the corner whose daughter, who was going to be a nun, would often join them. Joe still attended mass on Sunday, while Jose was now attending more often. Then Joe went to college.

Who was it that had been visiting them that spring? Not Carlos. Carlos had not come to California since World War I, never again since then ventured from his plot of corn and tomatoes and chili in Los Rafas. Nor was it Dandy. Jose and Dandy would have come to blows over nothing at all at that time; Theresa was certain they would not have had Dandy staying with them. Joe had just started college then; he must have been seventeen or eighteen. That would make it about 1948 or 1949, the year before Tomas died.

Yes, she remembered. Tomas and his wife. That spring. One of

136

their sons had been in the Navy stationed at Long Beach. They had come to see him before he was transferred to Hawaii— or maybe it had been Japan. And to visit Jose. A joyful visit between two brothers who had not seen each other for three years and whose relationship was almost as close as father and son. There had been a special warmth in that visit, as if Tomas somehow knew they might not see each other again. He had still been a young man, only fifty-five, but he had been gassed in the war and his damaged lungs were weakening.

'Remember,' Tomas said to Jose one Saturday evening after dinner, 'how it was thirty years ago when I left Los Rafas to be a doughboy? To be sent to France?'

'You told me to help papa take care of the farm,' Jose said. 'I remember the chickens most of all.'

Tomas reached into the neck of his shirt. 'I wore this the whole time I was overseas and ever since. A St. Christopher medal. It was blessed by the Archbishop of Santa Fe. It has always kept me safe. I'm going to give it to my son tomorrow. He'll need St. Christopher with him among all those orientals.'

'He's an officer,' Jose said. 'He'll be safe.'

'I never thought way back there in France that I'd have a son who would one day be in the Navy and go to the orient.'

'We're getting old, Tomas.'

A brief flash of anger. 'You, maybe. But not me.'

It continued as an evening of reminiscence, of remembering the farm long ago when it had been on the isolated outskirts of a small town. When there had been few Anglos in their lives, and they had lived innocently as Spanish-speaking Americans without the press of Anglo ambition and assertiveness. Finally, farm-early, Tomas and his wife rose to prepare for bed.

'What time is mass tomorrow?' Tomas asked.

'Let's go at eight o'clock,' Jose said. The wives nodded in agreement, and all eyes turned to Joe who had sat half asleep through much of the evening.

Joe's eyes widened, blinked, as if he had just come awake. Then his head shook. 'No,' he said quietly, almost apologetically, 'I won't be going.'

Stone silence. Then an awkward stirring, with people avoiding

137

each other's eyes. 'What was that?' his Uncle Tomas finally said in disbelief.

Joe looked from his father to his mother before he answered. 'I don't go to church anymore,' he said.

Jose's face turned past crimson to purple. It must have taken the greatest will to keep from shouting in anger. Tomas and his wife exchanged awkward glances. 'Good night,' they said in unison.

The bedroom door had barely closed when Jose turned on Joe. 'What is this about church?' he lashed out.

'I've decided to stop going to church. I don't believe it anymore.'

'Is that what they teach you at UCLA? Disrespect for God?' Then Jose turned to Theresa. 'It's your fault,' he said. 'You should have listened when Father Ryan said to send him to Loyola.'

'Father Ryan!' Joe said. 'That's what's wrong with the church. That's your man of God? Look at that big fat gut. How can he preach against gluttony with that stomach in his way? Get near him at mass. You could get drunk from smelling his breath. Then what does he preach about? If I hear his tirade against the Jews one more time— I don't know. This is Catholicism? Bigoted. Self-serving. Narrow. Well, it's not for me, thank you.'

'As long as you live in this house, you'll go to church!'

'Oh, dad,' a tone of exasperation.

'And you have to drop this little bomb when my brother is here. Half of Albuquerque will know about it next week.'

'Sure. There'll be neon signs all over town with letters six feet high saying, 'JOSE RAFA'S SON DOESN'T GO TO CHURCH. A FAMILY DISGRACE!'

'Don't get smart with me.'

'Both of you stop it,' Theresa said. 'Now, Joe. What is this all about?'

'I don't want to be a Catholic anymore. I just can't swallow all that crap. It's too narrow. Too confining. It isn't really catholic enough. Only Catholics go to heaven. Can you really believe that?'

'Don't you believe in God?'

'I don't know. All I know is that I can't accept the Catholic god. He isn't big enough. Good enough. If there is a God, he's for everybody. Catholic, Protestant, Jew, Buddhist, Mohammedan, whatever.'

'Is that what they teach you in college?'

'Oh, for Christ's sakes. No! It's just that the way to learn is to ask questions. And all questions are legitimate. Even: Is there a God?'

'We should have sent you to Loyola.'

'Oh, mom. It's too late for that. Next thing you'll be wringing your hands saying, "We should have kept you in parochial school." It has nothing to do with where I went to school. I've met some of those Jesuits from Loyola. They're so brainwashed it's like talking to someone from another planet.'

'Don't talk like that about God's priests,' Jose said, but his anger was spent.

Theresa and Jose looked at each other as if to say: Where did we go wrong? What did we do or not do that our son should turn out like this?

'I'm sorry I upset you,' Joe said. 'My not going to church has nothing to do with you. I hope you understand that.'

Theresa nodded her head yes, even though she didn't understand. Quietly, Joe turned and walked from the room, leaving her and Jose in the silence.

'It's all that college,' Jose finally said. 'All those Godless institutions. They're supposed to educate them, but look what you get.'

Blame it on college, Theresa thought. But what about those years when you seldom went to church? When you would tell me you had enough of that bull? Joe's college was this living room on Sunday mornings.

'Maybe he should quit school and go to work,' Jose said. 'What good is an education if it just teaches you to turn your back on everything your family taught you? He should be out earning a living. He's old enough.'

'You can't be serious?'

'Look at you. Having to go to work to help out. Look at me. I didn't go to college, and I still made something out of myself.'

Theresa looked at him, trying to comprehend. I didn't go; why should he? Was that what she heard: Jealousy? Had they left Los Rafas, worked hard for what they had, worked hard to give their only son—their hope—a chance and now this? 'No,' she said. There was a look on her face that threatened violence. 'The only way for him, for us, is for Joe to finish school. I'll work two jobs if I have to. To quit is crazy. Next you'll be telling me we should move back to the farm.'

'No,' Jose said. 'It's just that I don't know what to do with that boy.'

'Man,' Theresa interjected.

'Here is my oldest, dearest brother having to hear this kind of a family squabble.'

'What if Tomas hadn't helped you leave Los Rafas those years ago? What if he hadn't helped you go against your father's wishes and go to school? What then?'

Jose did not have a ready answer this time. A look of confusion, of pain, flickered across his face, and he sighed. 'No more of your bull please.'

'You don't want to think about it, do you?'

'Goddamn it! Leave me alone. All that is past. You don't need to dig it up.'

What pain there must be between estranged father and son, Theresa thought. To see yourself reborn, with another chance to set things right, then to see that reborn self go off in another wrong direction. Men were not allowed to show love and concern for each other. Or to cry when that love failed them. It was not like mother and daughter. Women could be close. But men— Never.

'You didn't really mean that about Joe quitting school?'

'No. For Christ's sakes, no. It's just my brother.'

'Tomas is very dear to you, and you want things to be right for him.'

Jose's eyes clouded, on the verge of tears. 'And for Joe, too,' he said. 'For him even more.'

Theresa took his arm, and they went to bed.

At least, Theresa thought, Spain is a Catholic country. Jose had reconciled himself to the Church about the time Joe had left. God had traded one soul for another. So whatever it was that her husband sought in Spain, he would be under God's protection. At least that much the years had brought.

As for the rest, life had sandpapered the rough edges of Theresa's and Jose's relationship so that from the vantage point of time it looked smooth and placid. The broad outlines remained like gentle curves that belied the abrasive conflicts of the past. In retrospect but one conflict stood out—like the two sides of a coin. Their very differences as people. Theresa was a fighter who wanted more, while Jose avoided conflict and sought tranquility. Yet, in contradiction, Jose who was obedient was autocratic, while the rebellious Theresa gave more freedom to their son.

The opposites finally met there. In their son. A grown man now. No longer a believer in the God that Theresa loved above all earthly things. College educated in spite of his father's reservations. Middle-class and un-Spanish in a sense that was both pride and despair to Jose. Torn from her body at birth, ever to move farther and farther from her until she had to realize that her son was not hers. A realization that came late, if ever, to Jose. For the separation was pain that one had to accept before it would go away. The only separation whose pain lasted a life time was the separation from God.

Jose, she thought. Take care and come back. Find whatever it is you are seeking.

22

How do you cure a headache? Take an Anacin. Visions of the cutaway drawing of a head with gears and wheels and pounding—pounding—pounding, flashed through Jose's mind. Only Bayer contains 100 percent aspirin. Bufferin prevents upset stomach. Excedrin contains more of the pain killer doctors recommend. All aspirin is alike. On and on these nightmare visions of American television ran through Jose's head to finally end in a pistol explosion. A bullet. Mexican aspirin.

The vision would not leave him. Hadn't he had enough headaches of his own? A lifetime of them. Working in an Anglo world. Learning to live with a pushy wife; if she'd been a nigger, they'd have called her uppity. Raising a son to follow in his footsteps who went off instead in some direction Jose did not understand. Life's headaches. But none of them bad enough for a Mexican aspirin.

Maybe there are Spanish aspirin, he thought. But all he could conjure of Spain were Captains from Castile in leather and shining metal breastplates, castanets, snapping fingers, and thundering big-horned bulls with shouts of 'Ole!' None of them were pain-relieving.

Then a tune flitted past his mind's ear, changed after a few bars, leaving him undecided between 'In a little Spanish town...' and the grand, almost pompous 'Granada.'

A hiss from the airplane's loudspeaker system, then the announcement in Spanish. He fastened his seat belt, ground his cigarette into the ashtray, and looked out the small window. 'Granada' had won, the half forgotten words flickering into recognition in clusters like listening to a weak radio station through heavy static... the snow clad Sierra Nevada... There was no snow covered mountain below. Here Spain was brown, monotonously so, with gentle rolls of hills and sparse greenery. Much like home. Like California or New Mexico, the arid high desert where nature's beauty was concealed in the subtle shades of brown and gray interrupted only infrequently by thin veins of life, the rivers.

Madrid. Another airport. Another frightening landing with grimfaced officials waiting at the end to scrutinize passports and stamp official stamps.

The young woman at the service desk at the airport reserved a room for him at a hotel on the Avenida Jose Antonio. A quick taxi ride along the busy freeway and he was in the center of the city. Bustling. Crowded. Old. Undistinguished. Like any large city. The hotel stood across from the Plaza Espana. It was relief to finally get a room, to finally stretch out after that long ride on the airplane.

If there were only a maid to unpack my bag, Jose thought. Or my wife or my mother. He tried to conjure in his mind's eye a likeness of his—he tried to envision wife, but it came out mother. The visions alternated faster and faster until what he saw was a blur that was both yet neither.

'Goddamn it!' He hurled his suit coat across the room where it hit a chair and slid to the floor. 'I would like someone to take care of me,' he said aloud, but no one answered. There was the telephone and room service. 'No,' he said. 'The hell with it!' He picked up his own coat and hung it in the closet.

Jose sat on the edge of the bed. Lonely for the sound of a human voice, he started to talk to himself. The sound was not real enough, so he started a chant of curses. It built up from a whisper to a piercing shout that left his throat muscles taut and voice strained.

A pounding from the wall behind the bed. 'Shut up!' Jose shouted. 'Or I'll do it in Spanish, and then you will have something to pound about!'

But the pounding accomplished its purpose. He sat quietly for a few moments, letting the silence cleanse his eardrums and soothe his throat. Then Jose started to laugh softly. 'I'm going nuts,' he said to himself. 'I need to get out of this room into the street. To the park. Someplace.'

It was siesta. The shops were closed, and after two stops for coffee, he walked back toward the hotel, crossing the street to the Plaza Espana. He took off his coat and sat in the warm sunlight in back of the huge monument. Across the pool of water the lifesize statues seemed to advance towards him. Don Quixote on horseback, lance in hand. And Sancho Panza on his donkey.

Only here, Jose thought, would you see in a public place the statue of a madman and his servant fool.

But then he thought about his mad, foolish self alone in the world. Lonely for— Lonely for someone. For something. Lately it had been airplanes, hotels, taxis, restaurants. Stewardesses, porters, desk clerks, drivers, waiters. 'Si, senor. Anything you say, senor.' He had been the boss. Wasn't that what he wanted?

But there had been no relationship. Only an exchange. Service for money. Like parts of his life, he thought. Not really living. Just a perpetual traveller with a bag in his hand, skimming through what he called life, leaving tips for services rendered.

'You're nuts,' he said to himself, looking across the pool at the statue on horseback. 'Bored.'

Of course bored, he thought, pouncing on the word like a drowning man to a life preserver. It was siesta. The perpetual siesta. So he could not see the man he had come to Madrid to see. He had even passed the street where the man kept his shop. Senor Gomez S. Numero cinco. Calle de Los Libreros. Number five. Street of the bookshops. Closed. Come back at four o'clock.

He leaned back on the bench and looked at the reality of Spain. It was in no way like his dreams. Madrid was just another big city. A wide main avenue. Tall buildings. Shops. Crowds. Yes, he thought. The people were different. For some reason he had imagined that they would look like the people in the Los Rafas of his boyhood. Distinctive types. Distinctive features. But no. The men here were short. Even shorter than those of Los Rafas. The women stout, at least the older women; girls were still slim girls. The features— What would he call them? Nondescript? No. Like Anglos. That was what startled him so. Few dark complexioned. No heavy Indian features. Just Anglos. Like—like probably any other European. Nothing of the New World about them. He could have been in Germany for all that it mattered. Or England. Certainly not in the Los Rafas of his dreams. Anglos speaking Spanish.

A shadowy figure hovered at the periphery of Jose's vision, then moved directly in his line of sight. A gigantic head smiled, as if at the joke nature had played on his dwarfed body. A visored cap perched on his head at a jaunty angle, his clothes a faded uniform of some sort whose original color was difficult to determine.

'You like that statue, senor?' The dwarf's voice boomed out a basso profundo.

Jose blinked at this amazing creature, peered around him at Don Quixote to see if something had really blocked his view or if he was having a hallucination. 'Si, senor,' he finally answered.

144

Acknowledged, the dwarf approached and sat on the bench, legs dangling like those of a child. 'A beautiful monument of a great country.'

A madman and his fool, flickered through Jose's mind, but he listened attentively. Was that some sort of military uniform the dwarf wore? Could a dwarf have been in the army? No, he thought. Certainly not.

'Have you read Cervantes, senor? You haven't lived until you've read Cervantes.'

Should I rub his head? Jose thought. Isn't that what you do for good luck? Rub a dwarf's head? Or was it a hunchback's hump? 'Yes. Yes. I've read him. In school. Years ago.'

'Where did you go to school? You're not Spanish, senor.'

A tune flickered through Jose's mind, and he smiled. In a little Spanish town, upon a night like this— 'Can you guess? From the way I speak Spanish, can you tell?'

A woman and her small child passed, the child pointing at the dwarf. Oblivious, the dwarf studied Jose's face as if the answer to where he went to school were there. His face brightened at this little guessing game. 'Well, senor. To begin with, you are not Spanish. At least I don't think so. The accent is— I can't explain. Not exactly Spanish. Yet your Spanish is very good. Excellent. It has to be your natural language. Like—a Latin American.'

Jose smiled with pleasure. An intelligent man this dwarf. But he was on the wrong track. Latin American.

'Well, senor,' the dwarf continued. 'If I had to make a guess, I'd say—' He hesitated, scrutinizing Jose for a long while. 'Well, senor. I would have to say Mexico. You went to school in Mexico.'

Jose froze. It was as if a knife had pierced his side. Even the pride in his knowledge of the Spanish language could not shield him from that thrust.

The dwarf laughed, a deep rumble that seemed to carry over the pool of water to the advancing Don Quixote and Sancho Panza, past them to the open stretches of walkway and grass to the busy avenue far beyond. 'That is correct, is it not, senor?'

'No,' Jose said, shaking his head in puzzlement. 'I'm a Norteamericano. A North American.'

'Norteamericano? Wonder of wonders.' The dwarf's arms

swept out, describing a half circle, a rainbow, the horizon, whatever miracle you could ascribe to such a gesture. 'Magnificent, senor. North America. I always dreamed about going to North America. Where the streets are paved with gold! I should have known! I should have used my eyes. Just look at your shoes. Your suit. Who else but a North American could dress like that?'

Jose started feebly to add, 'Of Spanish descent.' But the words would not come out. They ran into each other, a crumbled mass that stuck in his throat.

'You are on a holiday then, senor?'

'Yes. A holiday.'

'How magnificent. A holiday. Other than a few North Americans what we mostly see are rich Germans. Well, senor, if I can be of service.' Raised eyebrows. Surprise. The dwarf did not notice Jose's reaction. He had dropped to the ground where he stood adjusting the faded jacket of his uniform. 'I am an excellent porter, senor. Also a bearer of messages. I am strong.' He flexed an arm to show his muscle. 'My station is at the hotel on the corner of Jose Antonio just two blocks from here. Now siesta is over. I must go back to work. Adios, senor. It has been the greatest pleasure to make your acquaintance.' With a stiff, awkward bow, he turned and walked across the plaza.

Jose watched the diminutive figure disappear into the now increasing crowd of pedestrians. I never asked about his uniform, Jose thought. It puzzled him. One of those insignificant mysteries that occasionally flashed across his life like a shooting star.

His older brothers had worn uniforms, Jose realized. Doughboys in khaki. Even his son had quit college to join the army during the Korean War, but he didn't want to think about that. Only he, of all the men, had missed a war. No soldier hero he. And then the dwarf. No, he thought. I'm making too much out of nothing.

His eyes returned to the statues, to Don Quixote and Sancho Panza, and he asked himself aloud, 'Where are the monuments to the conquistadors?'

23

With siesta over, the streets were crowded. The shops were opening their doors. But the urgency to find Senor Gomez S. had dissipated. Fatigue settled in on Jose, and he realized that only today he had arrived from Mexico City on an airplane. Tomorrow. Senor Gomez S.

The next day he felt better. From his room high up in the hotel, Jose could look down on the Plaza Espana. Down on the streets not yet busy with traffic, just a few cars here and there in the fresh morning that was still too early for crowds. After a breakfast of coffee and churros, he walked the few blocks to the Calle de Los Libreros. The shops along the way were just opening. The TWA ticket office already had several customers waiting, tourists confirming or changing their air flights. The movie theaters were still closed, although lines would start forming for the eleven AM showing a bit later.

There was no prominent sign on numero cinco. Only the small gold letters on the door, the edges of several letters worn by time. Blas Gomez S. Old Books. A hand lettered sign above the gold letters stated: No textbooks here.

A glance down the street. Groups of students, they must have been of college age, entered one of the other bookstores. Jose walked into number five, a small shop with a large wooden desk near the entrance, a counter behind it on which were piled stacks of books waiting for their permanent homes on the already crowded shelves. The bell ring was answered by the sound of heavy footsteps from the back of the shop.

'Senor?' The smell of coffee floated in with a middle-aged woman.

'I'm looking for Senor Gomez.'

The woman shook her head briskly. 'He's not here.'

'I've come all the way from North America to see him.'

A look of skepticism. Her eyes studied his clothes before they searched his face. 'I'm sorry, senor. My husband is away from the city. He won't be back for several days. Is there something I can help you with?' Jose sank onto the chair beside the desk. Concerned, the woman approached him. 'Are you all right, senor?'

The nodding answer was slow, tired, 'I—I had no idea,' Jose finally said. 'I had counted very much on seeing Senor Gomez. But now—' He stared dully at her hands which held each other in support. The thin wedding band was almost lost, sunk into the fleshy finger.

'If it's about books—'

'No. No.' From his wallet Jose pulled the card: 'Alfonso de Sintierra. Geneology. Coats of arms. Historical consultant.'

Senora Gomez read it. Turned it over to see if there were anything written on the reverse side, then handed it back. 'I don't understand, senor.'

'I was referred to your husband by Senor de Sintierra. About a geneological search. Your husband was to help me.'

'He spoke of no search to me. I'm not even certain if he knows Senor de Sintierra. A North American isn't he? I don't know, senor. Are you a professor doing research? Or a lawyer looking for an heir?'

Jose smiled sadly. A lawyer, he thought, looking for an heir? Rather, an heir looking for a heritage. 'No, senora. It is family business. Important personal business.'

Senora Gomez shook her head as if she did not quite understand. 'I can sell you books,' she said. 'We have old books. On history. Geneology.'

Was this what de Sintierra meant? Jose thought. A bookseller who had hidden treasures on his shelves that might lead him to the source? But the senora did not know. Her husband would if he were here. Wasn't that the way?

'I am trying to find the history of the Rafa family that left Spain for the New World in the sixteenth or seventeenth century.'

'We have books,' she repeated, hurrying to a large, ancient ledger. She thumbed through, searching with a forefinger as if the titles were something that had to be felt. She read off the titles of several. At each Jose shook his head. Then from behind the counter, Senora Gomez lifted a huge volume, thick as the unabridged dictionary in an American library. Pages flipped. The reading forefinger searched down several pages. 'Here, senor,' she finally said. "Catalog of Passengers to the Indies during the 16th, 17th, and 18th Centuries." I knew that somewhere I had seen something.'

There had been too many titles. This one was like the murmur of words one heard at mass but did not understand. But the excited tone of voice, the animated expression of face, and Jose knew he had missed something. 'What was that?' Senora Gomez reread the title. A warm flush of pleasure oozed through Jose's body. 'That sounds like something,' he said, barely restraining the exuberant hope that made him want to shout. 'Do you have it? Is it for sale?' It was his good luck, he thought. Brought by that dwarf, even if he hadn't rubbed his head. His Spanish luck.

The look of disappointment on Senora Gomez's face gave him the answer. He did not hear her words. 'How sad, senor. No. And it is out of print.' Their disappointed eyes met. 'Perhaps, senor, you can find a copy in one of the bookstalls near the Botanical Gardens. Or at the Library. Surely they will have one at the National Library.'

'Yes,' he said, more to himself than to her. 'Certainly such an important book would be in the National Library.'

It was a short taxi ride to the National Library. Then a confusing search, with steps leading up, and various entries at ground level. Finally, after a few questions, Jose found himself in the reference section. Past the guard who directed him out again. There seemed to be students everywhere in the quiet, footstep-echoing halls. The line-up at the counter seemed to be the right place. Here, for two pesetas plus identification with his passport, he received a stamped visitor's ticket. Then back past the guard who nodded him in.

A confusion of indexes. Catalogs and dictionaries, authors, subjects. Each group subdivided again. A sense of panic overwhelmed Jose. Everyone else seemed to know what they were looking for. Pulling out card files and thumbing through with brisk assurance. He watched a young woman copy from a card onto a slip, then leave the reference room through a large door and turn up a flight of stairs.

'Catalog of Passengers to the Indies,' he said to himself. First a search through the section marked catalogs. Then through the section marked subjects. He found other books, yes. But not his book. His was an important book. Didn't they know that? Why— It should be on display somewhere. Prominently. In a glass case flanked by guards. Floodlighted. A burglar alarm in case anyone tried to tamper with the bullet-proof glass.

But no. Not even a footnote on a card. There were other books. Many. But none the right one. In exasperation he copied down the information on one: 'Spanish-American Surnames,' by Alfredo Souto Feijoo. Siler. Avenida Jose Antonio 55, Madrid 1957. With all the appropriate identification numbers. Then out the room and up the stairs to learn how this system worked.

Another counter. Busy. With young women taking slips from students and older men in blue smocks carrying books. Briskly his slip was taken, stamped, and a numbered slip returned to him. The next room, the young lady said. The table with the number she had given him.

Jose shuffled timorously into the huge study room. Rows and rows of empty chairs and tables stared impassively at him. Only a few, up at the very front, were occupied. He checked his number and made his way to the chair and table. He would have to see how this worked. There were very few books in the bookcases lining the walls. A blue smocked man came along the aisle and deposited a number of books on the table two rows ahead. The young man next to him sat working out a chess problem with an open text beside the board.

Oh, God, Jose thought. This is ridiculous. Where do they keep the books? Everybody seems to be waiting.

He looked at his wristwatch. Finally, a man in blue came by and deposited a book on the table infront of Jose. It took but a moment to leaf through the pages. M. N. O. P. Q. R. But no Rafa. Lots of Spanish-American surnames, but no Rafa. He slammed the book shut. The chess player dropped the chess man he held in his fingertips.

'Bullshit!' Jose said under his breath. A curious student looked up but obviously did not understand the English word. Jose's sense of frustration decreased as soon as he was outdoors. A mausoleum, he thought. A tomb. Where they bury books and station guards and attendants to make certain you don't try to

150

bring knowledge back to life.

Another taxi ride to the bookstalls near the Botanical Gardens. A long row of stalls up the slope. Magazines. Old books. New books. But not *the* book. Then another trip back to Senora Gomez's shop.

An elderly gentleman stood at the counter in an intense discussion with Senora Gomez. Her eyes acknowledged Jose as he entered. Impatiently Jose listened to their transaction. He glanced along the shelves on the wall as if the book he wanted might possibly be there. Footsteps. The customer had left.

'Have you found your book so soon, senor?'

Jose shook his head. 'I want to get in touch with Senor Gomez,' he said.

'He is away. For several days.'

'I could go see him. It is a matter of the greatest urgency. And I don't have much time.'

The senora frowned. He could see the questioning on her face. 'He is on business, senor. In the south. Looking at some books for sale.'

'I wouldn't interfere with his business. But in the evenings. Or at meal times. A few moments. A direction. A hint even. I have Senor de Sintierra's card. Your husband is the man he sent me to see.'

Her eyelashes fluttered. What was she thinking? A madman? A fool? She sighed and shook her head. 'Senor. You have come a long way. From North America. It is the least I can do. Senor Gomez travelled to Granada and Sevilla to view some private collections. I can give you his itinerary. You may want to telephone him at one of the hotels where he'll be staying to make sure you'll meet him. What more can I do?'

'I could ask no more,' he said. He watched, trembling, as she reached behind the counter for a ledger and carefully copied from it onto a piece of paper, which, at last, she handed to him. 'I'm forever grateful, Senora Gomez.'

Jose rushed from the shop as if the next train to Granada was waiting for him at the curb. He read the note as he walked quickly down the street. When he reached the corner breathless, the strength drained from him. The day had been too much. He

151

patted his jacket pocket. Empty. His damned pills were still packed in his bag at the hotel. Although it was but a few blocks distant, he took another taxi, knowing that what little strength he had should be hoarded to get himself into his room and into bed for a rest. Granada could wait until tomorrow.

24

I should have known, Jose thought. I should have taken a train or even a bus. It's bad enough being stuck behind some smudge pot of a truck for miles, but now this.

The driver peered out from behind the hood of the automobile. 'It's all right, senors. It shouldn't take long to fix. There's a garage in town and an inn not too far up the road.'

Jose and his fellow passenger exchanged skeptical glances. They had ridden in near silence since they had left Madrid in the chauffeured car. Senor Benetar, Jose thought. A strange, dark fellow. Very dark. Almost—no. Not that dark. Not like a Negro. Perhaps he was a gypsy. With that thought, Jose became conscious of the weight of his wallet and passport. He resisted the temptation to pat his breast pocket to check them.

No, he thought. Gypsies don't travel around in chauffeured cars wearing business suits. Senor Benetar is in imports, exports. On his way to Granada. Strange man. But accommodating. Offering to share the rented car on the drive to Granada. Sheer luck that. Not having to drive himself. Nor mess with the damned trains and their schedules and delays. But now this! Delays anyway. Damn!

'Do you know this country, Senor Benetar?'

A quick, repeated shaking of the head. 'I have to be in Granada tomorrow morning.' He sat silent for a moment, then spoke again. 'I have to apologize for this inconvenience, senor. You, too, have business in Granada.'

They were at the outer edge of a small town. The late morning air was warming, although there was still a cool edge to it. A road branched off the main highway. A short distance away a cluster of trees hovered around what might have been a park. It was quiet. Restful. Without that confined feeling of the city—where tall, faceless buildings stood shoulder to shoulder on both sides of the street, a canyon of brick and cement with anonymous goings on inside.

The road toward the trees was rutted, passing along fields and hedges and grape vines. Mothers were walking their small children. Slowly. In repose. For Jose it was like a road to the past. Quiet. Open. The country.

'What do you think, Senor Benetar? The inn or the park?'

A solemn glance at the countryside. 'The inn. Perhaps they are still serving breakfast.'

They walked past the park, turned on another country road that led past the bull ring. The air, the sun, the open fields lulled Jose into a rare state of relaxation. He felt drawn into himself. As if the outer boundaries of his flesh had tightened, concentrating the essence of what he was. His muscles and nerves and flesh seemed to hum in accord, in a sense of well being.

The smell of air, the green of the trees, even the benignly dusty road were incomparably beautiful. Had Los Rafas once been like this? In remembering his childhood, such quiet, peaceful dreams appeared. But Eden had turned harsh as he grew older. And when evoked again, memory was clouded with sentiment.

When I was young, Jose thought, I could only think of tomorrow. When adult, of today. But now when I am old, I think mostly of yesterday. Somehow, at all three ages, I have looked for the same thing; it must be somewhere back there in the middle of my life, where future, present, and past converge. But what is it?

They walked up to the old two-story inn. Jose stopped in the washroom. From the window he could see into the courtyard. A black and white kitten chased something in the dirt around a wheelbarrow. Two little black dogs came quickly out of an open door on the other side, barked, then disappeared back into the building. A rope strung between two trees supported tiny pajamas with feet that were drying in the sun. Just behind the clothesline two workers emerged from a large door that must have been a shop. One of them stretched and yawned, turning his face to the sun.

As he left, Jose tipped the woman attendant. He glanced quickly at the nearly empty sitting room, then walked past the desk toward the dining room. Senor Benetar was already seated alongside one of the wide windows that looked out on the countryside.

'This reminds me of my home when I was a boy,' Jose said. 'The country. The fields. I used to have a pet horse. A pony. I would ride him through the fields playing Spaniards and Moors. Or maybe I was a conquistador defeating the Indians.'

'I am of Moorish descent,' Senor Benetar said. His solemn, dark eyes peered over the top of his coffee cup as he drank.

Jose was startled. 'No offense, senor. You know how children are.' A short, slow nod. 'I hope you understand. It's just that the countryside took me back to my boyhood. Perhaps you played Moors and Spaniards as a boy.' Stupid! Jose thought the moment the words rushed out as if of their own accord. Why did I say that?

Senor Benetar smiled tolerantly. 'You are a North American, senor.' As if that explained something.

Well, Jose thought, there it goes again. The mouth from which comes words that I don't really mean. The putting off of someone whom I really want to care about.

The thought pierced Jose painfully. It had been years ago. One of those scars that never disappear. His son. What had his fool mouth said then? 'Mexican.' Yes. And there had been a girl. Pretty little thing. But crazy. She had run out of the house. Joe and she were going to be engaged. Yet she had run out of the house when Jose had said that word.

Well, that had been good riddance anyway, Jose thought. What had happened afterwards had been the problem. Damned stubborn kid. Just like the Rafas. Enlisting in the Army like that. When he only had a year to finish college.

'I can't take it anymore,' Joe had said. 'The sooner I'm out of this house, the better. I'd rather be in Korea than here.'

Yes, Jose had agreed then. To keep him away from that girl.

154

Not reckoning with the fears that would flood in on him later. What if he's killed? Jose would eventually think. In the middle of the night he would suddenly find himself awake, his eyes wide open, thinking: What if he's killed?

That would be the end of my line, Jose thought. No one to carry on the name. No other son. No daughter even. He would shift in bed and stare through the dark at Theresa, wondering. Maybe she doesn't want any more children with me, he thought. Maybe she could have them, but she doesn't want them. Then he would turn away, anguished. You're crazy, he said to himself. Absolutely nuts. Joe will be all right. You'll see. You'll see. But the anxiety continued all through his son's basic training, then on to more training, then overseas to Korea. Continued even through the pride when Joe had been awarded a medal. A Bronze Star. For heroism in action. Proud, yes. But what did pride mean if they shipped him home in a casket? Then one morning he picked up the newspaper and there it was in the headlines. Korean truce!

Was that all there was to the scar? Jose asked himself. No. It had been more than that. The letters his son did not write to him. Always to Theresa. (He did not think about the letters he did not write to his son.) The avoidance, the breech—which even Theresa could not heal. What had he, Jose, done that was so wrong? He had always wanted the best for his son. Only told him what to do so that things would be better for Joe. But it always seemed to come out wrong. As if wanting too much had worked against their relationship instead of for it.

Yes. That had been the wound that had scarred the deepest. A cleavage as if they were two creatures from warring planets. Had his son ever said: I love you, dad? Had Jose's father ever said: I love you, son? Here he was. Both father and son. And never hearing what he wanted to hear.

Stop it! Jose said to himself. In a moment you'll be crying in your coffee. He looked across the dining table at Senor Benetar. There was a man who would not waste his time on such silly thoughts. Stern. Solemn. The kind of look Jose remembered on his father.

Well, the hell with it. What was he wringing his hands for?

Not only did he have a son, he had grandsons. Two of them. One, his favorite, like a piece torn from grandpa's soul. He had to smile. Yes. The little skunk. He would let people know what a Rafa was. And probably have six sons of his own when the time came.

The waitress came by and refilled his coffee cup. Senor Benetar sighed, and Jose swore he could hear his flesh crack when the sigh became a smile. 'Ah. Now I feel human, Senor Rafa. What do you say to a leisurely stroll back to that park? Through the countryside that reminds you of your boyhood?'

They left word at the desk in case their driver came looking for them. Then they strolled along the country road. Along a field of grapes shielded from the road by a shoulder-high hedge. Past the bull ring again. Then into the shaded dirt promenade that was the park.

They walked along a wall until they came to the entrance, crossing a short bridge over a shallow gully to the grassy area beyond. There were small buildings here and there, some like stages empty and waiting.

'This must be the fairgrounds,' Senor Benetar said.

Jose glanced around, seeing a black silhouette against one of the small buildings. A metal profile of the Knight of the Rueful Countenance astride Rosinante. On some of the park benches were men his own age. Gray haired. Wrinkled. In remnants of uniforms. Some with canes or crutches. Survivors. Veterans. Past their days of glory. Fit now for sitting on park benches. Behind, at the edge of the grounds, was an encampment of military. Young men in their full vigor polishing the large trucks or ambling quietly from one place to another, purposeful while smoking cigarettes.

'Over there,' Senor Benetar said. 'A nice bench in the shade.' They sat, the two well-dressed men in business suits, among the veterans who hardly gave them a glance.

From behind one of the trucks drifted the song of a guitar. A lively air. Accompanied by the sounds of male voices. Ending in laughter. After a moment, a few chords, then it began again. This time only the guitar sang. Plaintive. A song of soul. A tremelo of notes overriding each other. In a minor key. Taking one back. To where?

Jose glanced at his companion. Tears flowed down Senor Benetar's cheeks. In the spell of the music himself, Jose could but watch his companion who looked as if the melody had captured his soul and transported it back to that beginning place where feeling once again joined the mind so that they were one.

The song drifted off slower and softer. Until one's imagination still heard it, still sought it in the silence, trying to call it back from the place it went to. Senor Benetar sighed and blew his nose into a large clean handkerchief, then folded it neatly and wiped his eyes with one edge.

'Are you all right, senor?' Jose said. He felt shaken by this breech of what he had decided about Senor Benetar. It did not fit the strong, stern, solemn man he had imagined him to be.

'Yes,' he answered in a hoarse voice. Senor Benetar sat silent for a moment, then looked at Jose. 'I never expected to hear that song in this place. It was a shock.' Then silent musing again. 'It is called "Recuerdos de la Alhambra." "Memories of the Alhambra,"' he finally added. 'It takes me back. Back. To when my people ruled this country.'

Well! My people rule it! flashed through Jose's mind. Conquerors! Conquistadors! But then his reaction dissipated, and he saw only this sad old man next to him. 'That was a long time ago, senor.'

Senor Benetar continued talking. Slowly. Sadly. Almost as if to himself. 'My ancestors were Spanish Moors who became Christians rather than leave Spain when the kingdom of Granada fell in 1492. Those who were expelled lost everything. Their homes. Their property. Those who were still alive went back to Africa. Those who stayed became Christians. Spanish citizens. All they lost was their religion—their souls. Although some practiced the Muslim religion in secret.

'My family was one who carried with them through the centuries the memory of the grandeur that was Moorish Spain. We gave this infidel land what culture there was at that time. It was from the Moors through Spain that Europe gained. Mathematics. Medicine. The guitar whose sad song awakens a flood of memories in me.

'My family thought always that some day the Moors would

reconquer Spain. Reconquer what was lost almost five hundred years ago. My father was one of those who saw reality. "This is foolish." he said, "to dream of reconquest. The Moors lost everything but their illusions. I have no more illusions. We have lost. The Christians have won—even our souls. So let it be. Winners do not have to learn any new lessons. Only losers. And the hardest thing for a loser to learn is to forgive. Both the winner and even more important—himself."

'So my father accepted himself as a Christian Spaniard. As a young man I moved to Africa, took up the old religion, became a trader. Where once my ancestors traded their religion for their lives, now I traded goods from Africa to Spain.

'But now. Now I am coming back to Spain. After all those years I realize it is my home. Tell me, senor. Will you stay long in Granada?'

'No.'

'A pity. You should see the Alhambra. Written there are the words that finally changed my mind. In Arabic, in the halls of the Alhambra. "Wa le ghalib il Allah. There is no victor but Allah." These words made me realize that my father was right.'

The guitar once again. This time a lively tune, and the young soldiers were singing lustily. Across the park a benchful of veterans nodded heads and dozed in the sun.

'So,' Senor Benetar said. 'This park reminds you of your boyhood.'

'It reminds me of what I dream my boyhood was,' Jose said. 'I don't know if it's a real memory or not. Maybe it's just the memory of a dream.' Jose felt a sadness settle over him, like a cloud passing in front of the sun. For a moment he felt the tears rise, much the way Senor Benetar must have felt but a short while ago. But he could not cry.

'Ah, Senor Rafa. Look what comes across the way to disturb our siesta. Our driver. A pity.'

'Yes,' Jose echoed. 'A pity.'

25

'No, senor,' the desk clerk said. 'There is no Senor Gomez registered here.'

'But he's supposed to be staying at this hotel. I telephoned this morning. He was out. The clerk took a message.'

'Ah, senor. This morning.' The clerk searched through more records. 'Senor Blas Gomez S. Room 507. He has checked out, senor.'

Jose looked behind the clerk at the rows of key boxes. 507. A folded slip of paper. 'Did he leave a message?'

Again the clerk searched through some papers on the desk. 'No, senor.' Jose pointed to box 507. The clerk read the slip. 'No, senor. This is *for* Senor Gomez. From Senor Rafa.'

Jose recited the message from memory. 'Car trouble. Will be delayed. Hope to arrive in Granada early evening.' The clerk looked at Jose in surprise. 'Thank you,' Jose said.

Nothing to do now but wait for the dining room to open, Jose thought. Then tomorrow the train to Sevilla. Too bad Senor Benetar was not here to join him at dinner. An interesting man. Morisco. Converted to Christian. The interesting things he said. How everything happened in that magic year. 1492. The Moors defeated and Christianized. 'Baptism or exile,' is what the king decreed. The Jews expelled from Spain. The New World discovered. When Catholic-Islamic-Jewish Spain had become one nation—politically and spiritually. While in the New World they had initiated another trilogy of culture—Spanish, Indian, and later Anglo. As if the one God, the true God, sought balance. What is taken away here is put back there. Senor Benetar was an exile of the old, and he, Jose, an exile of the new.

Still the Spanish leave, Senor Benetar had continued. Once to the New World to seek gold. Now to Germany or Switzerland or England to seek a living wage. Working as waiters or highway laborers. A far cry from the Captains from Castile.

Well! Enough! Jose thought. This is all too confusing. There is too much to think about. Too much thinking gives me a headache.

But was it so much better in the New World? a little voice whispered to him. Then, in a tuneless chant that he had not heard in forty years:

Mexico Joe.
Mexico Joe.
Crossed the river near the Alamo.
Go back Joe;
Not so slow.
Across the river back to Mexico.

A sense of panic assaulted him. His first job. That's where he had heard it. He didn't even remember from whom. In the fish cannery. Where a sense of rage would possess him, so that it took all the control he had to keep that sharp knife of his working on the fish and not seeking out the singer. He remembered the voice, but not the man—a nasal whine from Oklahoma or Texas. Mexico Joe's Anglo friend.

For Jose, going to the fish cannery in California had been like a young Spaniard going to Germany to build roads. Another language. Another culture. The same prejudices. *But in his own country.* That was what had galled him most. 'My country 'tis of thee, sweet land of liberty—'The song turned sour in his throat like spoiled milk. It was no 'Memories of the Alhambra.'

But he had shown them. They had let him help the timekeeper because he was able to speak Spanish to the Mexican workers in the cannery as well as English to the rest. He had done the work so well, known his numbers so well, that soon he was helping the bookkeeper. Then the Okie strains of Mexico Joe's voice had faded, lost in the cannery while he had moved into the office.

Five years he had worked at the cannery. He would have worked there longer, maybe even retired from there but for his wife. Sometimes she was a worse task master than the cannery boss.

'We can't live here anymore,' Theresa had said. 'Joey will be starting school this fall. The schools here are terrible. This neighborhood is no place to bring up your son. We might as well be living in East L.A. This is just another barrio. An Anglo barrio.'

'Christ. I'm tired. I worked all day. The end of the month report has to be ready by Friday. I've got a headache. Leave me alone!'

'We have to move,' Theresa continued. She never raised her voice. Never screamed like those Indian sisters of his. Soft voiced. Firm. Logical. It drove him mad! 'It's—it's not good enough. I want something better. Something more.'

'And I'm the donkey you're riding to the Promised Land,' he said. 'I can only carry so much. Goddamn it! Leave me alone.'

'I'll go to work if I have to.'

He had left the room then. His hands had automatically jumped out, thumb and fingers curled as if he already had her throat between them. An outrage. Absolute outrage. No self-respecting woman went to work while she had a husband to support her. No self-respecting man put his wife to work. Earning the bread and butter was a man's job. Woman's work was in the home.

The door behind him opened quietly. 'You never talk to me,' Theresa said. 'You give orders, then you run away. How can we ever settle anything if you never talk to me?'

This was more than Jose could bear. He wheeled around and was across the small room in two steps. His hand was up before he realized it. Smack! Right across the face. Her startled eyes widened and stared at him for just an instant before they flooded with tears, while the red handprint slowly developed on her cheek. Then her mouth twisted, and she sobbed.

'My God—' Jose started to say. But she had turned and gone before he could add, 'I'm sorry.' He followed her. 'Mi vida,' he shouted. 'I didn't mean it.' The answer was the slam of the front door.

She came back an hour later. The next weekend they had started looking for another place to live. In southwest Los Angeles. This took him much farther away from the cannery so that soon he started looking for a job closer to home—and found it. With a branch of the bank less than a mile away. Until much later, when they had transferred him to Boyle Heights because he could speak Spanish. And even much later, when he was promoted to headquarters in downtown Los Angeles to help with their Latin American work.

Well, Jose thought, that had been better than going to Germany to work. Counting fish maybe not. But counting money certainly. Yes, the New World was better. At least there was a chance.

And Theresa. She had finally gone to work herself. Not then. But later. Years later. To help send Joe to college. And then the crazy kid had gone off to the Army like that. Gone back to college afterward on his own. In Berkeley of all places. Well. The world changes. How the world changes. In his father's day— Never mind, he told himself. He didn't want to think about that.

'Senor.' Jose looked up. 'The dining room is serving now, senor.'

'Thank you.'

He rose from the overstuffed leather chair and walked slowly in to dine alone.

26

Now at last, fatigue settled in on Jose like heavy dark clouds of foreboding. Even a long night's sleep did not help, and the train ride to Sevilla drained him of what little energy he had left. He dropped onto his hotel bed and slept through dinner, waking only long enough to telephone the elusive Senor Gomez. Gomez was out again, and again Jose left a message. Then back to sleep until the next morning.

Senor Benetar visited him in his sleep. Briefly. Just before he awoke. 'We did not succeed in the Old World,' he said. 'The Christian and the Moor got together; the Jew and the Christian got together—at least Christians converted some Moors and Jews. But all three did not get together as equals. You have the chance in the New World to bring them together—Spanish, Indian, Anglo.'

'No,' Jose said. 'I am Spanish. A son of conquistadors. Maybe we can get together with the Anglos, but with the Indian dogs—never.'

Senor Benetar smiled. 'But that is why it is the New World. So there can be a new beginning. And besides,' and here his smile broadened, 'what about your grandchildren? They refute your denial.'

'No,' Jose insisted, shaking his head vigorously. 'My Anglo daughter-in-law has no Indian blood.'

'That's not what I mean.' Still smiling with that insolent, knowing expression on his face.

'No,' Jose said. 'Never. Never. Nev—' He awoke at the sound of the word coming from his own lips, his heart pounding. Christ, he thought. A nightmare.

He looked around, half expecting to see Senor Benetar. Thank God, he thought. I'm in Sevilla. No Moors here, leading back to Africa. No Indians either. No taint of those dark races that pollute the blood and make a man a slave. I'm Spanish. Pure Spanish. Son of conquerors. Architects of the New World. We beat the Indians. Conquered them.

But Senor Benetar's smile lingered in the air, mocking him. Jose answered the smile with a grudging admission. 'Well. Yes. In what is now the United States the Anglos defeated us. So, in a way, we are a conquered people. Like the Moors.' The smile did not disappear. 'The hell with you!' Jose said to the air. Then, realizing that he had been talking to himself, he hurriedly dressed and went downstairs for a quick breakfast before seeking Senor Gomez.

The streets of Sevilla were still sparsely crowded. Sprinkled with those cripples that surprised Jose. Twisted limb beggars on street corners. The legless. The armless. Dwarfs—reminding him of the little man in Madrid. His lucky dwarf.

In Mexico the beggars were Indians. Pitiful little brown arms and hands sticking out of huddled serapes on cold street corners. At home in the United States one did not see beggars nor many cripples. Was that what progress meant? Take the beggars off the streets and—and what? Hide them away, he thought. In institutions where they do not offend the public eye. A sublimation that

163

was no less vicious than Grandees hacking off Indian heads with Toledo steel.

Jose brushed aside a dwarf as he turned the street corner. He was thinking bad thoughts. Wrong thoughts. Thoughts he never considered before. As if that damned smile of Senor Benetar's followed him, suspended above him like a toy balloon. Mocking him.

The hotel was just across the plaza. He rang Senor Gomez's room on the house telephone, then hung up and asked at the desk. The clerk answered. Perhaps Senor Gomez S. was in the dining room. He was a man of business. An early riser. A thin man. Very thin. With a sharp, long face. Hair turning gray. Not tall. Not short. Perhaps a bit shorter than senor.

Luckily there were few people eating breakfast and only one man alone. Jose recognized him from the desk clerk's description. 'Senor Blas Gomez S.?'

The man looked up from his coffee and rolls.

'I hope you'll forgive me for intruding on you like this. I am Senor Jose Rafa. I talked to you by telephone when you were in Granada three days ago. I had hoped to see you the day before yesterday, but our limousine from Madrid broke down.'

Slowly a recognition lighted Senor Gomez's eyes. He pointed a hand toward a chair. 'Ah. The telephone message last night. Passengers to the Indies. You're the gentleman from North America.'

Jose nodded with an expectant smile. He handed Senor Gomez a business card. 'Alfonso de Sintierra. Geneology. Coats of arms. Historical consultant.'

Senor Gomez read it casually between sips of coffee, then handed it back. 'But are you not Senor Rafa?' he asked, puzzled.

Jose nodded. 'Senor de Sintierra sent me to you.' A questioning shrug. 'You do not know Senor de Sintierra?' A slow shaking of the head. 'I don't know what to say. This is all so ridiculous.'

'I understand that you want to buy a book. "Catalog of Passengers to the Indies during the 16th, 17th, and 18th Centuries."'

Jose shook his head. He was confused. Stunned by the infamous lying of that bastard de Sintierra. 'I—I am trying to find my origins. To find where I came from.' But then the words as they came out even puzzled Jose. As if he did not know who he was. 'To trace my family,' he explained. 'The Rafas. Back here to Spain.' *already has a notion of what he wants to find. Think*

'Sixteenth century, senor. That was over four hundred years ago.' The tone of his voice said more: What does it matter now? 'If there were an inheritance or a royal title—'

'I need to know. It's a matter of life and death.'

'Well, senor. So important. But how can I help you? I am only a seller of books.'

Jose did not know what to say. He slumped back into the chair and looked with confused eyes at Senor Gomez who had nodded to the waiter for more coffee. 'You mentioned the book,' Jose finally said. 'Out of print your wife told me. There must be something for me in that book.'

'Perhaps senor. At any rate, you have come to the right place. The Archives of the Indies are here in Sevilla. Logs. Papers. Records of the exploration of the New World. It was from here that Columbus sailed on his third voyage. And the ships from the fourth voyage started from here. This also is his final resting place. His tomb is in the cathedral.'

'And the book?'

'It was published by the Archives. Certainly they would have a copy. Perhaps you could even see it. I don't know. They conduct tours through the Archives. But to see the books? It's for scholarly research. It would require permission. Letters. I don't know.'

'But you, senor. Would they let you in to look at the book?'

'Perhaps. I have been of service to the Director. In my business I find old books. Meet librarians, scholars at institutes. Perhaps, senor. But I'm a very busy man. I have appointments today and tomorrow. Perhaps the day after that. Before I return to Madrid.'

'I will pay you,' Jose said. 'When one is descended from conquistadors, it is worth much to find some answers.'

'Conquistadors? Well, senor. All I can do is look in a book. That does not require money. As for conquistadors. You want Extremadura, not Sevilla. That is the country of the conquistadors.'

'Would I have come from there?'

'I don't know, senor. That is where some came from. Pizzaro.

Cortez. Balboa. deSota. DeValdivia. Hard men from the hard land of Extremadura. Toward the Portuguese border. A land that has seen many conquerors or would-be conquerors come and go. The Romans even. Conquerors that were in Spain for centuries. Extremadura has a tradition of conquest. The Captains from Castile were really the Captains from Extremadura. Castile was the name of the kingdom. Extremadura was the province. Go there, senor. To see the origins of your conquistadors.'

Senor Gomez folded his napkin and laid it on the table, meanwhile glancing at his wristwatch. 'I'm sorry, but I have to leave, Senor Rafa. It has been most interesting talking to you. I don't meet many North Americans.'

'When can I see you again? About the book.'

'The day after tomorrow. If you call for me here at the hotel. I will find out what can be done at the Archives. I will also have some small business to finish, but that should not take long. Until the day after tomorrow, senor.'

'Many thanks. You have been most kind.'

With a quick nod, Senor Gomez left the dining room. Jose remained in the chair thinking. Now Extremadura. Birthplace of the conquistadors. One time Roman colony. It was as if, in following the road back, every destination was not an ending but another beginning. Branching off again into other roads. Where he did not know which fork of the road to follow, and began to wonder how far back one should go. Or whether one should decide on one final crossroad and say to oneself, 'This is far enough. I stop here.'

Where would it all end? With Adam and Eve? Or up in the branches of some monkey's tree? God! It was all so confusing.

The waiter stood waiting to be called, but Jose left the table, walking thoughtfully through the lobby and out into the plaza. It was warmer now, and he gravitated toward a bench in the sun in the plaza.

Perhaps I shouldn't have started this crazy search, he thought. At every step nothing but confusion. Lies. Or ignorance. Blind leads. As if I was never meant to discover the source. Never meant to go back and pick among the fossils for one whose remains says Rafa.

After a while the sun began to loosen the tight muscles in his neck and shoulders, began to relax his body until his mind began to follow. He dozed off. Lightly. Still somewhat aware of his surroundings. Then deeper. Down that road that transported him to another world. Another time.

He was galloping across the high desert on Rosinante. The wind whistling past his suit of armor, the visor open so he could see the way. The trail up the Rio del Norte had been attacked again. Wagons destroyed. Cattle driven off. And the safety of the settlement still two days march away.

Well. He, Don Jose de Rafa, would take care of those Indian dogs. 'Just a little farther, Rosinante,' he urged. 'Up that rise so we can see which way they went.'

They stopped, Rosinante whinnying and pawing the ground, as Don Jose surveyed the landscape. To the east he could see the thin ribbon of the river winding along the desert. He could barely make out the wagon train, recovering from the attack. Then as he turned he could see farther north and west a trail of dust moving away from the river.

'There, Rosinante. Those heathen dogs. Hurry.' They set out at a gallop, following the trail of dust. It was late afternoon before they slowed their pursuit. There were signs that the Indians had slackened their pace, and some sixth sense told Don Jose that he was near their encampment.

The call of a bird. Then again. He pulled on the reins, steadying his horse. The bird call repeated. 'We have them, Rosinante,' he whispered. 'We must be very quiet.'

Don Jose dismounted and crept ahead through the low shrubbery. After a short distance the ground sloped down gently to a small creek backed by a high embankment. He could see the raiding party now—their several horses tethered to the small trees on the right. He sat for some time, watching them. Counting them. Figuring exactly how he would surprise them. They were talking and laughing among themselves, certain that no white man was anywhere near.

Back to Rosinante with a final check of horse and weapons. The lance he carried in his right hand. The sword hung in its scabbard on Rosinante's side. The dagger in Don Jose's belt.

Quietly, horse and rider moved to the most sheltered part of the slope, working as closely as possible before breaking into the open.

The long shadows of dusk were settling in, the light losing its fierce intensity and becoming that softness that was not yet dark. 'Brace yourself, Rosinante,' his whispered. Then, with a light touch of his spurs, 'Santiago! Death to the heathen dogs!'

Rosinante raced to cut them off from their horses. Down came the lance. The soft jolt. Rosinante stepped over the fallen bodies. Then to the sword, singing as it sliced through the air, severing an Indian head.

It was over in minutes. The last Indian bolted from the camp toward the thin line of trees at the edge of the slope. With a few powerful strides, Rosinante was upon him and Don Jose impaled him on his lance. Slowly he turned Rosinante and counted the bodies. They were all there. Then, to be certain, he rode up to the first body.

With a flick of the lance, Don Jose rolled the Indian over so he could check for signs of life. His glance moved up the dusty brown corpse. The face seemed to magnify under his gaze. He stifled a scream that started to well up from his gut. It was the face of his dead father. With a sense of panic he spurred Rosinante to another corpse. Again the lance. This time Don Jose peered immediately at the face. His brother Daniel! He leaped from his horse, ran to a third corpse and rolled it over with his boot. His brother Tomas!

Don Jose turned and looked at the bodies strewn across the wreckage that had but moments ago been an Indian camp. He was confused. This was madness. Chaos. As if something inhuman had swept in like a hurricane dispensing death impartially, without thought, without recognition. Fate in human form. Playing God.

As Don Jose wandered dazed at the edge of the camp, he stumbled over a body in the deepening shadows near the trees. He glanced down, bending over to see better in the fast fading light. Headless. Blood throbbing from the headless neck in powerful jets as if the heart still beat. A few feet distant in the clearing he saw the dark, melon shape that he knew belonged to the body.

He lifted the visor of his helmet to get a better look. The heavy metal helmet flew off at his touch, rolling with a clatter toward the severed head, where it twisted like a twirling coin on edge and fell over the head.

A chill pierced Don Jose. He strode toward the helmet to recover it. As he reached down and touched the metal, the visor flew open, and open dark eyes and brows burned at him almost as if they were still alive. He snatched the helmet by the visor opening, giving a shake to dislodge the head. The weight bumped against the inside of the metal, and he shivered. He turned his face away so he could not see it fall, but a ghostly laugh forced him to turn.

'It's crazy!' he said to himself. 'Imagination. Or the wind.'

The still air gave lie to the wind, and he was certain he was not imagining. Not a Captain from Extremadura. By now he had turned his glance back. A piercing shriek burst from his depths. The severed head that stared up at him was grinning. *And it was his own face!*

'Senor! Are you all right?'

The concerned voice was bodiless for just an instant before Jose came fully awake. Then he saw a small group of people staring at him from the plaza walk. Although it was bright sunlight, he felt a freezing chill and his moist clothes clung to him.

'All right,' he croaked, his voice still thick with sleep.

'Should someone call a doctor?' one of the crowd asked of a companion.

'I'm all right,' Jose repeated. 'Just a nightmare.' When his eyes cleared and he looked around, he could see that it was sunny daylight. Among the concerned passersby who watched were a few restrained smiles. Drunk, they probably thought. Embarrassed, Jose stood and hurried away on wobbly legs.

'Extremadura,' he said to himself. 'That's where conquistadors come from.' He resolved to take the next bus from Sevilla.

169

27

The bus had bumped along the two-lane highway that had climbed most of the curved way since it had left Sevilla. Although Jose had taken off his jacket, he still felt uncomfortably warm, especially now that the terrain had flattened and they were moving through vineyards that smelled fruity in the late morning sun. The bus had followed interminable smelly, smoking trucks during the ascent—moving at speeds that agitated him to impatience, like the slow moving traffic on crowded streets in suburban Los Angeles. Now the fruity aroma replaced the smell of truck exhaust and a slow moving, horse drawn wagon full of grapes became the impediment to fast travel.

The young Spaniard who sat across the aisle from him smiled shyly. Jose had been avoiding his glance during the drive, and the noisy shifting of gears and lurching of the bus had helped discourage conversation. Now, though, he nodded in recognition.

'You are North American. No?' The English words sounded strange to Jose after the weeks of immersion in Spanish both here and in Mexico. For a moment he did not understand because his mind was still geared to the other language.

'Yes,' Jose finally said.

'I could tell by clothes. Englishmen clothes do not look so good.'

'Where did you learn English?' Jose did not really care, but he did not want to be rude.

The young man beamed as if Jose had paid him a compliment. 'In London,' he said. 'I work in restaurant. I going home now. To marry my—' He searched for the word, his lips practicing in silence until, with a look of relief, it came out, '—my sweetheart.'

'A homecoming.'

'We be in Merida soon. My family be there for me.'

By now a few of the other passengers in the bus had turned and looked solemnly at this loquacious young man, glancing from him to Jose. The young man acknowledged them with a few words of explanation in Spanish. Jose felt uncomfortable at being the center of attention and turned his gaze out the window. But the young man was not to be dissuaded.

'You speak good Spanish, sir. I heared you at the bus station. Will you stay in Merida?' Jose sighed and shook his head. 'We do not see many North Americans here. On the Costa Del Sol yes. German too. And English. Are you on business?'

Jose shook his head again. The London restaurant must have unhinged the young man's Spanish reserve. He could see the smile, more restrained now, as the young Spaniard nodded and glanced at his stay-at-home countrymen who tried to look uninterested at the conversation they could not understand.

Up ahead Jose could see the crossroad with the wooden sign. When the bus stopped and turned right, he sighed with relief. 'The bridge!' the young man said, again demonstrating his English. 'We are almost there.'

There was a slight undertone of voices among the other passengers now. Ahead Jose could see the sequence of arches over the Guadiana River. Caesar's legions had marched across that bridge some two thousand years ago. The bus backfired and wheezed its way across as if it, too, knew that it was almost home.

'You should stay in Merida,' the young man said to Jose. 'There is a history, a side of Spain here that few travelers ever see. We are descendents of conquerors.' Then they had crossed the bridge and travelled down a narrow street into the main square. A small town. Old and tired.

When the bus pulled into the terminal Jose saw a grim, older couple standing solemnly alongside a poorly dressed young man and two girls. 'Hello,' the young man shouted out the window in Spanish. Then to Jose. 'My family. My brother there is going to Germany next month. To work in construction.'

Jose watched the young man rush off the bus and move swiftly toward the austere group. There were tears in the older woman's eyes, and the father extended a hard, rough hand. Jose looked away. There was something too familiar in that welcome of the world traveler come home. Like a regression in time to some forty years ago, his first return to Los Rafas from California.

'Over there, senor.' The bus driver pointed to a building. A half hour later Jose was on the road again, the chauffeur a dour man who raced the small Spanish automobile with cavalier abandon along the main highway that ran northeast. In less than half an hour they turned off the highway onto a country road, bumping along, raising dust that hung heavy in the early afternoon heat.

In spite of the heat and his fatigue, the faint stirrings of anticipation excited Jose. 'How far?' he asked the driver.

'Not too far now, senor.'

Jose smiled. This was a kind of homecoming for him too. A return for the world traveller who had set off generations ago for gold in the Indies and who now, generations later, had come back to the place where it all began. He had travelled a long road. Not just now, from California. Or even from Los Rafas. But through the centuries.

After another ten minutes the driver looked back at Jose. 'Just ahead, senor. It's not much.'

Peering through the windshield he could make out the arch supported bridge across the river. Above it, on a low hill, the squat castle stood guard over the brown countryside. They drove along the unpaved road past the flat houses with their tiled roofs into the main square, stirring dust that refused to settle, that hung suspended as if waiting for the law of gravity to be enforced in this desolate place.

The car skid to a stop, plumes of dust rising from behind it, and the driver turned off the engine. 'It's siesta, senor,' apologizing for the empty plaza. 'There is the statue.'

Jose looked around in disappointment. If it were not for the castle on the hill and the red tile roofs on the houses, he could be in the deserted plaza of some Indian pueblo in New Mexico. He walked toward the statue, thinking that whatever magic was in this place would be there. He stooped along the way, grasping a handful of weeds that desecrated it like an abandoned graveyard.

There he stood in bronze—Hernan Cortes, the conqueror of Mexico, holding a Castilian standard in one hand and some kind of a baton in the other. Below were inscribed the names of past glories: 'Mejico, Tabasco, Otumba, Tlaxcala.' Jose followed the conquistador's gaze out over the abandoned plaza.

Jesus, he thought. No wonder he left. Even Los Rafas at its worst is better than this. Maybe that's it, he thought in disappointment. The best thing about home is that it forces you to leave so that you can find a better life.

And yet, deep down, he felt that pang for home. That need to find a final place where one could lie down and say: 'This is all. There doesn't have to be any more. Now I can rest.' But this dismal place only gave him pain, only gave the lie to his hope that finally he would find home.

The driver followed Jose's footsteps at a respectful distance. 'He's not buried here,' the driver said. 'Mexico. He wanted to be buried there. We have his monument, but Mexico has his body.'

Jose nodded and walked silently across the square, tempted to clear the weeds from this graveyard of a plaza but finally shaking his head at the futility of it all. There were no monuments to Cortes in Mexico. Only a memory of infamy. A kind of awesome, grudging accord one gives a rapist whose victim gave you birth. The father one cannot acknowledge.

After a slow stroll around the ghostly plaza, Jose returned for one more look at the statue. 'Mejico, Tabasco, Otumba, Tlaxcala.' If Cortes was your father, Jose thought, then your mother was—He did not want to think the next words. They popped out anyway. Malinche. Never mind that the Spaniards called her Dona Marina. It was Malinche. An Indian. And you, child of the Old World and the New, are Mexican.

Mejico? No. Not Mexican. His visit here was foolish. This was the wrong town. It was not Cortes he wanted, but his followers who marched up the Rio Grande. Coronado. Or better yet, Onate or Vargas. Certainly no Malinche. If anyone at all it was a woman of the pueblos. Perhaps. But perhaps not even that. Spanish. Pure Spanish. Conquerors.

So not Malinche, a quiet voice continued. Perhaps Pocahontas. Or Desert Blossom. Mestizo. Child of the Old World and the New. A new race. The New Mexican.

One last look at the wrong statue of the wrong conquistador, and Jose turned toward the driver. 'I'm ready to go back to Merida,' he said. 'To catch the afternoon bus to Sevilla.'

The driver nodded, sensing a change in mood in the senor, his eyes warily studying the tired, fleshy face and slumped shoulders. The features that had begun to slur like a drunkard's tongue, as if

173

time were too many drinks taken too fast.

'It's just a little country town by a river,' the driver said. 'Not of much consequence.'

With a grunt, Jose climbed into the rear seat of the automobile. They drove slowly through the plaza. 'Senor,' the driver said. 'There is one more place. Over there. That's where his house used to be. By that plaque.' Jose did not even turn to look.

A heavy weight seemed to sit on Jose's chest on the drive back to Merida. He stared at the rear of the front seat, depressed, disappointed, puzzled that he should come all this way hoping to find the grandeur of history, his history, and to find only this— less than the home he had left for this journey. The fear came to him that he would go on like this forever—unfulfilled. That somehow through the warp and woof of his being, there would always be this one thread that was missing. Something that no one else could see but that he, himself, felt as if it were a limb that had been amputated, making him less than a whole man.

During the dusty ride, Jose looked up into the rear view mirror twice, both times seeing the noncommittal eyes of the driver watching him. Did he look that bad? he thought. But then the awareness dissolved, and he was back in that black state of despair.

The twenty-mile ride was over quickly, and Jose grunted with surprise when the driver said, 'Merida, senor.' The bag from the trunk was unloaded and a fee exchanged. Jose had planned to stay overnight in the parador, but there was no point now. He would be back in the hotel in Sevilla by suppertime. Then he could rest the next day before seeing Senor Gomez. This thought triggered a brief rise in his hopes, but then fatigue dragged him down again, and he had this terrifying cognition that he was going to die.

The bus moved back across the harsh land of Extremadura even more rapidly than it had come. As if it too were glad to have left the place. Extremadura, Jose mused. 'Hard extremes' was what it meant in English.

As he stared out the window of the bus, only half seeing, the landscape seemed to change, moving back in time to a happier place. There were cornfields now (the Spaniards disdained corn as food unfit for humans and fed it to their hogs). Cornfields that ran past the little adobe house for a long distance to the river. From the edge of the field he could see above the rows of corn the cluster of cottonwood trees that lined the Rio Grande, the Rio Bravo del Norte of history. The boy stood at the rise alongside the irrigation ditch, barefoot, his bib overalls faded and patched, a shapeless hat on his head.

'Herminio!' A wave of arm toward the rustling sound of movement in the cornfield. Then the small boy emerged, a crafty smile on his face softly lit by the sun fading into dusk.

'Old man Griego's melons are ripe,' he winked.

Jose looked around surreptitiously. 'Shh,' he said, then walked up to Herminio where their whispers could be heard only by each other.

'We can cut through the cornfield,' Herminio said. 'I have a beautiful one all picked out. As gorgeous as Lucy Gallego's behind. Then we can cut back toward the river and have a swim before we have our feast.'

'After dinner,' Jose said. 'I have my chores to do. I'll tell mama I'm going to your house to study.'

'And I'll tell my old lady I'm going to your house to study. If she believes that, she'll believe anything.'

Now he could smell distinctly the faint sweetness of the growing corn. The boy was moving crouched between two rows, not as fast as running but not as slow as walking either. 'Herminio!' The whispered call travelled a ghostly route and died in silence, unanswered. 'Herminio!'

'Over here,' the whispered answered finally came. 'This way.'

They were cutting across the fields now, picking their way through the barb wire fence that separated corn from melon. 'There,' Herminio said. 'That one.' Then an elbow to Jose's ribs. 'Doesn't that look like Lucy Gallegos?'

Trying to suppress his laugh, Jose followed Herminio who tucked the melon under his arms. The giggling Herminio tried to stuff down his own laugh and the pressure of the swallowed sound exploded into a high pitched fart. Then Herminio dropped the melon and fell onto the ground laughing aloud, while Jose, beside himself, let out a loud whoop that seemed to travel

175

through space toward the moon.

Then they were at the river, breathless from running, while they dropped off their overalls and slipped into the dark coolness of the water. Rio Grande. River of life. Feeder of cornfields. Sweetener of melons. Cooler of boys at the end of the hot summer days.

He could taste the sweet melon now. Juice running down his chin. Filling the stomach that seemed forever hungry, unfulfilled by beans and tortillas and chili. 'Don't swallow the seeds,' he warned the gluttonous Herminio. 'They'll grow inside of you into a melon.'

'I'd like to plant a seed inside Lucy Gallegos.'

And their laughter echoed along the banks of the quiet river. Flowed with barely a ripple, following the flowing waters toward the south. Toward the river's home, its final resting place—the Gulf of Mexico.

'Sevilla in thirty minutes!'

The bus driver's words only partially brought Jose back to the present. He was still with that river, flowing homeward. 'Hurry!' his mind said. 'Hurry! I want to be home.' Then a giant vise clamped on his chest, kicked him like a horse's hoofs, and in a last panic he knew he was going to die. 'Home,' raced through his mind. 'But where is home? Theresa! Mama!'

Blackness. Peace. Home.

28

Joe Rafa had collected his one bag after the airplane from Sevilla had unloaded, then checked it in again for the flight back to the United States which would not leave for a few hours yet. The wooden box with his father's body was already on its way, and they would come together once again at their final destination—Albuquerque.

All the business had been taken care of except for this one item: a note left in Jose's box at the hotel signed by Senor Blas Gomez S. with a Madrid address. There was enough time between planes that he could take care of the business with Senor Gomez S. That would make neat dispatch of everything here in Spain. Then on to the most important aspect—the funeral.

'Senor Rafa,' the note had read. 'I had to return to Madrid a day early. However, I have news about the Catalog. You may contact me in Madrid if you wish. I hope your trip to the land of the conquistadors was a pleasant one. With most sincere best wishes, Blas Gomez S.'

Joe had been tempted to ignore the note, fly back to the United States with not another thought for Senor Gomez S. until he had talked by telephone to his mother. Theresa had sounded farther away than she should have, even with the distance and the deficiencies of things mechanical. Disjointed. Confused. For one of the few times that Joe could remember, showing her age.

'Heart!' he had shouted into the telephone, as if his voice must travel those thousands of miles on its own power. 'The doctor said it was his heart. It was quick. On a bus. They pulled into the station in Sevilla and when everyone else had left, the driver went back to wake him up. There was a smile on his face as if he were having a pleasant dream.'

Then he had heard the sob, could almost see the tears, and he started to censor his words. He did not mention the note from Senor Gomez S. Why raise questions one could not answer? He did not mention the small notebook with the handwritten notes, words engraving the sheets beneath from the force they had been written with. Letters large and undisciplined. Driving. Confused. The nervous sputtering of energy betraying itself in the cryptic sentences and half sentences.

'No soy Mejicano.'

'Passengers to the Indies 16th-18th.'

'Biblioteca Nacional.'

'Alfonso de Sintierra.' That one Jose recognized. The shyster from East Los Angeles.

'Is it a matter of color?'

Two business cards pinned to a page. 'Luis Gomez,' and 'Blas

177

Gomez S. Old Books.'

'Memories of the Alhambra.'

There was more. Much more. All in a similar vein. With lists of places visited, monies spent. An orderly accounting recorded in that frantic handwriting.

So Joe censored himself. Told Theresa only that he had died painlessly and that all would be cleared up quickly and that they would be in Albuquerque for certain on Tuesday. Plan the funeral for Wednesday or Thursday.

In the rush of the past few days, Joe had barely had time to think of his father. The attempts to do something, he did not know what, to help Theresa. The frantic flight to Spain to arrange for returning the body—he could not say corpse. The officials, the papers, the telephone calls. All seemed a jumble of confused days that were indistinguishable.

Even now, as the driver weaved the taxi expertly on the wide streets leading toward the center of Madrid, the reality of his father's death had not come in on him. His mind was leaping ahead to Senor Gomez S. and that unknown. And he was aware that he was postponing what he would have to think about: Jose Rafa.

Today is not forever, he told himself. It will all calm down. He promised himself that on the flight back he would let himself go so it could all sink in. He would drop the energetic practicality that had sustained him these past few days. Thank God for his wife Margaret. She had taken Theresa under her wing while he had flown on wings of his own to settle the matters in Spain.

The taxi turned right on the Avenida Jose Antonio, past the shops and restaurants and hotels. The driver pulled to the curb, pointing to a street sign. 'Number five is just a few doors down, senor.'

When Joe entered the book shop, the man at the desk looked up. 'Senor Gomez?' The man nodded. 'I am Joe Rafa.'

Gomez stared silently at him, mulling something over before he spoke. 'I'm sorry, senor. You look familiar, but—'

'You may have spoken to my father, Jose Rafa.'

'Ah.' Senor Gomez's eyes brightened. '"Passengers to the Indies." We were to meet in Sevilla. But where is Senor Rafa?'

'He's dead.'

A stunned silence. Then, 'I'm sorry, senor. It must be a terrible shock for you and your family.' Senor Gomez looked at Joe gravely for a moment. 'You resemble your father very much. I was confused when you walked in.'

Joe nodded. Embarrassed, he said, 'Senor Gomez. Could you speak slower. My Spanish is not too good.'

A puzzled look, a slight shift as if the focus were now less direct—talking through a filter to someone who was no longer your exact equal. 'I forget. You are a North American.'

'I return to the United States this afternoon. I wanted to—' Not knowing quite how to say the words in another language, Joe thrust the note to Senor Gomez.

Gomez adjusted his glasses to read it. 'Yes,' he said. 'Your father came to me in my hotel in Sevilla. We had missed each other in Granada. It was about the book. An educated man your father. He was searching for the origins of the Rafa family here in Spain. We found reference to the book, "Catalog of Passengers to the Indies during the 16th, 17th, and 18th Centuries." It is out of print. But I checked at the Archives of the Indies in Sevilla. The book was published there. I sought permission for Senor Rafa to look at it.'

'I see.' Thinking: Is that all?

'Permission was granted. However—' Gomez lifted his arms from his sides, then dropped them in resignation. 'You, Senor Rafa. Are you interested in the Catalog?'

'Thank you, but no, senor. It was a—' How did you say hobby in Spanish? '—an interest of my father's. At one time in his life he was going to be a teacher. The Rafa history was important to him.'

'And now—' Again the lift of arms, the silent drop to his sides. 'It is a very sad thing to lose a loved one. Well—' Senor Gomez shuffled through the pile of books on the desk, signaling that that was all. There was no more he could tell Joe.

'Tell me, Senor Gomez. Do you know of a Luis Gomez in Mexico City?'

'Luis Gomez in Mexico City? I have never heard of the man. Gomez is a common enough name.'

179

'Is there anything else you can tell me?'

A shrug. A thrust of the lower lip. 'No, senor. I met your father once. Spoke to him by telephone once. Left him a note that you answered. Fifteen minutes in all I spoke to him.'

'Did he owe you any money for your services?'

Senor Gomez' face seemed to stiffen as if flinching from a blow. 'No, senor. There is no money in this.'

For an instant Joe considered apologizing for the mention of money. But something of that stiff pride piqued him. It reminded him in a way of his father. So instead he thanked Senor Gomez for his time and his help, and left.

Joe turned onto the main avenue. There was time before he had to board the plane. Time for a cup of coffee. For a few quiet minutes alone. To think of pride and death.

29

The key, Joe thought, was in that Hispanic pride. Pride born of—of what? Part poverty. Part social status. Part sensitivity to the gap between what a man was and what he wanted to be—or of what others thought him to be. It was there in the scribbled notes in his father's notebook.

'No soy Mejicano.'

'Is it a matter of color?'

'Passengers to the Indies 16th-18th.'

It was the wholy crazy thing of being in Spain, the father country of the Americas, to find some ancient thread to the past that would somehow justify this pride.

Joe had seen it in himself. In growing up. In accepting his Mexican ancestry in contrast to his father. Then, as he grew older, to rethink what he had thought settled once and for all. His Mexicanness. His father had a valid point, he came to realize. But was it so important? Did it matter what someone called you?

Then, rethinking that, he said to himself: 'Yes. It matters.'

It had to do with the forgotten promises of America. With the unspoken assumptions people had that were wrong. That had to be changed before the promises could be fulfilled.

It had to do with winning. For history only remembers winners, while losers fade into forgetfulness as if they had never existed. The truth of the matter is: for every winner there is a loser. And America's history, his North America, was strewn with the bodies of losers who did not stay dead.

The Bible was wrong, he thought, when it stated that pride goeth before a fall. Or rather it was incomplete. For pride also remains after a fall. A pitiful compensation for the loss that one cannot accept.

And there were more losers than the Colonial Spanish stock from which the Rafas came. There were the first losers, the American Indians, from whom the land was originally stolen. Joe shared of that loss, too, because his Spanish ancestors married (a euphemism?) American Indians to form the North American version of the New World mestizo. The new race forged of Old World and New. A promise of what the future had to bring if the earth's people were to learn to live in peace.

There were other losers, just as pained, just as prideful—striking out in their pain into the melee that was modern America. The black. In the New World longer than most. First brought from Africa to the Americas by the Spanish when the native Indians died or ran away when enslaved. Then imported to the United States by the arch-exploiter, the epitome of prejudice, the early English, the ultimate Anglo. Until those black losers became the pawns that were freed in a struggle over an institution—over an organization—a government—a country. Preserve the Union. And incidentally, you slaves are free.

That led to the final ironic loser. At last an Anglo. The southern Confederate. The rebel. So that finally American Anglos as a group knew what it was to lose. The pantheon, the rainbow of humanity as losers: red Indian, brown Spanish-Indian, black African, white Anglo. The brotherhood that could not be forged in peace had been forged in loss. If they could only recognize it.

Well, Joe thought, it was in that maelstrom of losers that his

181

father had held to his pride. The first Rafas must have come to what was now the United States in the seventeenth century. Rafas were among the founders of Albuquerque. 1706. Seventy years before the Liberty Bell would be heard across the continent. Spanish colonials. Pioneers. Who had come across the Atlantic following the route that Columbus had discovered. Overland from Mexico on foot, on horseback, in caravans, with carts hauled by oxen or mule. To found a new outpost of the Spanish empire. The northernmost reaches of New Spain.

It was the pride in that pioneer ancestry that remained. For the Rafas had settled and stayed in that isolated outpost, in the same place, for three hundred years. The first almost two hundred as citizens of the Spanish empire. Some twenty plus years as citizens of the Republic of Mexico. Now over one hundred years as citizens of the United States. And during that time the world outside slowly encroached—finding a feudal culture still anchored in the way of life that first came with the Spaniards.

It was strange how men from the outside world—Anglos— treated the Spanish Colonials. Joe remembered reading a history of New Mexico written by a well-known New Mexican—an Anglo New Mexican. It started with the Spanish settlement. The explorations by the generations of conquistadors that followed Cortes. Chronologically one could sense the change. The settlers started out Spanish. In 1821 with Mexico's revolt from Spain they became Mexican. In 1846 with the annexation by the United States after the Mexican War, the settlers remained Mexican. Fifty years later they were still Mexican. Decades after the homes in which they had lived for almost two hundred years had become part of the United States, they were still not written about as Americans. Much less Spanish, their pioneer stock. But Mexican!

That would not have been bad if it were true. It was not a statement of fact, but an accusation. A sign of prejudice. A kind of putdown that winners often use, especially if there is guilt for whatever misdeeds they have done to take what was not theirs. The Spanish did it to the Indian. The Anglo did it to the Spanish Colonial. If I steal from you, knowing it is wrong—then I can bury my guilt by thinking you less than me and therefore not deserving of better treatment.

And there were other, subtler implications. Modern day implications. Part of it had to do with relations between Spanish Colonials and Anglos. Joe had seen it in his own life. When someone had asked him his ancestry (Why was it that only certain groups were always asked this question while others never were?) and he would reply, 'Spanish,' there was that certain reaction. A knowing smile. That said: 'He's ashamed of being a Mexican, so he says Spanish. But he doesn't fool me.'

The other part had to do with the same question asked by an American of recent Mexican ancestry. 'Eres Mejicano?' Again the reply: 'Spanish.' The reaction this time not a knowing smile but one of anger. One that said: 'You're putting me down, brother. You're denying me. You're ashamed of being a Mexican and at the same time you're prejudiced against Mexicans. A Judas. a Malinche. Worse than an Anglo.'

So that finally in his own life, Joe found it easier to say: 'Mexican.' The Anglo would nod, his smile now one of confirmation of what he thought he already knew, and then drop the matter. They were on common ground. Things were OK. The American Mexican would nod and smile, thinking: 'Brother. We are brothers. Let's drop this thing now that we know where we stand.' Things were OK.

For Joe it was simpler this way. It saved talk and explanation that in the end resolved nothing. But things were not OK with his father, Jose. Not like this. Because the word 'Mexican' had been (and still is in some places) one of prejudice in the southwestern United States. It was a derogatory word rather than a statement of fact—applied to the poor, the hungry, the unemployed, the accented, the powerless. And when his father heard the word applied to himself, that was how he took it, with the added dimension of his Colonial pride. 'If you demean me, then you are recognizing me. If you recognize me, I want you to recognize me properly. Spanish!'

So it turns. Words. Feelings. Wheels inside of wheels inside of wheels. With the need for different words. Accurate words. Accurate not only in fact but more important, in feeling. For his Colonial Spanish-Indian self was a brother to all the other Hispanos. To the Mexican. The Cuban. The Guatemalan. The Salvadorean. Panamanian. Argentinian. Chilean. Columbian. To every one. The common roots flowing back to the common language, religion, customs. To father Spain. Grafted like half of a Siamese twin onto the native Indian cultures throughout the Americas to flower into a new breed. Hispanos. The new race. The way of the future.

So Jose, his father, had held onto his pride, perhaps not really knowing what it was. For the United States was not a Hispano country like most of the rest of the Americas. But Hispanos had their place there too. And his father, moving into the Anglo world, had earned for Joe the opportunity to succeed. And Joe in turn, wanted whatever success he had to earn for his children the right to fail. To fail and still be accepted. To fail and not be outcast, not be second class. For history may forget losers, but life does not and God does not. While life can disdain losers, God does not. For we are all, winners and losers both, God's children and deserving of His love.

30

The funeral was over. Even members of the family had gone. Only Joe and Margaret remained with Theresa inside grandmother Rafa's little adobe house. Joe could hear from outside the hushed voices of their three children with one remaining cousin who was Grandma Rafa's nurse. He took Margaret's hand and squeezed it. His mother sat quietly, eyes closed, perhaps in prayer. Grandma sat in her rocking chair, her tiny body almost lost in the shadows of the dimly lit room.

Theresa spoke without opening her eyes so that at first Joe did not realize that she was talking to him. 'Why do you suppose he went on that crazy trip?'

'He wanted to find himself,' Joe said. Theresa turned and

looked at him questioningly. 'He was trying to trace the Rafa family. To find out where they came from.'

'I don't understand,' she said. 'They came from here. From Los Rafas. He didn't have to go halfway around the world to find that out.'

Joe turned away from her gaze. It surprised him to realize that in his entire life he had never talked to his parents about what underlay his father's quest. That everything he had learned from them about prejudice had been indirectly, through a kind of osmosis.

'It was prejudice he was trying to understand,' Joe said. 'He had been trying to sort through the things that must have pained him all his life. Trying to find in the family tree that limb that said he was all right and that the pain had all been a mistake.'

Theresa's face came half alive now, and she nodded slowly. 'It wasn't easy for your father. He had to work. To go out into the world and meet people. To brush up against people's prejudices. People he worked with. Or neighbors. There were not many raza where we lived or in the banks where he worked. He was among the first. It was hard on him. But then you wouldn't know about that.'

Joe turned sharply toward her. Had that been an accusation? But she had turned her gaze out the window. No, he answered himself. I'm just tired. Jumpy. 'No,' he said aloud. 'I never knew how hard it was. It was much easier on me.' Thinking: Easy enough that I could drop it by the time I finished college while Jose carried it with him all his life. 'And it's getting easier,' Joe continued. 'It's gotten almost fashionable to be a Chicano. You can get special privileges for enrolling in some colleges or in getting some jobs. What was prejudice for Jose became almost neutral for me and is becoming pro-judice for your grandchildren. The world changes.'

Theresa remained silent for a long while before she spoke again. 'Do you think your father found what he wanted? Learned that it was all right to be of la raza?'

'I hope so.'

'Do you think there was a priest somewhere near him at the end?'

'I don't know,' he said. 'In any event, we'll pray for him.'

'Jose.' Grandma Rafa's old voice wavered with the insistence of a petulant child. Tears flowed slowly from Theresa's eyes down her cheeks.

'She thinks you're your father,' Margaret said.

Joe rose and walked to her, squatting beside the low rocker. 'Yes, Nana,' he said, placing a hand on her frail little arm.

'Bring your mama a nice glass of water, Jose. From the pump.' Joe went to the kitchen and turned on the faucet; the pump had disappeared when he had been a small boy. He rinsed a glass and carried it freshly filled to his grandmother. 'That's a good boy, Jose. You always were a good boy. My favorite. You never fight with the other boys and you always do what your mama tells you.'

Theresa had closed her eyes, though the silent tears were flowing faster now. Margaret moved her chair next to Theresa and placed an arm around her.

'You're a smart boy, Jose. A bright boy. Your teacher told me. "Jose is a bright boy. He will be something special some day. A teacher. A lawyer." Yes. That's what she told me. He will be something special for a little Spanish boy.' She pushed the half empty glass back to Joe and smiled. After a moment her head began to nod, the rocking slowed, and she was asleep in the chair.

'I don't think she even realizes she went to a funeral today.' Joe said. He was thinking of all the funerals this family had seen. First Uncle Tomas. Over twenty years ago. From a disease of the lungs, weakened by gassing during World War I. Then Uncle Daniel. Ten years ago. An accident while drunk in his bathtub. Grandfather Rafa, old Carlos. Just a few months past. Now his own father, Jose. All the old men were gone except Uncle Carlos. All of the women still survived, including his grandmother who was over ninety years old.

Margaret handed Theresa a handkerchief. 'Mother. Do you want to take a rest here or would you rather go with us to see Carlos?'

'I think I'll stay.' Theresa's voice was soft and teary. 'You go ahead. He's expecting you.'

186

Joe went outside for his cousin, Juanita. 'Is Grandma often like this?' Juanita nodded. 'We're going to see Carlos for awhile. She's asleep now, but then you never know—'

'Daddy. Daddy. Do we have to go? Can't we stay?' His nine-year old daughter, Terry, bounced up and down pleading while her older brothers, Joe and Bill, stood quietly watching.

'Joe. I'd like you to drive us.'

'Oh, dad.'

'Bill. You help Juanita watch grandma.'

'Nobody has to watch me,' Terry said.

Joe went back into the house for Margaret. 'Will you be all right?' he asked Theresa.

She wiped her eyes dry and nodded. 'I want you to promise me something,' she said to them both. 'You know your father wanted to be buried here. He even wrote it into his will. Well. When I die—'

'Now, mother.'

'No. No. It happens to us all. When I die, bury me in California. I left here long ago—for good.'

Joe and Margaret's eyes met. 'Certainly,' Joe said. 'You don't even have to write it into any will.'

'I'm going to anyway. Not for you. But for all the others. I wouldn't want them bothering you just because you'll be keeping a promise to me.'

'Whatever you say,' Margaret said.

Joe and Margaret joined hands and walked solemnly out to the automobile where their son was waiting. 'How long are you going to be, mama?' Terry asked.

'Not very long.'

Joe handed the keys to his son and slid onto the passenger's side of the front seat. 'You be careful, Joey,' Margaret said.

'It's Joe, mother.'

'Don't go running over any curbs,' Terry mimicked. Young Joe quickly flipped a middle finger at her, then turned on the ignition.

'You know the way to Uncle Carlos' house?' Margaret asked. Young Joe nodded.

They drove west along the paved road, Los Rafas Road, toward the river. The same way Jose, as a boy, would have ridden his horse. The road would have been dirt then. The houses fewer and farther apart, with more fields for planting.

His father had not been so old, Joe thought. Sixty-five. Carlos was over seventy and still going strong. Grandfather Carlos had lived to ninety-five. But then the number of years of a man's life was not always the same as the experience he had had, the pains he had felt, the stresses he had endured. Hadn't he known much younger men, his contemporaries, men in their forties, who had dropped before going along the path too far. Strange, mysterious dyings that only at the end mirrored the intense inner churnings that had propelled them early to their graves. Heart attacks. Cancers. Suicides. As if life were too much to bear, and they took an easy way out—overt or subtle. In the end it was all the same: what one cannot endure, one removes himself from. Even life itself. And to endure is an achievement.

'Up there. At the next road. Take a right,' Joe told his son. They were heading north towards Los Chavez. 'A long time ago,' Joe said, 'all this belonged to the family. Not recently. Maybe a hundred years ago. During my great-grandfather's time. Rich land. With the Rio Grande not even a mile from here. They were well to do for their time. Not much money. No one in the territory of New Mexico had much money. But they had their land and their crops and their livestock. They were a family to be reckoned with.'

Joe could see the expression on his son's face: Oh, not this history crap again. History was boring to young people. Until the time that they finally could see themselves as a part of it.

'But things change,' Joe continued. 'The old Spaniard-Mexican was looking toward yesterday. To his heritage. His tradition. Manana was something to ignore because it was going to come anyway. So why worry? It took the Anglo to face toward tomorrow and shape it to his dreams—good or bad.

'So it has changed here too.' He pointed across a field toward the new buildings that rose incongruously from what his memory saw as corn fields. 'There's the new high school,' Joe said. 'Uncle Carlos used to own that land.'

Just down the road beyond the large white house, Joe nodded

and pointed to the dirt drive that ran along the smaller white-washed adobe house. Young Joe drove down the long narrow driveway and parked facing the adobe walled corral. Aunt Cleofas stood at the back screen door waiting for them.

'I have some coffee,' she said as she ushered them in. 'Papa's waiting in the living room.'

Carlos rose to greet them. They sat on the old-fashioned furniture that was still as neat and clean as if it had just been uncrated. It matched the house. A comfortable house that time had passed by.

'It's a sad day,' Carlos said. There were tears in his eyes. Until now Joe had never realized how much Carlos resembled his father. A small man. Still thin and wiry where his father had added weight because of a more prosperous life. But a striking resemblance nevertheless. The large nose. The one eye slightly turned in, like Grandfather Carlos. A certain bearing. Maybe it was that more than the physical resemblance. An attitude. As of men who, in their own element, were born to command—to lead ghost armies that no longer marched to the sound of the future.

'You saw the high school?' Carlos asked. His voice faded in intimations, the words that could have followed remaining unspoken: That land was once mine. 'That's one of the things I wanted to speak to you about.' He meant land, not the high school.

Aunt Cleofas brought the tray with filled cups on fragile old saucers, the little silver pitcher filled with evaporated milk, a plate of biscochitos alongside the sugar bowl.

'Your mama must be going through a terrible time,' she said gently. Joe nodded.

Uncle Carlos' face brightened, captured by a fleeting thought, and he turned toward young Joe. 'You're a fine looking boy. A regular Rafa. Do you know how old this house is?'

'No, sir.'

'Fifty years old. I built it myself. Adobe. Thick, thick walls. Cool in summer and warm in winter. They don't make houses like this anymore.'

The walls, Joe could see, were worn smooth by years of coating and recoating. Even from inside he knew that it belonged to the earth. He felt from it a solid, heavy inertia that said: This is where I belong. No stone castles as in Spain on this new frontier, but the earth itself. Leaving no monuments after man has gone. For then the elements will erode what was manmade, giving it back to the earth from which it came. It is proper that it should be so.

'You were telling us about the high school,' Joe said.

Carlos looked thoughtfully out the window toward the front yard filled with flowers. 'It is not easy to say.' Joe waited, his silence giving permission. 'At one time,' Carlos continued, 'all of this,'—he waved a hand toward the outdoors in a sweeping general gesture,—'all this belonged to the Rafas. The land where the high school is was mine.' Carlos paused again, as if deciding whether or not he should continue; he looked at Joe as if the answer were on his face. 'Your father still owns a small plot up in the mountains. In the Sandias.' Joe looked at Margaret in surprise; he hadn't known about that. 'Some day he was going to build a cabin there. For vacations. When your mother feels better—when she is over all this dreadful thing that happened—will you speak to her for me? I would like to buy it. To keep it in the family.' Carlos sighed as if in relief.

'Yes,' Joe said. 'I'll speak to her.'

Now the talk drifted to lesser things as they drank their coffee. When Aunt Cleofas had cleared the cups, Carlos turned to Joe once more. 'How is mama?' he asked, meaning Grandmother Rafa.

'Old,' Joe said.

'She doesn't always remember, poor thing,' Margaret said. 'She thought Joe was his father.'

'She is very old,' Carlos said. 'She's become like a child. When she understands, I tell her to come live with us. But she doesn't want to. She wants her own little house. So Juanita or one of the other girls stay as her companion. It won't be long before one of us will have to take her in. She can't take care of herself.'

After a few more moments, Joe looked at his watch and rose to leave. His aunt and uncle followed slowly through the house to the yard. From the field behind the corral came the laughing undertones of children's voices.

'They're in the tomato plants again,' Carlos said. 'Hey! Back there! Babosas!' he shouted. 'Get out of there!'

'OK, papa,' came the voices of two little girls. Then, still giggling, the voices drifted away.

'Those grandnieces,' Carlos said, shaking his head.

As they were climbing into the car, Aunt Cleofas put a shy, tentative hand to Margaret's arm. 'I'm so glad you were here,' she said softly, as if the men were not supposed to hear. 'Although it's a terrible time, we had a chance to talk. You know. You're not really like an Anglo. You're just like one of us.'

Margaret threw her arms around Aunt Cleofas and hugged her. When she turned around to enter the car, Joe could see that there were tears in her eyes.

Young Joe backed out of the drive and turned the car toward his grandmother's house amid the exchanges of 'Adios!' As the car rose over a main tributary from the river to the irrigation network, Joe could see west across the planted cornfield toward the cluster of cottonwood trees that lined the Rio Grande. He thought of his father and his grandmother. His uncle. His son, Joe. The grandnieces.

Like the river, life flowed on. Its head waters replenished by the winter snows. Its winding course fed by the freshets of early spring. Surging with gathering strength toward the ocean where storm and sun sent it upward to the sky and moist clouds drifted back toward the source to begin the cycle again.

So it is from generation to generation. Through the slowly changing landscape, life runs its deep, familiar course—in spite of all adversity.

Nash Candelaria is a descendant of one of the pioneer families that founded Albuquerque, New Mexico, in 1706. Although he was born in California, he considers himself a Nuevo Mejicano by heritage and sympathy. His parents and sister were born in New Mexico, and one ancestor, Juan, was the first known writer of the Candelaria family, penning an early history of New Mexico in 1776.

A graduate of the University of California, Los Angeles, with a degree in chemistry, Mr. Candelaria has been a science writer and editor and most recently has worked in advertising. His short stories have appeared in *The Bilingual Review/La Revista Bilingüe, De Colores, Puerto del Sol, Revista Chicano-Riqueña,* and *Riversedge.*

Memories of the Alhambra is the first of an integrated series of historical novels about the Rafa family. The second novel in the series, *Not By The Sword*, has also been published by the Bilingual Press. *Not By The Sword* goes back in time to the period of the Mexican War, when the Rafas became Americans by conquest, to continue the saga of the New Mexican Chicanos initiated in *Memories of the Alhambra.*